Barefoot

on the

Cobbles

a Devon Tragedy

Barefoot
on the
Cobbles

a Devon tragedy
by

Janet Few

Blue Poppy Publishing

Published by Blue Poppy Publishing 2018
info@bluepoppypublishing.co.uk

Printed by Short Run Press Ltd., Exeter

ISBN 13 : 978-1-911438-54-0

To Martha and Rebecca
who taught me all I know about being a mother

Acknowledgements

There are so many people who have helped me in my *Barefoot* journey. Firstly, thank you to my characters' relatives for letting me lay bare their ancestors, in all their frailty. Thank you to The Clovelly Archive and History Group for their assistance and for permission to use the photograph that appears on the cover. I am grateful to the publishing collective Blue Poppy Publishing for taking me into their fold. I would like to pay tribute to Dan Britton for the truly amazing song that he wrote to accompany this story. The lyrics appear at the end of the book. Details of his evocative music can be found at www.chrisconway.org/dan.html. The lovely ladies of my writers' group have been unfailingly helpful, providing advice and support to a comparative novice, at least as far as writing fiction is concerned. I owe a huge debt to those who have scrutinised drafts of *Barefoot on the Cobbles,* being constructively critical, chasing errant commas across my manuscript and ironing out the clunky bits; any that remain are entirely my responsibility. Finally of course, thanks to my nearest and dearest who have had put up with me as *Barefoot* took over my life.

Author's Note

Barefoot on the Cobbles is based on a true story. All the main events and many of the minor ones, are rooted in fact. This means that, unlike most novels where you find a disclaimer about the characters being fictional, all the people that you meet in these pages actually existed. A few have had their first names changed but this was purely because there were rather too many Marys or Williams. I have made every effort to contact the living descendants of the principal characters and have had their blessing to write this book. I do hope they feel that I have done their ancestors justice. For some of the characters, I had an overabundance of information, including, in some instances, the actual words that they used. In other cases, it was difficult to uncover many details, so I had to use my best judgement. I have tried to be faithful to the historical record and where I have had to fill in the gaps, I have endeavoured to invent scenarios that I feel sit well with the characters' personalities, as I perceive them.

For more background information about the creation of *Barefoot on the Cobbles*, its characters and its setting, including many photographs, please look for the link at bluepoppypublishing.co.uk or refer to my own website thehistoryinterpreter.wordpress.com.

The Folk you will Meet as you Wander down the Cobbles and Beyond

A Family Touched by Tragedy

Polly - a desperate mother
Albert - her husband, a fisherman
Daisy - their eldest daughter
Leonard, Bertie, Violet, Mark, Nelson, Lily and Rosie - their other children

In Court

Mr Lefroy - solicitor for the defence
Richard Ottley - a jaded reporter
Mr Brown - the coroner
Mr Cruse - foreman of the coroner's jury
Mr Duncan, Mr Cock and Mr Fulford - magistrates
Mr Carnegie - presiding over Bideford county sessions
Mr Warlow - appearing for the Director of Public Prosecutions
Superintendent Shutler
Police Sergeant Ashby

In Bucks Mills

William - Albert's father
Mary 'Mrs William' - Albert's mother
Fred - Albert's brother
'Crumplefoot Tommy'
Aunt Ellen 'Mrs Tommy' - his wife and Albert's aunt
Eadie - their daughter, Albert's adopted sister and cousin
Sammy, Evie, Peg, Alice, Dol and Gilbert - their other children
Captain James 'King of Bucks' and his wife - Albert and Eadie's grandparents
Aunt Matilda - a deluded soul, Albert's aunt

Aunt Agnes, Aunt Lizzie and Uncle John - Albert's other
aunts and uncle
Walter - Eadie's husband
Captain Joe - a householder
'Takey' - a fish merchant
'Johnnie Adelaide' - a neighbour
Norah and Gertie - his daughters
'Daft Bob'
George - Albert's cousin and Ada's intended

In Peppercombe
Richard Wakely - Polly's father
Eliza Wakely née Found - Polly's mother
Arthur - Polly's brother
Lydia, Jane, Ada and Ethel - Polly's sisters
Mrs Pine-Coffin - Lady of Portledge Manor, Polly's
employer
Winifred - her daughter

In Bideford
Susan Prance née Found - Polly's aunt
Joe Prance - a fishmonger and grocer, Polly's uncle
Minnie and Athaliah – their daughters, Polly's cousins
May - another daughter, recently died in Wales
Willie and Hilda - May's children, lately arrived in
Bideford
Mr Hopson - an ironmonger
Frank Holwill - an ironmonger's assistant, Athaliah's
suitor
Mrs Newman - a superior dressmaker
Mrs Emily Powell - a struggling gentlewoman
Captain Thomas Powell - her profligate husband
Frances, Rosamund, William and Margaret - their
children
Florence Powell - another daughter, much mourned
Reverend Roberts

Reverend Page
The Misses Ley - schoolmistresses
Mr Tardrew - a creditor
Temperance Lloyd - a supposed witch
Philip Waters - an Appledore boatbuilder

At Clovelly Court

Mrs Hamlyn - Lady of the Manor
Mr Frederick Hamlyn - her husband
Mr Caird - her agent
Hon. Betty Manners - heiress to the Court
Herbert Henry Asquith - the Prime Minister
Mrs Asquith - his wife
Hon. Arthur Asquith - their son
Lord Northcote - a guest
Lord Hugh Cecil - another guest
Lord Cromer - another guest

Clovelly Villagers

Granny Smale aka Granny Pengilly - a tea-shop owner
Captain William Pengilly - her first husband
Harry Smale - her second husband
Annie Stoneman - her granddaughter
Ben and Mabel Stoneman - Annie's parents
Susan, Hettie, Norman and Fanny - their children,
Annie's siblings
Mrs Emma Stanbury - Polly's neighbour, a witness for
the prosecution
Mrs Hannah Davies - her daughter
Stanley Davies - Mrs Davies' son
Mr Edward Laurence Collins - an outsider
Mrs Amelia Collins - his wife
Alice, Mary and Bella - Daisy's friends
Mr Tuke - a gardener
Mrs Tuke - his wife
Abraham Tuke - their son, a reluctant soldier

Mrs Jones - a lodging house keeper
Eli - a carrier and a relative of Albert
Samuel Harris
Mrs Harris
Oscar Abbott
Mrs Abbott
Sid Abbott
Tom Pengilly - coxswain of the lifeboat
Will Harding
Rose Harding - his wife
Billy Harding - his son
Frank Badcock
Merelda Badcock - his wife
Wilf Badcock - his son
Richard Foley
Jack Foley
Mrs Foley
Mrs Bushell
Steve Headon
Dick Cruse
Captain Charlie Bate
Tommy Bate - his son
Catherine Bate - Tommy's wife
Captain Jim Jenn
Captain Jenn senior
Mr Moss - publican of the Red Lion
Tom Finch - gardener and organist
Will Oke - an unfortunate elderly man
Mrs Oke - his wife
Reverend Simkin
Miss Lott and Miss Hazard - schoolmistresses
Mr Ellis - a shopkeeper
George Reilly - a photographer
Postman Branch
Mrs Howard - a postmistress

Encountered in Clovelly
Vera Wentworth, Jessie Kenney, Elsie Howey and 'Mrs Pond' - women with a purpose
Dr Crew, Dr Kay, Dr Toye and Dr Ackland
Thomas Sanders - the relieving officer
Mr Dennis - a magistrate
Frank Ifield - a singer

On the Western Front
Major Shilland
Corporal Squance

In Torquay
Mrs Gilley - proper gentry
Mr Gilley - her husband
Laura Kate Cornelius - a former servant with social aspirations
Percy Cornelius - her husband, a butcher
Kathleen Cornelius - their daughter
Mr Meyers - Mrs Cornelius' father
Francis Meyers 'Mr Francis' - Mrs Cornelius' brother
Owen Meyers - another brother, a fallen soldier
Mrs Alice Meyers - Owen's widow
Mrs Miller - impoverished gentry
Agatha Miller - her daughter, a dispenser
Winnie Hamm - a servant, Daisy's friend
Louisa Taylor - superintendent nurse at Newton Abbot workhouse
Dr Cook
Eugene O'Brien and Mary Pickford - film stars
Charlie Chaplin - a comic genius

Prologue
January 1919

The magistrate was saying something. Polly, with throat tightening and heat rising, struggled to focus. He repeated his question but she was transfixed, unable to answer. Images and incidents from the past kaleidoscoped before her eyes. She saw her childhood home in the secluded Devon valley, her courtship with Alb, her firstborn being put into her arms. Her daughter, Daisy, skipping barefoot down the Clovelly cobblestones, living, loving, laughing. Daisy, bone thin and dying. Daisy, whose passing had somehow, in a way that Polly couldn't comprehend, led to her being here in this crowded, claustrophobic courtroom, with every eye upon her. She must compose herself, pay attention, escape from this nightmare. All she wanted to do was dream of the past, both good and bad times but somehow more certain, safer, predictable. Times before everything began to spiral terrifyingly out of control.

Mr Lefroy, the solicitor, had assured her that she wouldn't hang; this was a manslaughter charge not murder. Nonetheless, phantom gallows haunted Polly's

1

restless nights. Even when she calmed and the hangman's noose receded, there was still prison. Prison meant Holloway. Polly's hazy and fragmented impression of Holloway was gleaned from the terror-ridden stories of suffragettes' force-feeding, that the pre-war newspapers had revelled in. Or would they say she was mad? Echoes of insanity had touched her in the past. There were barely acknowledged tales of people she knew who had been locked away. When compared to the prospect of prison, the asylum at Exminster was somehow more familiar but no less formidable.

Polly knew she must concentrate, breathe slowly, think about what she should say. Mr Lefroy had explained that all she needed to do was to keep calm and tell the truth, so difficult in this alien environment with all these well-to-do folk looking on. Faces. Faces whirled and blurred in front of her. There was Alb, shuffling in his chair and running his finger round the restrictive collar that she had helped him to fasten only this morning. He looked lost and bewildered, barely recognisable without his beloved trilby hat. Faces of the villagers, reproachful and remote. Mr Collins, her accuser, cold and self-possessed. Mrs Stanbury, gossiping neighbour, once a friend maybe but now here as a witness for the prosecution. Then, overlaying all of these, the vision of Daisy. Daisy looking like a young lady in her new hat, proudly setting off for her first job beyond the security of the village. Daisy fighting, screaming, twisting her head away from the spoon that held the broth that might save her. Daisy dying.

Was it really her fault, as they were saying? Polly wondered. Could she have done any more? She was a mother; mothers should protect their children. She had tried, she really had, struggled in vain to shield them all from harm. The enormity of her many failures consumed her. There was Bertie, not quite the full shilling, Violet and her troubles, the worry over Leonard while he'd been away at sea during the war. Nelson, poor little Nelson and now, Daisy. If she and Albert were sent to prison, what would happen to young Mark and her two little flowers, Lily and Rosie, hardly more than babies in her eyes? Violet was scarcely old enough to look after them all. Would the children be allowed to stay in the cottage? There would be nothing but the workhouse, forbidding and final, a fortress of despair.

⚖

At the back of the courtroom, in the seats reserved for the press, sat Richard Ottley. He had been expecting it to be merely another day in court; yet more hours of listening to melodramatic tales of insignificant people's lives. His forty years as a journalist had exposed him to tragedy, to violence and to despair. He'd seen defendants who were angry, who were terrified, who were blatantly lying. It was all one to him. Empathy was long-buried, part of his nature no more. He was there to record, to report, to remain impartial and aloof. There was something though about this case, these defendants, these witnesses, that had caught his jaded attention.

The evidence unfolded, the confident tones of officials interspersed with the hesitant whispers of those for whom court was an intimidating experience. Ottley found himself uncharacteristically caught up in the events and emotions that were being laid before him. He looked at the magistrates, the counsel, the prosecutors. His gaze swung from the accusers to the accused. How had they all been drawn inexorably, inevitably, to this day, to this courtroom, into this horrific situation? Were there clues in what had gone before, harbingers of this dreadful moment? What events, what actions, what hurts in the tangled web of their pasts had brought them, inescapably, to this appalling instant?

1
Summer 1890

In the little fishing hamlet of Bucks Mills, the street sloped steeply down to the square. On the step of Captain Joe's substantial house sat a weeping child, dishevelled and dirty, her tears tracked by the grubby smears on her sun-stained cheeks. A young fisherman was walking towards her, on his way up from the shore. As Albert approached, the girl's hand scrubbed across the bottom of her nose and she sniffed heartily. The other hand failed to push her dark hair from her eyes. Her faded ribbon had long since ceased to perform its duty.

'Why tears maid?' asked Albert, moved by the plight of one of Crumplefoot Tommy's ever-increasing brood.

'Me da fetched me one.' The tone was philosophical but she scarcely stifled a rising sob. 'He said I woke the bebby but I niver.'

The child's statement was broken by a sharp intake of breath and a hiccup as another sob surfaced. At twenty seven, Albert was well aware of females, in a way that was circumscribed by his god-fearing, chapel-going upbringing but girls of this age rarely crossed his horizon. He was uncertain how to still the distressing sounds that were emanating from this scrawny specimen. He extended his hand, dirt engrained and calloused from rowing. The child regarded it suspiciously. Albert judiciously wiped the offending hand on the back of his trousers and proffered it again, pulling her to her feet. Albert knew the child was one of his assorted collection of cousins, this one a daughter of his Aunt Ellen but to be truthful, there were so many of them that he was never quite sure which was which.

He gave up trying to recall the correct name and asked, 'Which of Tommy's maids be you then?'

The child seemed unperturbed by her anonymity.

'Eadie,' chirped the mite, already brightening at an exchange that was not accompanied by blows.

She was obviously expecting something of Albert now but he wasn't sure what the appropriate course of action would be.

After a moment's thought, he came to a decision, 'You come along with me maid. 'Tis Friday and ma will be frying fresh caught pollock for dinner.'

Trustingly, Eadie looked up to where Albert loomed over her and she gripped his hand tighter, her fingers barely reaching round his palm. Together, they began the walk up the road towards Albert's home. Resolutely, Eadie tried to match her stride to his, determination on her narrow face. She stumbled occasionally but was smiling now. A few villagers looked askance at the roughened fisherman, hand in hand with his incongruous companion. Daft Bob, who lived with his aunt at the Coffin Arms, waved and grinned amiably. He was harmless enough but Eadie was wary.

The pervading scent of fried fish reached them as they approached the bend in the road and turned towards the path that led to Rose Cottage, near the top of the street. Albert had struggled to keep the conversation going on their walk up the hill but Eadie was clearly impressed that an adult was talking to her at all.

Emboldened by interaction that was a sharp contrast to the indifference she encountered at home, Eadie said, 'Da says there be too many maids in our house and we ain't no use nor ornament.' The statement was laden with stoicism.

The cottage that they were approaching was quiet; could there be houses where there weren't too many children? wondered Eadie. There were five girls in Ivy Cottage, where Eadie lived, the stairs leading directly on to the bedroom that she shared with her sisters. The new baby slept with their parents in the room beyond. Her older brother, now sixteen, had a palliasse downstairs when he was home from sea. A world where there could be solitude and silence was foreign to Eadie.

Curious and with the candour of childhood, Eadie asked, 'Do you have too many girls in this house?'

Albert's mother, Mary, came to the door in time to hear Eadie's question.

A wistful expression crossed her face, 'No,' she said, 'No girls. Just Alb here and his brother Fred, both full grown now and their da and me.'

Unlike most of her neighbours, Mary did not struggle to fit many children into three or four rooms. She had had only the two sons; two sons and many disappointments. Secretly, she'd longed for a daughter. A daughter could be a companion, they could sew together, bake together and a daughter would be a comfort as she and William tumbled into the strictures of old age.

At chapel, the minister said, 'Thou shalt not covet' and Mary was not by nature prone to envy. It did seem unjust though, that Tommy's wife had presented him with so many girls, girls who appeared to be an unwelcome encumbrance, whilst she had such a yearning for a daughter. She was too old now of course, past childbearing these five years gone. Past those days of expectation and joy, days that ended in heartrending sadness, as yet another pregnancy faltered when she had hardly had time to begin to hope. She remembered that Eadie's mother was newly delivered of a boy. Mary was conscious that Mrs Tommy had had that mental trouble not long after Eadie's birth; mental trouble that had meant she'd spent months in Exminster asylum. Having children sometimes turned the brain. She hoped it wasn't happening to her sister-in-law again.

'How's your ma and the new chile?' she asked.

'Not too special,' Eadie was eyeing the spitting frying pan, to which Mary now turned. 'Ma says 'tis harder to get back to work after lyin' in now she's older.

8

Evie and Peg can do plenty but 'tis hard for Alice and me to carry the buckets from the well or manage the heavy cook pot. I can turn the mangle though,' she said with pride. 'And mind Dol and jiggle the bebby's cradle when he cries. He's sweet. 'Twill be harder when school starts next week as we will have to do our chores before we go but ma says she will be glad to get us out from under her feet and just be left with Dol and bebby Gilbert to do for.'

Memories of the alleged misdemeanour that had led to her unjust punishment surfaced and Eadie's bottom lip trembled. She sucked it between her teeth to stop herself crying again before these nice folk. She knew Mrs William of course, her ma sometimes stopped to pass the time of day and she'd often watched Albert head down to the beach with his father and brother, to man one of the small fleet of fishing boats that put out from the shore. This was the first time she had been inside their cottage though. Eadie was overwhelmed by the neatness, by the order, by the silence. No baby's napkins drying on a clothes horse, hindering whoever was trying to stir the cooking pot. No sisters squabbling, pulling hair and laying claim to prizes that Eadie herself had found tossed up by the sea.

Albert was explaining to his mother how he had rescued a distressed Eadie from the square.

'Mebbe you stay here for a day or two maid, 'til your da calms down,' said Mary.

There was reassurance in the words but who was the more comforted, Mary or this dark-visaged child with sadness in her soul? Mary turned to her son, who had unwittingly presented her with a few days of companionship.

'Albert, when you've had your dinner, you must tell Mrs Tommy her maid be here. Mayhap she will worry else.'

Mary's mind was racing; unlike her heart, the cottage lacked space for a small girl. Could the child perhaps sleep on a mattress in the scullery? wondered Mary. Invigorated and hardly daring to think how long she might extend the stay of their unexpected visitor, Mary heaped crispy, golden fish and a pile of boiled potatoes on to a thick china plate. Eadie stuffed the food in her mouth with a voracity that suggested she was used to fighting her siblings for a share. Two plates were loaded for the absent William and Fred and set to keep warm in the Bodley. Relieved to have passed the responsibility of Eadie to his mother, Albert sat absently at the table, his thoughts elsewhere, occupied with wondering if he would meet the Wakely girls after chapel on Sunday. The eldest, Lydia, always approached him with a proprietary air but he preferred Polly, feisty too but still over-shadowed by her pushy elder sister. He'd heard their brother was now a coachman in Scotland. Scotland; it was another world. Albert was restless in Bucks Mills, would he ever escape? Maybe not as far as Scotland but many a man his age was married and set up on his own. Here he was, with his brother Fred, still crewing his father's boat like a youngster. His mother's voice drew him back to the present.

'Eat up son.'

A steaming syrup pudding, anointed with thick yellow custard, was set on the scrubbed wooden table.

Mary turned to Eadie, 'Tuck in maid. Your da will be in soon, tide's on the turn.'

Unaware of her slip of the tongue, Mary was already letting the child put down tenacious roots, roots that were to weave their way into the fabric of this home like the ivy that was embedded in the walls of Eadie's own cottage. Had Mary been able to see into the future she would have been surprised and gratified to know that these bonds were to tether Eadie to Rose Cottage for the rest of her life.

Hobnails clashed and sparked on the cobbles outside and the menfolk filled the small room with their bulk and the scent of the sea.

'Good catch?' asked Mary.

'Plenty enough,' replied William. 'Takey's off to Bideford with a cart load. We were late in, so he was already pretty full and we've some left he wouldn't have, so they'll need salting down.'

Mary suppressed a sigh. Although she was brought up in a farming family, she'd been the wife of a fisherman long enough to have accepted the tasks that were her lot but her hands were increasingly cramped from years of cleaning and gutting fish. She could get Eadie to help perhaps but she baulked at subjecting those still soft, starfish hands to the cuts and the pain of the salt water that would impregnate them. Eadie, replete with the unaccustomed good food and the warmth of the welcome, remained unobtrusive in the shadowy corner. Turning, William spotted the smock-bedecked child whose bow, now re-tied, was almost as large as the face beneath it.

'What's Tommy's maid doing here?' he asked.

Eadie, sensing that her reprieve might now be on an uncertain footing, shrunk down and tried to make herself invisible. As the gaze of this giant of a man raked her, instinctively, the child looked up, dark eyes widening and she smiled broadly, lightening her sharp features. Her loose top teeth had been unceremoniously yanked from her mouth by her father earlier that week. String had been duly tied round the troublesome incisors and attached to the open door before its sudden slamming. Memories of pain and a blood-filled mouth had already dimmed in Eadie's consciousness, eclipsed by other hurts. Unbeknowing, in the split second of that disarming toothless smile, Eadie secured her future in this family unit.

Firmly and before she could be gainsaid, Mary answered, 'She be staying put. There's too many of them down at Ivy. I could do with some help in the house now me arthritics be so bad and she will walk up to school with Johnny Adelaide's girls. Norah's about her age and Gertie can keep an eye on them both on the way. She won't be no trouble.'

The words sounded like a plea but the tone was decisive. William shrugged. Children, especially female children, were women's business. He guessed Mary knew what she was about, he wasn't going to argue. He didn't suppose such a small scrap would stop him supping tea and dozing by the Bodley of an evening.

Mary took mothering Eadie in her stride and as the weeks went by, both woman and child flourished, enfolded in the comfort of their budding relationship. The villagers shrugged their shoulders and minded their own business, unquestioningly accepting that Eadie now belonged to Mr and Mrs William instead of Crumplefoot Tommy and his wife. Casual comments, exchanged as neighbours passed in the street, paid tribute to the mutual benefits of the new arrangement.

'Mrs William's looking well. Niver seed her so cheery.'

'That there Eadie's growing apace, she be a pretty maid with her hair all combed.'

'I saw Mrs Tommy out with the bebby. She's perked up a bit. Not like all that trouble she had after young Eadie was born. That must be a relief to Tommy an' all.'

The spectre of the asylum was a pall that hung over every one of them. That Eadie's mother had spent time there was acknowledged but rarely vocalised. It was alluded to in hushed tones or conveniently ignored. It was as if refusing to name their fears would spare them from the grasp of that dreaded building in the south of the county. Their silence would grant them immunity. If the words remained unspoken, madness would not reach out and claim them, as it had claimed the poor overworked woman at Ivy Cottage, whose only crime was to have another child. Sometimes the comments delved a little deeper, as the chattering women sought to show off a more intimate knowledge of their neighbours.

'Well Mrs Tommy could niver quite take to the maid you know. She came back from you know where when Eadie was just a tiny mite and next they knew they lost their young lad.'

'Apple of Mrs Tommy's eye he were. Don't think she ever quite forgave Eadie for being spared when their Sammy was taken.'

'Them've all been left to run wild down at Ivy if truth be told.'

'Well, they did have a time of it.'

The tone made it sound like a plea, but the words were decisive. Mary took pride in fashioning a Sunday bonnet and new smock for the child. She derived a welcome contentment from having a girl about the house. Here was someone she could cook with, knit with, even confide in. The child's bubbling chatter was a refreshing antidote to the rough, monosyllabic masculinity of her husband and sons. Eadie submitted to Mary's ministrations with equanimity. She was comfortable in her new home; its serenity encircled her. It was a far cry from the muddled, cramped inefficiencies that had been an integral part of life at Ivy Cottage. Her mother, Ellen, had seemed glad to have one fewer mouth to feed, one fewer offspring to cope with. Although Eadie sometimes regretted not being able to mind the baby, she did not miss her sisters. She was free from the arguments, the noise and the clutter. Solitude suited her. The minute hole that Eadie had left in the chaotic life of Ivy Cottage had filled imperceptibly, as if she had never been.

There was a reassuring rhythm to Sundays in the cottage at the top of the street. Mary would spend the morning cooking, whilst William dozed in the kitchen chair; rarely stirring as his wife tutted and flustered round him, pans banging on the stove. Albert and Fred, uneasy in their Sunday clothes, would be fidgeting restlessly, aware that there were nets to mend or pots to make but knowing that these were not tasks for the Sabbath. Sometimes, the young men might stroll down to look longingly at the sea, skimming stones and watching the tide swirl over The Gore, as the boats lay idle above the reach of the waves. In between scrubbing carrots and basting potatoes, Mary would help Eadie to learn the verses that she would be expected to recite at Sunday school in the afternoon. Sunday school brought Bible stories, carefully coloured texts, and gusty renditions of *Jesus Bids us Shine* in unformed reedy voices. Then it would be home for a tea of cut-rounds and cake. It was the family's habit to attend the early evening service at the Methodist Chapel. Such an emphasis on chapel-going was something new for Eadie. Under her parents' regime, religious observance had been sporadic at best.

The quiet of the August Sunday enveloped the village but all was bustle in Rose Cottage, as Mary straightened her best bonnet and wiped jam from Eadie's face. At Mary's chivvying request, reluctantly, William put on his newly shined boots, Albert slicked back his hair and Fred reached for his waistcoat. Then they were ready for the few yards' walk down the hill to the chapel, ready to hold their heads high in front of their neighbours. Some weeks, in the thunderstorms of summer, hammering rain would beat a soothing rhythm on the tin roof, drowning the preacher's voice but on this particular Sunday, the sky was cloudless. The long hot day had made the atmosphere inside the tiny hut stifling. Kneeling on a coarse hassock between Mary and Albert, Eadie's mind wandered as the words of the prayers washed over her. The walls of the chapel echoed back the phrases with an eerie resonance. For Eadie, the sermon was the hardest part. The dust motes swam in the sinking sunlight and she struggled to stay awake as the preacher spoke of sin and salvation. As her thoughts began to drift and her head sank on to Mary's shoulder, a gentle nudge jerked her awake. She blinked her eyes deliberately, in an attempt to stave off sleep. Respite came when the preacher called for a hymn. Eadie struggled to follow the words in the red-covered hymn book but the music revived her.

Sometimes, Albert would walk Eadie down to the sea when the service was over. They would call in to greet their grandparents in the cottage on the cliff. Eadie loved the cottage. Even the gate was exciting, having, as it did, a ship's wheel at the centre. Eadie's small fingers would proudly trace the name that was engraved in the wooden frame: King's Cottage. She smiled; her granfer was a king. Thrilling though that thought was, Eadie was in awe of the creaking couple who inhabited this cottage of wonders. The grandfather, Captain James, was held in high regard by the villagers, most of whom were relatives of one kind or another. He could no longer row out to pilot boats in over the bar, or rescue ships in distress, these glories were now merely memories to be shared with the next generation. The old man might still potter in the bay, handline for fish from the shore or sit in the porch and ponder on the past. He would raise his telescope to scan the sea that had been his love and his master for more than eighty years. The telescope was another delight. When Eadie visited, it would be hung proudly above the fireplace. She longed to be allowed to peep through it but it remained in place, its leather lovingly worn and its brass gleaming.

Two things blighted these Sunday visits for Eadie. Firstly, King's Cottage was also home to Aunt Matilda, their grandparents' youngest daughter, who cared for her parents in their old age. She was a strange little woman, slight and swarthy, with rotten teeth and the faintest suggestion of a moustache. The poor woman was inoffensive enough but she dwelt in the corners of Eadie's nightmares, chilling and dark. Then there were the terrors of the privy to overcome. The privy was a talking point in itself. Not that there was indoor plumbing, that would be unheard of for ordinary folk but here there was no long dark walk to a spider-filled hut in the garden. Eadie would have welcomed the spiders, they held no fears for a country child. She had, after all, grown up in the dust and debris of Ivy Cottage. Her grandparents' privy however stood resplendent in a tiny room at the back of the cottage. It held horrors for

Eadie. Aunt Matilda insisted on plying her with cups of strong tea and Eadie did not know how to refuse. Soon she would be wriggling and squirming, trying to ignore the discomfort of her full bladder. She would look anxiously at Albert, hoping that he would say it was time to go home. Anything to avoid having to heave her small buttocks on to that gaping hole in the high wooden seat and hear below her the rushing of the stream, over which this part of the cottage was built. Once, she had made the mistake of peering down the hole at the dizzying water flowing swiftly past.

This week though, Eadie was spared the agonies of embarrassment and fear that accompanied her visits to King's Cottage, as Albert did not suggest a walk to the sea. Instead, he seemed eager to be off on his own as soon as the service was over.

'I'm walking up to the late service at Goldsworthy ma,' Albert called back to Mary, as he strode off up the hill.

Mary's lips pursed and a worried frown crossed her brow.

'What's he off up there for?' asked William. 'What's wrong with a godfearing Wesleyan service that he wants to go gallivanting up to the Bible Christian Chapel as well?'

'It'll be them Wakely girls,' said Mary. Tales of Albert's interest in the family had reached her in the way that only insidious village gossip can.

'Hmm,' replied William, frustrating Mary by his lack of concern.

'He can do better than those Wakelys,' said Mary, with a mother's defensiveness. 'They're no better than gypsies with their bold eyes and brazen ways.'

William felt that his wife was overreacting. He was aware of the rumours surrounding the Wakely family from the neighbouring valley but any hint of gypsy blood was generations ago and they seemed relatively harmless. It wasn't like Mary to take against someone with little reason, thought William. The crux of the matter was not so much the Wakelys' origins but the fact that they came from outside the village. Marrying a Peppercombe girl brought with it the danger that Albert might decide to leave Bucks Mills and Mary would be distraught if he moved away. William glanced at Eadie, skipping now, freed from the strictures of chapel. Perhaps this small girl could help Mary to come to terms with the thought of their sons leaving home. It was high time Albert took a wife. William looked forward to teaching a grandson the ways of the sea, as his own grandfather had taught him. William shook himself. Why were they worrying when, as far as they knew, Albert wasn't even walking out with one of the girls?

'Let's wait to fret when he brings a maid home, mother,' he soothed.

Albert panted up the hill in the day's lingering warmth. It was a fair step to Goldsworthy and he didn't want to be late. Maybe today he would pluck up the courage to ask Polly if he could walk her home after the service. This would not be the first time that he had attended Goldsworthy Chapel, as well as his own, in the hope of engaging the Wakelys in conversation. As he walked, he cast his mind back to his first encounter with the sisters. It had been a few months ago, when a temperance rally had been held in Bideford and various local congregations, of the different Methodist denominations, had arranged charabancs to the town. Albert had gone, not really because he had strongly held convictions about temperance, more because it was an opportunity to escape the confines of the village. He had signed the pledge at a young age of course but did not find abstinence irksome. Since the Coffin Arms closed to customers decades ago, there was no ale-house in Bucks Mills, so alcohol was not a temptation.

It was a large but rather boring rally, with platitudes from the platform that Albert had heard many times before. At the end of the afternoon a tea was served and Albert suspected that he was not the only member of the audience to prefer the prospect of refreshments to the preceding lectures. As he queued to take his place at the long tables, Albert became aware of a group of three dark haired girls immediately in front of him. In the crush, one of them stepped back suddenly, landing heavily on Albert's foot. She twisted round.

'Oh, I'm sorry,' she said.

The girl was about to turn back to her companions when her gaze took in Albert's height, his muscularity and his piercing blue eyes. Here was someone who might be worth getting to know. She looked around hastily for signs of a female companion. Establishing that Albert appeared to be alone, the girl boldly struck up a conversation.

'I'm Miss Wakely, Lydia Wakely,' she said, 'and these are my younger sisters, Jane and Polly.'

The emphasis on the word younger did not escape Albert. Miss Wakely was clearly expecting that Albert would consider her sisters too childish to warrant notice.

'Have you come far?' asked Lydia, after Albert had introduced himself hesitantly. Before he could respond, she went on, 'We come from Northway, it's nowhere much. We are with the group from Goldsworthy Chapel. You won't have heard of that either.'

As it happened, Albert had been aware of the recently rebuilt chapel, belonging to the Bible Christians, that nestled in the back lanes of Parkham but he didn't correct Lydia. Instead, he explained that he was from the neighbouring hamlet to their own. At this, Jane Wakely, who was plainly the shyest of the trio, put her hand to her mouth with an ill-disguised gasp of alarm.

'You come from Bucks?' she whispered, blanching.

At this point, the queue shuffled forward and the Wakely girls were being ushered to their seats. Albert wondered if he should try to avoid prolonging the discussion with these young women but a matronly sort, who was obviously part of the organising committee, guided him towards the next available chair and he found himself sitting next to Lydia. Lydia meanwhile had turned on her sister and was shushing her.

'Don't be silly Jane, those tales of Spanish pirates are rather romantic,' she was saying.

Albert knew that folk sometimes said that the residents of Bucks Mills were the descendants of Spaniards who had been wrecked off the North Devon coast hundreds of years ago during the Armada. Certainly, his own dark hair, swarthy skin and flashing eyes, gave veracity to the legend. He didn't know no sense to it himself but he was aware that his granfer and the other old men of Bucks Mills, liked to keep the legend going because it encouraged folk to leave the little village in the valley alone. In any case, Lydia seemed unperturbed by his family's reputation.

Despite Lydia's outspoken manner and tendency to monopolise the conversation, Albert did manage to exchange a few words with Polly, the youngest of the three sisters. It was from Polly that he learned that there were two more sisters at home, Ada and Ethel and a brother, Arthur, who was making his own way in the world. He heard about their home in the cottage at the top of Peppercombe Valley and how their father worked in an Appledore boatyard. She explained that she and her sisters usually attended Goldsworthy Chapel in the evening but that her parents preferred the early service. To his surprise, Albert found that he was enjoying himself, in a way that he had certainly not expected when he had set out from the village that morning. The tea was over all too soon and after a few more exhortations about the dangers of the demon drink, it was time for Albert to find his seat on the charabanc home. A few of his fellow passengers were known to Albert but he sought to avoid them, wanting to relive the events of the afternoon. He recalled Lydia's rather obvious attempts to attract his attention. It was difficult to form an impression of Jane, who had kept her eyes on her plate and hardly said a word throughout the meal. By the time the horses had dragged their load past Hoops Inn, on Albert's homeward journey, he had realised that it was Polly who troubled his thoughts.

Over the weeks that followed, Albert had struggled to make opportunities to speak to Polly, without the presence of her overbearing sister. Tonight though, he promised himself, tonight would be different. He could tell her how young Eadie was settling in and how the mackerel had been running well. Albert's day-dreaming was curtailed as he reached East Goldsworthy Farm and the rutted track swung to the right towards the chapel. A few other stragglers were hurrying towards the door, where the steward was gesticulating to encourage them to make haste. Albert eased himself into one of the back pews, pleased to catch sight of all five Wakely girls a few rows in front of him. His journey had not been wasted.

Although the Wesleyans and the Bible Christians maintained a healthy rivalry, there was much that Albert found familiar about the service. Tonight's voluble preacher was keen to see that the congregation were not short-changed but Albert was impatient for the service to be over. At last, the final blessing was pronounced and the worshippers congregated outside in the thickening twilight. Bats fluttered beneath the emerging stars and in the distance, a cow lowed mournfully. The chapel steward was offering to light the oil lamps that many of the chapel-goers had brought with them, a weapon against the encroaching darkness. Albert stood awkwardly to one side of the chattering groups, wondering how to approach Polly. At that moment, Lydia noticed him and stepped purposefully in his direction.

'Lydia you can't,' Jane was saying, putting a restraining hand on her sister's arm. 'He's one of them from Bucks, you know what they say about the lads from Bucks. They be wild and fierce and don't let no outsiders down the street.'

'Oh, rot,' replied Lydia, tossing her head imperiously. 'Think what folk say about us, always calling us gypsies and all. If I want to talk to a young man, I shall talk to him. He's got something about him that you won't find in the dull Peppercombe boys.'

Jane, always the most conservative of the sisters, hung back with the two youngest girls but Lydia approached Albert, with Polly at her side. As they drew near, Lydia pushed in front of Polly, almost knocking her from her feet.

'Hello Miss Wakely,' said Albert politely, removing his hat and looking desperately over her shoulder, trying to catch Polly's eye.

'How do you do?' Lydia responded archly, her tongue running across her top lip in what she hoped was an alluring fashion.

'I am very well, thank you,' responded Albert, conventionally, as he tried to edge his way sideways and include Lydia's younger sisters in the group.

'It's err, been a beautiful day,' Albert was struggling to think what to say but Lydia was undeterred.

'This will be my last time at chapel,' she said. She paused, disappointed that Albert had not expressed his regret but then she carried on regardless, 'I am off to work in Bideford next week. I feel so sorry for these girls,' she waved her hand expansively to encompass her four younger sisters, 'having to stay in Peppercombe. Fearfully tedious. I shall live with my aunt and meet such a nice class of people in Mrs Newman's shop. She is the best dressmaker in Bideford you know.'

Albert didn't know, nor indeed much care but inwardly he breathed a sigh of relief. At least in future he would not have to run the gauntlet of Lydia in order to speak to Polly. Lydia's inconsequential chatter rattled on but Albert had ceased to absorb what she was saying. He looked intently at Polly. They were surrounded by people, yet they were somehow alone.

2
Summer 1891

Polly walked up the road to the main highway, inhaling the scents of the fine summer's evening. Her new button boots were unsuitable for the pitted, muddy track, with its surface hardened by the recent dry weather. The local farmers, ever pessimistic, had been muttering about the likelihood of thunderstorms ruining the harvest but so far, the ripening crops stood bravely in the fields that lined Polly's route. The lane was edged with pungent cow parsley; red campion and rose-bay willowherb set the hedgerows aflame. The cloudless sky had a shimmering intensity that comes only when a hot day tips inexorably into eveningtide. The gentle insect hum, the birdsong and the surrounding beauty, raised her spirits and gave renewed purpose to her stride as she struggled to catch up with her father.

As he had done every Sunday evening for the past thirty years or more, Richard Wakely was walking to Appledore, to spend the week lodging there. This enabled him to ply his trade as a carpenter in Waters' boatyard, before returning home the following Friday. Although this was part of an uninspiring routine for the old man, for Polly it was a novelty, an excitement, a holiday. She shifted her battered canvas bag from one hand to the other; the thick leather handles had formed ridges in her palms. Her father's tar-stained holdall was slung across his shoulder and thudded on his back with each successive step. It receded into the distance, as he gained more ground. Richard seemed unaware of his daughter's presence, let alone her exertions. Lost in thought, he spat a plug of tobacco into the bank and kept his gaze firmly forward, glad that the heat of the day was abating for the journey. Richard contemplated the long walk ahead of him. Next week it would be July and soon the year would begin its descent towards autumn but for now, even at this time of the day, the air's warmth was stifling, making the journey uncomfortable.

Polly's feet were sweating and swelling; it really was too warm for a five-mile walk to be a pleasure. Wistfully, she thought of the times she'd seen Colwill's brake, clattering on its daily route from Hartland to Bideford. The five-shilling return fare was an exorbitant sum. Her father wasn't going to spend perfectly good coin on being bounced around as the horses descended past Hoops Inn. Polly knew that it wasn't only the money, even if a farm cart were to stop and offer them a lift, Richard would decline. Godfearing folk shouldn't be driving carts on the Sabbath. Aside from that, someone might see him and think he was getting soft, that he was too old to stand the rigours of his job, even suggest that he made way for a younger chap.

Once in Bideford, Richard was to leave Polly at the top of the town and she would walk down to Uncle Prance's shop in Mill Street. Aunt Susan had done well for herself to marry Joe Prance, a well set up man, with his own business. Somehow Susan, whilst in service in Bideford, had managed to snare a husband who was unaware of the rumour of the family's gypsy taint. Susan was spoken of with awe, as the member of the family who had gone up in the world. True, Uncle Prance walked with a pronounced limp, one leg being considerably shorter than the other, following a childhood accident but he was still considered a catch. Polly's sister, Lydia, always thinking herself somehow superior, had been intent on following the same path as her aunt. It was nearly a year since Lydia had left to lodge with the Prances, making her own way, working for Mrs Newman in the nearby dressmaker's shop. Despite her sister's condescending attitude, Polly was looking forward to seeing Lydia again and to spending time with her cousins. Like her own family, the Prances had a surfeit of girls, so, with Polly, there would be seven young women in the house. The prospect of a few days' stay in the bustling port, with its shops and other diversions, helped to take Polly's mind off her aching feet.

The thought that tomorrow she would not be sweeping out fireplaces or dusting furniture delighted Polly. Mrs Pine-Coffin, Polly's employer, was mindful that she had three unmarried daughters needing husbands and that the eldest of these had already reached the dangerous age of twenty-one without yet the hint of a spouse. Etiquette dictated that Winifred, as the first born, should really marry before her sisters and Mrs Pine-Coffin was displaying signs of desperation. Much as she hated visiting London since the death of her husband, she had decided to make the most of the end of the season and put her girls on parade in the hope that someone might focus on Winfred's portion and not on her slightly protuberant teeth and unfortunate tendency to be scholarly. So Portledge was shut for the month and the staff who lived-out, like Polly, were told that they were not required.

For Polly, at nineteen, the enormity of being out of a place, of being uncertain how she could bring money back to the family, was subsumed by the thrill of the unknown. As far as her parents were concerned, Polly was to visit Lydia until the end of the week. She was then expected to return home to find some work, helping with the harvest perhaps, to fill in the time until the Pine-Coffins returned and she could resume her post as under housemaid. Unbeknown to her family, Polly had escape on her mind. Her intention was to do as Lydia had done and find employment in Bideford. Surely, she thought, five days would be enough to secure a position in the town.

Polly pushed recollections of Albert to the back of her mind. She knew her parents did not approve of the attentions of the young fisherman. It wasn't that she and Albert were walking out exactly, her mother, in particular, would not condone that. Over the past months though, Albert had seemed to single her out in a special way; he'd offered to accompany her back from chapel and to hold her prayer book. Mr and Mrs Wakely were rarely seen at the evening service, so, beyond the scrutiny of parental eyes, Albert and Polly's relationship had progressed a little. Albert was certainly good looking, with his dark hair and disquieting smile. It was too soon though, for settling down as a fisherman's wife in a cob cottage in Bucks Mills, with a power of babies at her feet. Polly craved adventure, novelty; most of all, she wanted to be free of the boredom of restrictive routine.

Aunt Susan greeted Polly warmly. 'You'll have to shout,' she said, as Polly thanked her for letting her visit, 'I'm a bit deaf now'.

Certainly her aunt had aged in the few years since Polly had last seen her. Apart from her own brood of girls, Aunt Susan was now custodian of two young grandchildren, following the recent death of Polly's cousin, May, in Wales. Running round after young children, even with the help of her daughters, was clearly taking its toll on Polly's aunt. Polly was soon swept away upstairs by her cousins, keen to show off new bonnets and whisper about potential suitors. As Polly unpacked the few spare clothes that she had brought with her, her cousins kindly refrained from commenting on her yellowing undergarments and unfashionable attire. Instead, they offered to loan shawls, refurbish petticoats with lace and trim her dress with new ribbon. Lydia remained tight-lipped in the background, seemingly worried that her younger sister might show her up in some way. Lydia saw herself as the epitome of the sophisticated town-dweller now and was intent on severing ties with her rural background.

After the initial excitement, the cousins drifted away, tactfully leaving the sisters alone in case any private family news needed to be exchanged. Polly broke the awkward silence.

'Aunt Susan looks tired,' she remarked, 'is she unwell?'

'I've no idea,' replied Lydia after a pause. She had evidently not considered her aunt's state of health worthy of notice.

'I suppose it is looking after May's children,' said Lydia. 'They arrived just after I did. Little Hilda did nothing but cry for her mother for weeks and Willie ran off, trying to get back to his father.'

'Oh but they are such sweet children,' said Polly. She had been quite taken with three year old Hilda, who had shyly held up her doll for this new adult's approval.

Lydia snorted. 'They are such a nuisance,' she said, 'forever careering about and getting sticky fingers on one's gown.'

Wherever had Lydia learned to talk like the gentry? wondered Polly. Perhaps it was mixing with Mrs Newman's customers. She sounded more like the Pine-Coffins than one of Polly's own family.

'Don't you want children of your own?' Polly asked, genuinely curious. Surely everyone wanted children, maybe not yet but one day. Why did Albert suddenly intrude on her thoughts at this point? She shivered involuntarily.

'Gracious no,' exclaimed Lydia, 'the whole, err, children thing is so distasteful.'

Polly raised her eyebrows. No one could possibly grow up in the country, as they had, without having grasped the basic principles of procreation. It was the natural way of things.

'It was a problem, ummm, down there,' said Lydia, gesturing vaguely in the region of her lower abdomen, 'that killed cousin May. She was only thirty. Married at nineteen before she'd done anything, been anywhere. Well of course, it's no secret that Willie was a six-month child.'

'But surely you want to be wed?' said Polly.

'Well, married, yes, perhaps,' replied Lydia, 'but I am a senior assistant at Mrs Newman's now. I don't know what she would do without me. Don't you think I can be having time off to traipse round Bideford with you while you're here. Mrs Newman relies on me so much. We have such a superior class of patrons you know. If I were to marry,' Lydia returned to the question in hand, 'he would have to be respectable. Maybe an older gentleman, or a widower perhaps, with a private income. One who wouldn't be interested in the beastly side of marriage.'

You were interested enough in that sort of thing last year when you were trying to catch Albert's eye after chapel, thought Polly. They had always been the least compatible of the Wakely sisters but the gap that separated Lydia's life and aspirations from Polly's was now wider than ever.

Despite Lydia's attitude, Polly's time in Bideford was every bit as enthralling as she had hoped. Lydia and their cousin Minnie were working at Mrs Newman's during the day but Athaliah, the cousin closest to Polly in age, had been allowed time off from helping her father in the shop to show Polly the town. The young women had gazed in the shop windows, admiring hats and haberdashery and strolled along the quay, watching the ships unloading. Athaliah insisted that their walks took them past Hopson's ironmongery. She even took Polly inside, pretending to take an interest in the array of brooms and brushes on display. In truth it was Mr Hopson's young assistant who had caught Athaliah's eye. He had blushed scarlet as the girls had entered the shop but he was punctiliously polite to the other customers, one of whom was being particularly difficult about a loose handle on a pan lid that she had purchased the previous week. Polly was not averse to furthering this budding romance. She quite approved of Frank Holwill, who lived up at Coldharbour, as a suitable person to walk out with the painfully shy Athaliah. Polly was confident enough to stand up to a domineering older sister such as Lydia and find her own role in the middle of a family of girls but Athaliah was constantly eclipsed by both older and younger, more vibrant, excitable sisters.

Tuesday brought market day, with its feverish hubbub and bustle. From early morning, eager sellers arrived with their produce, by rail, by cart, or with panniers slung across the back of a horse or a donkey. Farmers' wives walked to the town from the surrounding villages to sell eggs, cheese or succulent pies. The smell of the butchers' stalls with their carcasses of meat and hanging game, caught the throats of the more fastidious. Squawking chickens in stacked crates and the shouts of the stallholders, vied with the chatter of gossiping women and the squeals of children clamouring for sweetmeats. Even though Polly wasn't much interested in buying produce, she was captivated by the commotion and the intensity of the occasion. The fast-paced activity of so many people gathered together in one place was overawing. This was much better than the languid lifestyle of Peppercombe. She paused by a fish stall selling mackerel and wondered if somewhere on a stall, there lay fish that Albert had caught. Polly reprimanded herself. She really must not let thoughts of Albert intrude. This was the adventure and exhilaration she had craved. She wasn't going to let it go now. All she needed was employment. Polly studied notices in the shop windows as they roamed the town but found nothing suitable. She could hardly be a delivery boy or serve ale in the Newfoundland Inn on the quay. She would have to hope that there would be something amongst the advertisements in Friday's *Gazette* that would be her gateway to a new life.

Polly stirred early on her last day in Bideford. Friday already. She needed to find a good reason not to return home when her father called for her in the evening. She dressed quickly and descended to the kitchen at the back of the shop, where her aunt was stirring porridge. Uncle Prance was at the counter arranging the dried goods to his satisfaction and awaiting the delivery of crabs, lobsters, and shimmering bass to lay temptingly in the window. A young lad passed the doorway, whistling shrilly and drawing a newspaper from the hessian bag that was slung across his shoulder.

'*Gazette*'s in Mr Prance,' he called.

Joe Prance took the paper and set it to one side, ready for reading when he enjoyed his pipe after his mid-day meal. Polly glanced sideways at the front page, which displayed details of forthcoming auctions.

'May I look at the paper please uncle?' she asked.

'Don't know why you'd want to look at that,' he replied. 'Go ahead if youm a mind.'

Polly took the paper through to the back yard, where she would be undisturbed and fought the breeze as she tried to lay it flat on a broken wooden packing case. She turned the pages, heart racing, this was her last chance. She took a deep breath and drew her finger slowly down the columns. The *Western Gazette* wasn't really a local paper, it covered much of the south of England, so the likelihood of a nearby post being advertised was remote but it was worth a look. Reading was a laborious process for Polly but she worked her way through requests for dairymen and gardeners until she reached those beginning "Girls wanted". Yeovil. Bournemouth. Plenty needed in Bournemouth, wherever that was; this was hopeless. She glanced apprehensively at the back door. If she was much longer someone would come to find out what she was doing. Polly began to read countless pleas for general servants. One for a post in Barnstaple was encouraging, at least it was a place Polly had heard of. Finally, two adjacent adverts seeking servants in Bideford. One required the respondent to apply via the Miss Williams' Library. Polly wasn't sure where this was and it seemed unlikely that she would get a response that day, so she looked again at the other advertisement. "General Servant (good) wanted, who can do plain cooking; and a house parlourmaid. Chudleigh Villa, Bideford." Polly felt that plain cooking might be beyond her but house parlourmaid, perhaps.

Polly casually walked back through to the shop. Her uncle had turned the sign on the door to "open" and was busy weighing out raisins into a paper cone for the first customer of the day. Whilst he was diverted, Polly secreted a piece of brown wrapping paper and the stub of a thick pencil into the pocket of her apron. Hastening through to the back yard, she licked the end of the pencil, turning her lips purple and began to painstakingly copy out the details from the advert.

Ten minutes later, with her apron discarded and the newspaper returned to her uncle, Polly stepped out into the warm morning sunshine, bound for the newsagents to purchase a card. On her return, she went up to the room that she was sharing with her sister and two of her cousins. Fortunately, Lydia and Minnie had left for Mrs Newman's and Athaliah was running an errand for her mother, so Polly had the room to herself. Trying hard to keep her writing straight and neat, she wrote the address on one side of the card. On the reverse she carefully inscribed her uncle's address and the message, "I have been a housemaid for Mrs Pine-Coffin. I culd come this pm if it wuld suit," followed by her full name. Polly licked the rust coloured ha'penny stamp, wincing slightly at the sour taste of the gum on her tongue. Slipping back outside, pretending not to hear her aunt's enquiry as to where she was heading, Polly went to put the card in the letter box at the Post Office. The finality of its drop made Polly shiver with excitement-tinged nervousness. It might be early afternoon before a reply reached her. Now all she could do was wait. She needed something to quell her nerves, to take her mind off the enormity of her actions; perhaps she could take Hilda to feed the swans on the river.

Polly held tightly to Hilda's hand, as the little girl bounced and hopped up Mill Street, not pausing to glance in the shops. Hilda, not yet old enough for school, was delighted by the prospect of the individual attention and Aunt Susan was glad of a few hours reprieve from the lively child. Polly was beginning to find her way around the town by this time and she confidently guided Hilda down Bridgeland Street, unable to suppress a smile. Life was good. The pair passed Lavington Chapel and the imposing merchants' houses, as they headed towards the river. Polly's basket contained stale crusts of bread and pieces of broken biscuit for Hilda to cast upon the waters of the Torridge. If the swans were absent, there should be gulls who would accept the child's offerings. They crossed the small stream and went in search of birds for Hilda to feed.

The morning passed by surprisingly quickly and it was soon time for Polly to return an eagerly chattering Hilda to the shop for dinner. It was as Polly was helping Aunt Susan to clear the plates after their mid-day meal, that the postman called for the third time that day. Uncle Prance took the small pile of mail and Polly held her breath. A neat, white card, with an address embossed in blue, was at the bottom. Polly hadn't really thought about this part of the proceedings. Of course, any reply would be by card and cards would be read by whoever took in the post.

'What's all this then young Polly?' asked Uncle Prance.

Polly held her breath, awaiting the storm but her uncle was smiling genially.

'Seems a Mrs Powell wants to see you up at Chudleigh Villa. Have you been looking for a new place?'

Lydia, home from the dressmakers for her meal, looked up sharply and then glowered at Polly. Polly tried not to sound defensive.

'Mrs Pine-Coffin's away for the summer. I felt in need of a change,' she said.

'What's all this about the range?' asked Aunt Susan, who had missed most of the conversation.

'Change, mother,' bellowed her husband. 'Change. Young Polly here is going for a position over East-the-Water.'

Susan still looked blank.

'Is it live-in?' asked Lydia. 'Only I really don't think I can possibly share my bed if she's going to come back stinking of grease from doing dishes.'

'It didn't say,' replied Polly.

Her spirits plummeted, she knew full well that, if no scullery maid was kept, the duties of a house parlourmaid might extend to washing-up. She hadn't considered that the job might not come with accommodation.

'Typical,' barked Lydia. 'Why couldn't you just wait for the Pine-Coffins to come back? They are such a well-to-do family. Has anyone even heard of the Powells? Are they anybody? She doesn't come to Mrs Newman's for her gowns.'

Clearly, for Lydia, having a sister who was in service was only made bearable if the employers were the Lords of the Manor.

'Well, she wants you at 4.30pm,' said Uncle Prance, handing Polly the card. 'Should you send word to say you'll be going do you think? A card might just get there before you do.'

The heatwave of the last few weeks showed no sign of abating and as Polly made her way down Mill Street, she was shocked by the strength of the sun. It was hard to believe that it was only a few months since the area had been gripped by storms and snow. Polly knew that she would need to walk slowly if she was to arrive looking cool and neat. Lydia had, grudgingly, offered to lend Polly her second-best gown, which was an enviable shade of blue. Aunt Susan had vetoed this, saying it made Polly look as if she was trying to get above her station, so she was wearing her own serviceable poplin. Even though the hottest part of the day was over, its practical dark colour added to Polly's discomfort. Unusually, there was not a gasp of a breeze coming from the river as Polly turned to walk across Bideford bridge, narrowly avoiding the brewer's dray that was heavily laden with barrels for the inns on the quay.

The sight of the red-sailed boats on the river reminded Polly once again of Albert, whose day's fishing would now be over. Perhaps he would be mending pots or showing young Eadie how to gut fish. Polly smiled to herself. It was a strange relationship, that between the reserved young fisherman and the little girl who had been adopted into the family. It was reassuring to see that he was so good with young children. Polly shook herself. This was not the time for romantic notions. She was off to start a new and wonderful town life. The days of dreaming of courting humble fishermen were, if not abandoned, then at least put aside. She did wonder though if Albert would miss her if she secured this position and she was not in chapel on Sunday. That at least would be one thing that would please her mother. If Polly was to be working in Bideford, it would be difficult to nurture her burgeoning relationship with Albert.

Beginning the climb up past the station, Polly could hear the whistle of the approaching train and she caught a whiff of acrid steam on the still air. She passed under the railway bridge, glad of the momentary shade. Pigeons cooed from the metal girders above her head and Polly took care not to get their droppings on her boots. Aunt Susan knew Bideford well; Prance's handcarts and cycles could be seen all over the town, delivering to customers. Over the years, Aunt Susan had been responsible for ensuring that a succession of slightly scruffy delivery boys took a selection of dried goods to the correct destinations. Her aunt's instructions had been clear, Polly was to go across the bridge, walk past the Royal Hotel and the station, heading towards the old fort, then take a sharp left-hand turn to approach the large villas on the Chudleigh estate. Polly repeated the directions over and over in her head as she walked along. Although she had wandered around the main town of Bideford during the week, this side of the river, East-the-Water as the townsfolk called it, was new to her. The exertion of her walk on the hot afternoon, coupled with rising trepidation, set Polly's heart racing. She was beginning to appreciate the significance of what she had done and to wonder how she would pacify her father, who was expecting to collect her for the return journey to Peppercombe later that day.

The imposing villas at Chudleigh could be seen from the far side of the river. Polly had noticed them as they stood sentinel over the white-washed town below. As she drew nearer, they seemed even more intimidating. Polly was wondering which of the pair of cream-bricked houses in front of her was the Powells' when a telegraph boy emerged from the right-hand house and retrieved his bicycle from where it lay in the hedge.

'Are you lost miss?' he asked, seeing Polly's confusion.

'I'm to see Mrs Powell,' she said, 'but I don't know which house it is.'

'That's easy', said the boy. 'I've just delivered to the Reverend Roberts here, so the Powell's must be that one.' The boy pushed back his round cap to wipe his hand across his sweaty forehead, winked cheekily at Polly and pointed to the house to their left.

'Thank you,' responded Polly.

She was grateful but even aspiring house parlourmaids didn't engage telegraph boys in conversation. Her lips set primly, she walked towards the house with a purposeful step. She could hear the shrill whistling of the telegraph boy fading as she descended the area steps and knocked tentatively on the door to the lower ground floor. There was a long pause and Polly was wondering if she was, after all, in the wrong place, when the door opened. Much to Polly's surprise, the slightly faded woman in her forties who bade her come in, introduced herself as Mrs Powell. Mrs Powell was tall and thin with swept back, wispy, fair hair, and a harassed expression. She was dressed in the deep lilac of half-mourning. Polly knew, from having spent a week listening to Lydia's raptures about the latest fashions, that Mrs Powell's gown, although elegant, was not new. She followed Mrs Powell's erect back and tapping footsteps up the stairs and into an airy drawing room. Polly was invited to sit on a high-backed wooden chair with a hard, stuffed seat, covered in rough material. Wringing her hands nervously, Polly cleared her throat and glanced around the sparsely furnished room. There were faded patches on the brocade wallpaper, as if pictures had recently been removed. On the piano in the corner was a large bowl of roses and a photograph of a young girl, in a heavy silver frame. Mrs Pine-Coffin would be horrified, thought Polly, one of her earliest lessons at Portledge had been that, on no account, should anything be set upon the piano. Faint echoes of children's voices could be heard from the upper floors and Polly wished that she weren't so hot. She fidgeted in her chair as she waited anxiously for Mrs Powell to begin. Polly did not know what to expect. She hadn't been interviewed for her post at Portledge, it had been enough that her mother was known because she helped out when the Pine-Coffins had guests and needed additional staff.

'We have no servants at present,' Mrs Powell said. 'We were to have employed two, as the advertisement stated but errr, ummm, circumstances', Mrs Powell spoke the word "circumstances" as if it were in capital letters, 'have dictated that there will be only one.'

Polly was too naïve to find it odd that a family who were clearly gentry should currently have no servants but her heart sank, if there was only to be a cook, then she would not be taken on.

'We are looking for a house parlourmaid, who might perhaps manage cooking nursery teas,' Mrs Powell was saying. 'Mr Powell often eats at his club and when he does not, I will prepare the food for the dining room. A daily will come in to do the rough and we hire a cook to help out when we entertain.'

Polly felt that some form of response was required.

'How many children are there in the nursery ma'am?' she asked, for want of anything else to say.

A shadow passed across Mrs Powell's face, as if recalling some sadness. She glanced at the piano. 'Just the two younger girls, Rosamund and Margaret, now that Frances eats with us,' she said. 'William is away at school in term time. You will find the girls very quiet and biddable. They go to the Misses Ley's School in Bridgeland Street, although Frances will leave in a few weeks.'

Polly stood up hastily as a gentleman breezed into the room. His red face and bulbous nose reminded Polly of Mr Punch in half-remembered childhood puppet shows. She sketched a bob as Mrs Powell introduced her husband. Captain Powell was affable but old, as old as Polly's father. He studied her appraisingly then walked to the sideboard and poured himself a generous glass of wine, before returning to his own affairs elsewhere in the house.

Polly accepted that she knew very little about how servants might be interviewed but the conversation that followed over the next twenty minutes was curious. It was almost as if Mrs Powell was trying to persuade Polly to take the post, rather than assessing her suitability. Surely, thought Polly, there should be questions about her previous experience and explanations of exactly what the post entailed. She hadn't even been asked for a character. Polly had been worried about her lack of a written reference from her time at Portledge. The need to keep her impending departure a secret meant that Polly had not dared to ask the Pine-Coffins to recommend her. It was all too likely that, had she done so, her mother would have got to hear. Mrs Powell's apparent lack of interest in Polly's former employment, averted this potential difficulty. Polly nodded and yes ma'amed in what she hoped were the right places. The post was live-in, Mrs Powell explained. Polly tried to hide the relief from her face. That will please Lydia, she thought, with a wry smile.

'I will show you the room', Mrs Powell said and led Polly up the narrow servants' staircase to a room under the eaves.

It was stiflingly hot and a fly buzzed incessantly as it banged against the dusty window. A narrow brass bedstead, with a flowered chamber pot peeping out from under the worn but clean counterpane, took up most of the space. There was a wooden chair and a small chest, that did duty as a wash-stand. A strip of rag rug covered the worn floorboards. Mrs Powell was apologising for the size of the room, as if Polly was a prospective tenant, not a servant. The room was at the back of the house and as Polly glanced through the grimy glass, she caught a glimpse of the river, with the town rising up beyond. Surely, Polly thought, Mrs Powell would not have shown her the room if she was not to be taken on. The room was wonderful and it would be all her own. Polly had never had a bed to herself before, a whole room was beyond imagination.

'When would you be able to start?' Mrs Powell asked.

'I would need to go home to collect my things', said Polly, thinking quickly. 'I could walk back with my father on Sunday evening if that would suit.'

'Indeed, you could commence your duties on Monday.'

The area door shut behind Polly as she left the house. She took a deep breath and rested back against the peeling paintwork for a few seconds, pausing to savour the moment. Had she really managed to find a job? She wanted to sing, to run, as she had when she was a child, to call out her good news to the unsuspecting passers-by. She struggled to walk sedately up the drive, to assume the decorum that befitted a newly employed parlourmaid. Turning, Polly looked back at what was to become her home, the arched windows gave the façade a benign air. Polly smiled. Those who had taunted her at school had claimed that the Wakelys could tell fortunes, had the sight, passed down from their gypsy ancestors. It was all nonsense of course but just this once, as she was about to begin a new life, Polly wished that she could see what awaited her.

3
1892-1893

Polly felt a child's chilly hand slip into her own; the thin silk gloves were no protection from the wind blowing up from the river. Margaret, sombrely clad and fighting back tears, gripped Polly's fingers tightly. She watched as her mother placed a bunch of rusty chrysanthemums on the long, wet grass in front of a forlorn gravestone. The name, Florence Louisa Powell, was deeply incised in the slate; a short life marked by the stark dates 1877-1890. The family was paying homage at this tangible reminder of a daughter, of a sister, who was forever frozen in time.

Polly dreaded the monthly ritual that saw the Powell family walk solemnly up to the new burial ground, to honour their dead child. The whole household were expected to join in the ceremony at the graveside. The two years since Florence's passing had done nothing to assuage her mother's heartache; Mrs Powell's crushing grief was palpable. Captain Powell endured the proceedings, aided by the imbibing of several stiff whiskies beforehand. Polly had learned to replenish the decanters on the sideboard before and after these visits. William was frankly bored, he barely remembered his sister. His mother's unbecoming public show, after all this time, was an embarrassment. He kicked at the gravel on the path and had to be reminded to remove his hands from his pockets. Frances and Rosamund assumed an air of sadness but in reality, were too self-absorbed to do more than give their departed sister a fleeting moment's attention. Young Margaret though, found these expeditions especially distressing. She had been seven when the rheumatic fever laid its sinister hand on Florence; old enough to be bereft but too young to understand. Florence had been the first person to be laid to rest in the new graveyard and Polly knew that Margaret fretted that her sister might be lonely up on the hill, away from her family, in the sparse cemetery. For Margaret, each freshly-dug grave was a relief, a signal that Florence had a new companion.

Polly had grown close to Margaret, the youngest of the Powell children. Frances was quite a young lady, only four years Polly's junior but the obligatory barrier between servant and served prevented any familiarity. Margaret though, was as yet untrammelled by the social superiority that had been acquired by her older sisters. On several occasions since her arrival at Chudleigh Villa, Polly had been woken by Margaret creeping into the room; the child shaken by unspeakable nightmares and seeking reassurance. Gradually, as Polly gained Margaret's confidence, the little girl shared the fragmented memories of her sister's last weeks. She was haunted by visions of Florence jerking and trembling as she lay shaven-headed on the chaise, striving to shake off the effects of the fever that had weakened her heart beyond repair.

Her time at Portledge meant that Polly was used to the habits of rich folk. She was well aware that it was customary for parents and children to live in such a way that their paths rarely crossed. Yet Polly had swiftly realised that Mrs Powell's demeanour in the presence of her children was unusually dismissive, even for the gentry. There was something too about the formality of the cemetery visits that was disquieting. Grief was normal, losing a child was a great sadness but Mrs Powell's absorption with her dead daughter, to the exclusion of her surviving children, was unnerving. Frances, nearing adulthood, was expected to spend most of her day in the morning room, embroidering, or painting delicate, floral watercolours that Polly much admired. Mrs Powell sat in solitude in the drawing room and rarely acknowledged Frances. When Rosamund and Margaret came back from Misses Ley's school each day, their presence was a sobering reminder of the aching void left by Florence. The girls were encouraged to scuttle upstairs to the nursery and remain there until bedtime. That way, their mother could forget that she now had three daughters, when once there had been four.

The autumn was the worst, the shortening of the days marked both Florence's birthday and the anniversary of her death. This year, as soon as the rites at the cemetery were over, Mrs Powell took to her bed with the vapours. The children tiptoed round the house, terrified of exacerbating their mother's anxiety. Mr Powell spent increasing hours at his club. Polly would hear him returning home late at night, occasionally stumbling and uttering expletives as he crashed into the furniture. Each day, Polly brought more wine bottles up from the cellar and the drawing room decanters depleted with alarming rapidity.

Taking some smelling salts upstairs to her prostrate mistress, Polly was alarmed to hear a desperate weeping from behind the door. She hesitated and waited for the sobs to subside before knocking. Responding to her mistress' whispered command, she entered. Mrs Powell looked at her through swollen eyelids.

'Do you have a sweetheart?' she asked.

'No ma'am,' replied Polly, guiltily disregarding the vision of Albert and wondering why Mrs Powell should pose such a question.

The words tumbled from the tormented woman, 'Never have children. Never love a child. You get too close and they're taken from you; then there's no escape from the heartbreak.'

The prospect of parenthood had been in Polly's thoughts of late. Despite her move to Bideford, her carefully nurtured relationship with Albert had grown into a vital part of her life. She hugged the secret to her, recalling the first Sunday she had returned to Peppercombe, after taking up her post with the Powells. She had managed to have a long conversation with Albert, as they lingered on the way home from chapel, somehow shaking off Polly's younger sisters. Despite Polly's determination to lead a new life in Bideford, they had come to an understanding. Since then, Polly and Albert snatched brief meetings when she visited her parents and lately, Albert had taken to walking out to Bideford to see her when he could. Polly was struck by the power of Mrs Powell's words. This fleeting exchange pierced her consciousness, casting an enduring shadow over the prospect of her future with Albert.

The spring brought hope. Polly enjoyed walking with Albert through the woods beyond Bank End. They marvelled at the snowdrops, the primroses, the fluffy catkins and delicate wood anemones. Polly was glad to get away from Chudleigh Villa; Mrs Powell's sorrow stifled them all. The Captain's army friends came to visit and Polly would have to serve sherry or brandy whilst they became increasingly jovial before descending into irritability. The Captain's drinking did nothing to lighten the mood and aroused the wrath of his wife. Polly, going quietly about her duties, would hear raised voices as Mrs Powell complained and her husband blustered. Then the door would crash yet again, as he left the house for the more congenial atmosphere of his club. Polly tried not to eavesdrop but sometimes it was impossible not to overhear.

'But we've not the money Thomas, you know we haven't. Goodness knows, we should be comfortably off. You sold your commission and frittered it all away. Two thousand five hundred pounds Thomas, a small fortune, enough to set us up for life, all gone. It was a blessing that your mother came to our aid. We wouldn't have this house if it weren't for her.'

'It was my right Emily, you know I got nothing from my father's estate.'

'No. And why was that do you think? Because he knew it would all be gambled away. I've sold all the pictures and the good silver. There's nothing of any value left. Even the beds we sleep in belong to your mother. It isn't fair on the children. Frances should be at finishing school but no, she's here all day with nothing to occupy her but her painting. We can't afford to bring her out, so she doesn't meet anyone suitable. She's destined to be an old maid. I've given the Misses Ley notice that Rosamund will leave at Easter. It is far earlier than she should but we can't afford to keep her there. At least we are saving on William's schooling now he is taking lessons from Reverend Roberts.'

Official looking letters arrived, letters that Polly would place on the papier-mâché tray that had replaced the silver one. This she would hand to Captain Powell who would glance at the envelopes and toss them, unopened, in the wastepaper basket. Then furtive looking men would call, asking for the Captain. Polly had been instructed to say that he was not at home. Fortunately, she was rarely obliged to lie, as her employer spent as much time away from the house as he could. More rows ensued. The atmosphere became unbearable. Polly found herself flinching at every harsh word, every door slammed. Shouldering their problems as if they were her own, she became increasingly unhappy. She had been here nearly two years now, she could go back to Peppercombe without any sense of failure but the thought of abandoning Margaret prevented her from giving notice.

The drawing room door was ajar. The Powells' words clearly carried to where Polly was polishing the hall floor.

'Court, Thomas. The shame of it. We shall never hold our heads up again. We've already had to leave Plymouth and then Tavistock. Now we shall have to move away from Bideford as well. Only this time it means leaving Florence. I cannot bear the thought of that.'

Above Mrs Powell's sobs, Polly could hear the decanter clashing against the glass and the glug of the whisky being poured.

Ignoring his wife's distress, Captain Powell responded unfeelingly, 'I quite fancy a change of scene. I wouldn't want to return to Plymouth of course but Portsmouth perhaps, or Southampton.'

Mrs Powell regained her composure and resumed her tirade, 'Why couldn't you just have found enough to pay off Mr Tardrew? If you'd only done that, all this might have been avoided. Then there's that money you owe to Tanton's Hotel, how could you have run up such a bill? Your mother has been more than generous, we should be able to live comfortably on the three hundred pounds a year that she gives us. What on earth will she think? We cannot expect her to keep making us an allowance if you are such a spendthrift. It is no wonder that your brother has washed his hands of you.'

'What's done is done, eh Emily,' Captain Powell replied. 'Like as not I shall be declared bankrupt again.

It will be as it was when I first left the army. Mother will come up trumps, she always does.'

Her husband's inability to take their plight seriously frustrated her.

'Can't you see Thomas, she shouldn't have to. What kind of man lives off his mother? I should have listened to my father. He said you had no prospects but I was a foolish girl who had her head turned by a man in uniform. I thought things would change when we moved away from all your cronies at the barracks but I should have known better. You will always be profligate. I try to run the household as economically as possible, making do with just one servant and there you are, off to Tanton's Hotel again playing cards. Then there is your drinking. I am happy for you to entertain your gentlemen friends here. I thought it preferable to you frequenting the club but then I chanced to go to the cellar because Polly was unsure which wine to bring to the table and I find we have only a few bottles left. You must have been very liberal with your hospitality. Then, when you are in drink, you enter into more rash bets.'

'Now Emily, I won quite a sum just last night, you know I did and the atmosphere is convivial. A man needs the company of other fellows.'

Mrs Powell's sign of exasperation was audible, even to Polly.

'That's not the point Thomas. You may have won yesterday but think of all the times when you have lost. It seems you can't even play a hand of bridge without gambling heavily on the outcome.'

Polly gathered up her polishing cloths and moved so that she could no longer hear the angry exchanges. It sounded as if the family might leave Bideford. In a way it would be a relief if her post came to an end. Regardless of how much she wanted to be able to comfort Margaret, working for the Powells was becoming intolerable.

Albert and Polly sat in the shelter on the northern edge of Bideford quay, looking across the river towards Chudleigh Fort. The occasional cart rattled by, as it turned the corner past the Science and Art School. In a few months, the heat would make sitting on the edge of the marshes unpleasant but in early March, with the faint spring sunshine rending the high white clouds, they were content with this as a meeting place. Polly poured out her concerns to the young fisherman who sat decorously beside her. She had been unsettled by the upheaval of Captain Powell's trial.

"Tidn't right that you be there any longer. 'Tis upsetting ee,' said Albert. "Tis time we be wed. We've waited long enough.'

'What'll your ma and da say?' asked Polly. 'I know they aren't best pleased that we be walkin' out.'

'Nor your folks neither,' replied Albert. 'They believe all that fierce Spaniard nonsense.'

'I don't think they'd be happy, whoever we'd chosen,' said Polly, sagely. 'They just want us to bide at home, with nothin' changin'.'

'Seems, as you get older, you forgets what 'tis like to be young.'

'Will my da give his say so, do you think?' asked Polly. 'I can't be wed without his permission. I just want to get away from the Powells. 'Tis proper miserable up there, what with Mrs Powell weeping for Florence, that gets no better. Then there's all this trouble with Captain Powell being up in court. There's no money for anything. I doubt they can afford to keep me on much longer in any case.'

'We will be wed afore long,' reassured Albert. 'Don't fret about your da. You'll soon turn twenty one, 'tis not long to wait, then none can gainsay us. Yes, that's it, sometime after Easter it'll be, as soon as we can get everything arranged.'

In the end, they settled for the Saturday after Whitsun. Polly gave notice and Mrs Powell expressed regret but barely disguised her relief at the thought of a wage saved and one fewer mouth to feed. Forsaking their home villages, Albert and Polly married at Bideford's Bethesda Chapel. Their parents, still mildly disapproving, stayed away but they were not lacking family to watch them exchange their vows. Albert's brother Fred stood up for him and Polly had her sister Ada and cousin Athaliah as bridal attendants. Athaliah had finally broken through Frank Holwill's reserve and she too was to be married later that year. In the few days before the wedding, Polly returned to Mill Street to stay with the Prances and the cousins chatted excitedly about their plans, jokingly comparing the merits of their sweethearts.

Ada arrived from Peppercombe on the Friday bringing family news.

'Ma sends her love,' she said. 'She wishes you well, 'tis in part the journey, you know she's never liked the town. 'Tisn't that ma hasn't taken to Albert so much but he is from Bucks and that's hard for her to swallow. She wants us all to settle down in Peppercombe and not go no further.'

'And shall you?' asked Polly.

Ada reddened.

'Well,' she said hesitantly, 'who knows? Maybe I'll be wed to a man from Bucks too one day.'

'Oh,' replied Polly, curious now. 'Who might that be then?'

''Tis too soon to say,' said Ada, 'but there's one who's shown an interest.'

Polly was saddened that her father was not going to see her as a bride. Unlike her ma, he could not use the journey as an excuse. He still walked in to Waters' boatyard each week. If their ma wanted the five Wakely sisters to marry Peppercombe lads, it seemed that their da didn't want them to marry at all. No one would ever be good enough in his eyes. Nonetheless, he called in to see Polly after finishing his week's work and pressed coins in her hand.

'I'll not be there maid,' he said. 'Always vowed I'd not set foot in any chapel but a Bible Christian one and I be too old to change my ways now.'

So it was Uncle Joe who walked Polly up the aisle. Aunt Susan had puffed round the corner from Mill Street at the last minute, not wanting to leave young Willie minding the shop alone for longer than was necessary. Lydia had claimed she was unable to get the morning off from Mrs Newman's but Polly knew better. Lydia still sought the rich, older gentleman of her dreams and was resentful of a younger sister beating her to the altar.

Reverend Page pronounced them man and wife. Polly's gold-flecked eyes looked up to Albert, where he stood at her side, tall and reassuring. She was relieved to be sharing her life with a man who was so very different from her reckless, unreliable employer. Their families had foresworn strong drink years ago and Albert would no more think of gambling than he would of jumping from the parapet of Bideford Bridge. Polly had found her safe harbour.

Young Hilda, now a grave five year old, proudly preceded the couple out of the chapel after the ceremony. Polly looked wistfully at the wilting foxgloves that the child carried in a wicker basket. She was glad to have spent these past two years in Bideford. It had opened her eyes to the wider world but now she longed to be back in a place where the wildflowers bloomed and she could breathe the country air.

Polly's time at Chudleigh Villa had left its mark. It was not principally the fear of the effects of alcohol,

Polly's temperance upbringing had already ingrained this in her. Although she shrank from the thought of debt, women of Polly's class were used to conserving coins and took pride in living within their means, regardless of the personal cost. The deepest scar that she carried with her from the old life to the new was the dread of allowing herself to love a child.

4
1894-1909

Polly was watching the chaotic clouds and the unceasing rain that pounded uncaringly on the pitted panes. Mrs Hamlyn had promised that the windows would be replaced but for now, the scratched glass, in its rotting frame, rattled and clanged with each succeeding gust. On the shore, sea-birds huddled on cliff-side niches, with their backs to the storm, feathers ruffled and chicks fledged. All week, the restless fishermen had watched gloomily, unable to check their pots for the sea's bounty, much needed during this poor summer. The storms of the past weeks had left them landside all too often and shore-bound tasks were done. Purposeless, they yarned under the shelter of the archway outside the Red Lion or plagued wives, already short-tempered and strained from eking out meagre supplies.

Polly had been pleased when Alb had announced that their first home together should be in Clovelly, a bustling fishing village just along the coast from Bucks Mills. It was only fitting that they should strike out on their own and not live under the oppressing eye of their families. All the cottages that straggled up Clovelly's cobbled street were owned by

Mrs Hamlyn. Her husband, Frederick, was a shadowy consort, it was she who held the power. Albert was used to fishing alongside the Clovelly boats, so, anxious for independence, he had sought an audience with Mrs Hamlyn's land agent, Mr Caird, enquiring if there was a suitable home available in the village. They had been granted the opportunity of renting the two-roomed cottage known as Rat's Castle. This tiny dwelling near the quay was reserved for newly-weds and it had suited them well for the past year. Now, with the impending arrival of their first child, they had moved to a larger cottage, near the Methodist Chapel. Albert was content working his fishing boat from Clovelly; putting out from the shelter of the harbour was preferable to the unforgiving Bucks Mills' shoreline. Here, if necessary, he could handle a boat alone. Usually though, he fished with his brother Fred, who had joined him in the move. Fred was unmarried still but he had settled in the Bow, with their distant cousin Eli. Albert was pleased to have his brother close at hand, reassured that young Eadie was firmly ensconced in Rose Cottage to lighten the lives of their parents.

Polly had not found it a wrench to leave Bideford; she had tired of the busyness of town life. She had had her adventure, it was time to settle down. The force of Mrs Powell's dire warnings had receded; Polly was ready to be a mother now. As her pregnancy advanced, Polly longed for companionship, for a confidante. The days dragged whilst Albert was at sea. She wished that one of her sisters was nearer to hand. It could not be the supercilious Lydia, who was still revelling in her senior post at Mrs Newman's, nor the retiring Jane, who would be flustered and nervous when Polly's time came. So, in the end, it was Ada who came out from Peppercombe, to help with the move to Chapel Street and to aid her elder sister in the final weeks of her confinement. Ada, at eighteen, was old enough to be a real support, a reassurance, as Polly embarked on the uncharted pathway towards motherhood. Not having had a child herself, it would not be seemly for Ada to help with the delivery, so it was agreed that, as soon as Polly's first pains started, Eliza Wakely would put aside her reluctance to leave Peppercombe and come to oversee the birth of her first grandchild. Polly and Albert's parents had mellowed with the news of impending grandparenthood. Both sides of the family were now reconciled to the spouse that their offspring had chosen.

The old women had been gnashing their gums and nodding wisely for weeks, commenting that Polly was carrying well. It must be a boy, no, it must be a girl. Ada had brought strict instructions from their mother; Polly was to walk a little each day. So, despite the weather, the sisters took regular strolls down to the quay. Worrying though the cool summer was, at least Polly was spared the heat as she hauled her heavy body from shore to home. Polly and Ada busied themselves with preparations for the baby. Napkins were cut from rough towelling and diminutive nightgowns were smocked. Polly's father had fashioned a cradle and Lydia had sent impractical embroidered coverlets.

Poor weather deterred the tourists, although the fitful sunshine on Bank Holiday Monday encouraged resolute visitors, hopeful that the clouds would disperse.

Albert spent the day bringing trippers ashore from the steamers that were moored beyond the bay. They arrived from Bristol, from Cardiff and from along the coast in Ilfracombe, adding to those who had journeyed by charabanc from Bideford railway station. They were eager to see Clovelly's quaint cobbles and to gawk at the residents, as if they were there on show for the sole benefit of the holidaymakers.

The stormy summer crawled on and Polly lurched from excited expectation to restive boredom. As harvest time approached, a throbbing pressure in the small of her back developed into a constant ache and Polly forewent her usual Sunday chapel attendance. She huddled inside, wondering how many more days it would be before she could cradle her first-born. Albert went to haul his lobster pots as the Monday dawn broke. Polly smiled when she saw him off but barely managed to disguise a grimace, as discomfort gave way to pain. Polly knew that it was time to send her sister scurrying with the message that would bring their mother. So here she was, watching the rain, trying to ignore the pains that were gripping her and hoping that her mother would reach Clovelly in time.

When Eliza arrived, early in the afternoon, Polly had taken to her bed, with Ada hovering anxiously around her. Thunder threatened. The sky dulled and the birds ceased to sing. The wind had dropped and a bronze shimmer streaked the sea. Albert had sensed the impending storm and come ashore in good time but Eliza soon dispatched him down to his brother's. Men were superfluous to this task. Ada was relegated to the kitchen where she was to ensure that water was boiling and towels were ready.

Beads of sweat spotted Polly's brow. The window was fastened, in case she should cry out and the neighbours might hear her. The room was stifling. Polly clenched her teeth, determined not to scream and gripped the knotted sheet that her mother had strung between the bed posts. The humidity consumed her. No longer could she focus on the anticipated pleasure of holding her baby. Her whole world was a wrenching agony and somewhere on the edge of consciousness, her mother's voice was telling her to bear down. A primeval instinct invaded her unwilling body and Polly prepared to give birth to her child.

The day had darkened into evening before a reedy wail was heard. Ada looked up. The intensity of her sister's labours had sobered her. Perhaps she would think again about encouraging the advances of Albert's cousin, George, if this was how bad it was. Polly seemed happy but maybe marriage and childbearing were not for everyone. Her mother came down the stairs, blood-stained sheets in one hand and a lidded bucket in the other.

'Tis a girl,' she said, 'and both doing well. You'd best nip down to the Bow and tell Albert. If I know men, he'll have been unable to settle down there. Pol could do with a tidy up, you can see her and the chile when youm back.'

Albert was transfixed by the swaddled bundle in his wife's arms. He gently stroked his daughter's reddened cheek. He was concerned by the mis-shappen head, barely disguised by the cloud of dark hair. Polly saw his expression and was quick to reassure him.

"Twill right in a day or so, ma says. She's a lusty cry on her, there's naught to worry about.'

They sat in silence for a few moments, overawed by the untouched innocence of the child that they had created.

'What will we call her?' asked Polly. 'Folk will expect Mary, or Eliza perhaps but I want her to have a name that's hers alone.'

Albert recalled how Polly loved walking amongst the flower-strewn woods above the village. 'How about Violet?' he said, 'or Primrose?'

'She's so new, so clean,' said Polly, 'if 'tis to be a flower, it should be a white one.'

'Lily then,' suggested Albert. 'No, Daisy, that should be it, pure and starry but not too fragile, more robust like. What do you think?'

'Yes, Daisy,' said Polly contentedly, "tis just right.'

Polly was fighting exhaustion now, it had been a hard labour, though not excessively long for a first.

'She'll grasp your finger if you let her,' she said.

Albert pushed his roughened finger into the tiny fist. He knew a moment of absolute, untainted love, as the miniature fingers curled round his own. Just for an instant the baby revealed the night-blue eyes of the newborn, before slipping into a doze once more. He'd felt affection for young Eadie, had been keen to protect her but nothing, nothing had prepared him for this. He vowed that Daisy should want for naught, that he would shelter this precious mite from all that might befall her; his role now was to defend his daughter from harm.

These were the happy years, free from fear. On Daisy's third birthday, Leonard was born. Again Polly had resolved to avoid family names. She relented with her second boy, calling him after his father but the child was always known as Bertie. Albert was content with his sons and looked forward to handing down the lore of past generations and teaching them the ways of the sea. 1903, another summer, another baby and Violet joined Daisy in the family posy of flowers. Daisy had grown into a leggy child, often roaming the Clovelly street alone, self-reliant and inscrutable. Mr Hamlyn breathed his last but the Clovelly villagers were largely untouched by his passing. Mrs Hamlyn, matriarchal and resolute, abandoned mourning and embarked on a programme of restoration of the Clovelly cottages. Polly took pride in her newly refurbished home and in her growing brood. The wider family expanded too; Fred was married now, with children of his own and two years ago, Ada had put aside her reservations and finally married George, although there was, as yet, no sign of a pregnancy for her.

Especially in summer's balmy days, Clovelly schoolchildren forwent the pull of fried fish and floury potatoes, in favour of bread and scrape wrapped in waxed paper. This they would take down to the rocky shore and they would spend the dinner break skimming stones, or, stripped naked, the boys would dare each other to leap off the end of the quay into the retreating waves. By some unexplained instinct they would be aware when their freedom was nearly at an end and by the time the raucous school bell rang out over the valley, they would be dressed and ready to hurtle up the cobbles back to the unwelcome shelter of the schoolhouse. Being first to reach the school door, held open by Miss Lott, was one of the small triumphs of childhood. They would settle on to the uncomfortable forms, ranked according to their relative abilities and pass sunny afternoons resentfully, longing to be freed from the classroom's restraints. Leonard tolerated his lessons, giving them just enough attention to ensure that he escaped the wrath of his teacher. Bertie struggled with schoolwork but his cheerful disposition won him friends. Daisy sat with Alice, from the Red Lion, with Mary and with Bella, although Bella's sharp tongue could make her an uncomfortable playmate. Occasionally, someone would recall that Daisy's ma had been born a Wakely and everyone knew what they said about the Wakelys. Daisy and her brothers were largely impervious to the gypsy taunts. Those who mocked, moved on to softer targets like Abraham Tuke, who could be relied upon to take their bait. A tall, scholarly boy, with thick glasses, Abraham was the archetypal victim but the intellect that provided his persecutors with ammunition eventually led to success in a scholarship and removed him from their orbit.

Baby Mark lay gurgling contentedly in the wooden cradle, as his siblings had before him. He had lost the wrinkles and redness of the newborn. Two girls and three boys, Polly thought, with a self-satisfied smile and she was still young yet. Maybe there would be others in the years to come; others to tug at her heartstrings and bring her such joy. How ridiculous Mrs Powell had been, motherhood was fulfilling, pleasurable, not something to be feared. During the school day, there was only Violet and now the new baby, Mark, for Polly to care for. Bertie was coming to the end of his first year under the care of Miss Hazard. Daisy was stolidly studious, winning awards for attendance and enjoying her studies as she and Leonard moved into the higher standards with Miss Lott in charge. Miss Lott was more severe than Miss Hazard but unfailingly fair and keen that her charges should be well prepared for whatever their futures might hold.

Deep brown, fresh caught prawns jumped on the oil-cloth as Polly filled the bucket to be taken down and sold to the Red Lion. A few more catches like this and there would be enough coins in the pot on the mantleshelf for Alb to buy a better boat. He hankered for a ledge boat, such as they used at Bucks Mills, preferring it to the heavier picarooner favoured by the Clovelly men. Polly looked up at her husband.

'There's nigh on three pounds ten in the pot now,' she said. 'You could send word to Philip Waters, over to Appledore. By the time the boat's ready, us'll have enough.'

Polly was always careful that they had sufficient money ready for rent day. Albert trusted her to ensure that they did not get in to debt, not an easy task when a fisherman's income was so uncertain. He knew that she remembered Mrs Powell's anguish and fretted when their savings ran low. The carefully harvested shillings in the brown jug were their nest-egg, something to fall back on in hard times.

"Twill not be for long Pol,' he assured her. 'The fishin's been good of late, so I'll soon earn enough to pay it back.'

Polly cut a thick, uneven slice from the loaf that she held close to her waist. She wielded the knife in a sideways motion, sawing the sharp blade back and forth towards her own body but Albert was not alarmed, this was her normal habit. She smeared a generous dab of dripping across the rough surface and handed it to her husband with a smile, thankful that Alb was such a good provider. She had chosen well.

By the time the message came to say that the boat was ready, Polly was able to give her husband a pile of florins and half crowns to take to Appledore. Albert left early to walk the fourteen miles to the ship-builders' yard. Strapped to his back was a pair of oars, he would need those for the return journey. Polly's father had worked for Philip Waters for years, this would be a sturdy boat that would suffice for as long as Albert was able to put out to sea. He had years left to him yet, his grandfather had hauled pots until he was in his eighties and was still hand lining until his death, a few years ago.

True to his word, Albert proudly rowed the new boat back from Appledore and worked her for the week. The mackerel were running well and the lobster were plentiful that year. By the Saturday, Albert solemnly returned four pounds to Polly to be placed back in the jug, insurance against the unknown calamities of the future.

No family remains untouched by pain. Albert and Polly's pleasure, as their third son grew to toddlerhood, was tempered by the death of Albert's father. Then there were worries over Bertie, as Miss Hazard took them to one side and explained how he was struggling, even on the lowest form of the infants' class. Despite this, the summer of 1907 began well, school books were set aside until September and Polly's children, along with their classmates, basked in their liberty. Visitors crowded into the Red Lion and the New Inn, guest houses hung out their "no vacancies" signs and queues formed outside the tea-shops. Leonard enjoyed the long school holiday fishing with his father, he was no longer a hindrance but old enough now to bait pots and gut fish. Even Bertie earned a few coppers holding the donkeys that waited uncomplainingly, ready to carry the next burden up the street.

Daisy was a child of the season, delighting in the heat and the chance to discard her boots in favour of skipping over the cobbles in her bare feet. She loved the feel of the hard stones as she curled her toes round each pebble, like a bird poised for flight. Then she would take

70

off down the hill, her bonnet bobbing on her shoulders as it slipped back from her head. That was when Polly's heart was fullest, watching the joy of her exuberant, elfin child. No one could call Daisy pretty, her skin was too sallow and her hair was too dark but her tawny eyes and her cautious smile were arresting. A visiting photographer, attracted by her difference, persuaded Daisy to pose, fetching water from the village pump, sitting dreaming amongst the hollyhocks and smiling up at Samuel Harris, as he stood smoking his pipe outside the cottage next to Daisy's own. As she reached her thirteenth birthday, Daisy was unable to define her feelings for Samuel but the married fisherman found the innocent schoolgirl crush mildly amusing.

The harvest was all but over, aided by a long dry spell. The newspapers began to report record temperatures and all but the hardiest sought shade. Polly opened every window in the cottage, seeking the elusive breeze. Bertie tucked in to his usual breakfast of fried bacon but the heat suppressed the appetites of the other children. Daisy listlessly picked at her portion and Polly agreed that Leonard could leave food on his plate and head off up to the cooling woods. She persuaded Mark to take some milk-soaked bread but Violet ate nothing. The child complained of stomach ache. Polly dismissed this, blaming the heat and the cream that was on the turn.

As the sweltering day unfolded, it became clear that Violet was unwell. The usually contented four year old grizzled and grumbled of pains in her joints and her chest. She sat at the table with her head on her folded arms. It was airless in the girls' room under the thatch but Polly thought Violet would be better lying on top of the counterpane, perhaps with a damp flannel to cool her head. As the child struggled to her feet, her nose began to bleed copiously. Polly rushed for a towel but Violet's smock was ruined. Polly would put it to soak in salt water but the stain would remain.

The next days were a frenzy of fear, as Violet lay, feverish and lethargic, in the bed that she shared with Daisy. Daisy squeezed in with the boys, so that Violet was undisturbed but still the little girl whimpered and moaned. Reluctantly, they sent for Dr Ackland, whose solemnity betrayed the seriousness of Violet's condition.

'I am afraid your little girl has rheumatic fever,' he said. 'With careful nursing and plenty of rest you should pull her through but I have to warn you that, even if she recovers, her heart will be damaged and she will never be strong.'

Rheumatic fever. The words were an icy brand. It was rheumatic fever that had stolen Florence Powell and left her family bereft. For the first time, Polly began to comprehend what Mrs Powell had meant when she said that having children could bring intolerable heartache. Echoes of Margaret's tortured accounts of her sister's last days reverberated round the cottage in Chapel Street. In Polly's quiet moments, unbidden visions of the lonely memorial in Bideford's new cemetery intruded.

The birthday that Daisy and Leonard shared went unmarked, as Polly devoted all her energy to caring for Violet. She wept when they had to crop the child's hair to allay the fever. Daisy's straight wisps struggled to grow past her shoulders but Violet's thick, dark locks reached almost to her waist. There was no need to wind her hair in rags on a Saturday night, to encourage the ringlets that Sunday chapel dictated. In the end, it was Albert who wielded the heavy scissors; Polly did not have the heart for it. Unseen, she secreted a curl in the back of a drawer; a brave reminder of the sparkling, prattling little girl who now seemed lost to them.

With aching slowness, Violet began to improve. Gradually the child was able to sit up in bed for longer periods, she began to take light meals but the mildest exertion tired her. She might never be able to join the others at the school at Wrinkleberry. Perhaps, thought Polly, she should not have been so complacent. Forever now, if things went well, she would be dreading that the scales would once again tip out of their favour, bringing more anguish and anxiety.

The birth of a fourth son, Nelson, in the summer of 1908, sent Polly's spirits soaring. Perhaps it was a reaction to the year of worry over Violet but somehow Polly felt closer to Nelson than she had to any of her other babies. He was a contented child, whose toothless smile made all seem right with the world. Although she was not yet able to walk more than a few yards without becoming breathless, Violet was growing stronger; that was another blessing. Then the pendulum of fate swung against them once more, as further tragedy stalked Polly and Albert's families. After seven years of marriage, Ada had finally had a child but the news came that there was something dreadfully wrong. Something that made Bertie's slowness seem as nothing. Water on the brain they called it and it was likely he would never walk nor talk. Ada was bravely nursing him at home but they'd been told that he was not long for this world.

As the family was reeling from this news, the postman brought a letter to Chapel Street. It was rare that folk wrote letters, postcards were usually sufficient to say what needed to be said. Albert took his knife from his pocket and sliced through the envelope. He withdrew two flimsy sheets of paper and began to read.

'Eadie's to be wed,' he said. 'Seems she's expecting. I'd no notion she was in the family way but she's five months gone. Ma isn't best pleased but there 'tis. Walter will move into Rose Cottage once they're married.'

'Well they've waited long enough,' replied Polly.

'There's those that won't approve of course,' went on Albert, 'and not just because they've anticipated the ceremony. With them being cousins, they will be afeared for how the baby will turn out.'

Neither of them voiced their thoughts of Ada's little son.

'Won't be a chapel wedding o' course, things being the way they are. Off to the register office in Bideford they be, it was all arranged as soon as she started to show. They've asked me to stand up for her, give her away like, now da's gone. Her real ma and da have had naught to do with her, since she was a little maid.'

'Shall you go?' asked Polly, knowing that Eadie was like a sister to Albert.

'"Tis a Saturday,' said Albert, 'I can spare time from the herring. I don't see as how us can both go, what with the littl'uns and all.'

'No, 'tis not as though it's in the chapel. I shall bide here but you've to go. Happen your ma will be there and 'twill be good to give her the news. You've not seen her since you went over to let her know Nelson had been born. You can say as how Violet's a mite stronger and that Daisy be working now. You'll be able to tell her Leonard's doing well. Even Bertie got a medal for attendance this term, she'll be pleased to hear.'

'I'm glad Eadie will still be at Rose Cottage to keep an eye on ma.'

'I know,' said Polly, 'The old folks are a worry. I fret over my ma and da, now there's only Ethel bringing money into the house.'

Polly was glad that her youngest sister, as yet, showed no inclination to marry and move away, leaving their parents needing care.

'Arthur sends what he can,' she went on, 'but with all the rest of us girls wed, 'tis hard for us to help. Lydia could do more, in that big house over to Bideford, with her fancy husband and no children.'

Just as she'd always planned it thought Polly, ruefully but without resentment. She had no wish to exchange her life for Lydia's.

'They will be glad of this new pension the government's going to be paying,' said Polly. I know father will be pleased to get it, seven and six a week, it's a tidy sum.'

Age was gripping them all, thought Polly, her own parents, now in their late seventies and Alb's ma not much younger. Alb himself had turned forty five this year. The fishing kept him fit for his age and there wasn't an ounce of fat on him but they were no longer young. Maybe they deserved some years of quiet now. She was relieved that Violet was so much better and that Bertie seemed to be managing, though he'd never make a scholar. Walter was going to do the right thing by Eadie. Perhaps their worries were behind them.

Two months after Eadie's wedding another letter arrived, this time from Albert's Uncle John. Albert read it with mounting trepidation.

''Tis Aunt Matilda,' he said, turning to Polly, 'Ma was saying when Eadie was wed that she was becoming stranger than ever. She's not been the same since Aunt Agnes went and of course, Aunt Agnes wasn't always right in the head either. They was doing so well together, selling teas from King's Cottage. Aunt Matilda's lived there all her life but it's been difficult for her since she's been there on her own. She says she's got roaring in her ears and she can hear voices and folk is out to kill her. Daft old girl.'

Albert continued reading. 'Then she's complaining of pains in her legs. Good job Eadie's was a quiet wedding, she'd have expected an invitation else and Uncle John says her language is something shocking. Her excuse is the devil's got her tongue. Sounds like she's gone proper mazed. She used to go to chapel regular, now she's saying she's going to hell. Uncle John's been having a right time of it. Aunt Lizzie keeps an eye on her best she can but she's pushing seventy and can't get down the hill like she used.'

'I'm not sure there's aught we can do,' said Polly, 'what with your fishing and I've the children to do for.'

'Uncle's had her put in the asylum,' Albert replied as he turned the page. 'They couldn't be minding her no more. She keeps trying to hurt herself, her face was all over scratches and last week she tried to climb out the top window. They were afraid she'd do away with herself. There was naught else they could do.'

Polly felt frozen fingers grip her heart. She was well aware that Matilda's sister, Albert's Aunt Ellen, had spent nigh on a year in the asylum, when Eadie had been a year old. They'd blamed that on child bearing. Polly glanced involuntarily at Nelson in his cradle. Was she immune to this affliction that struck at mothers unawares?

In the shadow of the asylum wall a diminutive figure crept across the moonlit grass, searching for the sea. She looked much older than her years, she was not yet sixty but her face was heavily lined and a slight shadow of a beard graced her chin. She pushed back the sleeve of her nightgown and dug her dirty fingernails into her arm until the blood ran. She was oblivious to the pain but she let out an expletive as the blood dripped on to the shapeless garment that flapped round her skinny legs in the sharp December breeze.

The woman lifted her head and sniffed like an animal. It was all so unfamiliar, everything felt wrong, she needed to find the water. Where was the water? Surely she only had to look out of her window and there would be the waves, breaking over The Gore? It hadn't been easy, getting out into the grounds. She wasn't sure why there were so many others sleeping in her room. She hadn't shared a room since she and Ellen and Lizzie were girls but despite all the people, it had been possible to slip out once snores surrounded her. The woman had wandered the darkened corridors aimlessly, spurning the chapel, which made her uncomfortable now. She had no place in heaven. God had abandoned her. The steamy laundry was more comforting, with its stench of damp linen. She did not know what had made her try the door to the drying yard, nor what had tempted her outside when it opened at her touch. All she knew was, that at all costs, she had to get away from those who were hunting her down; the sea would be her salvation. Her ma and da used to protect her, they were gone now of course, she knew that but where was Agnes? It seemed such a very long time since she'd seen her older sister. Agnes should be here. They needed to lay the tables for the visitors. If she could just climb that fence she would get to the sea, she knew she would.

A sheen of frost clung to the icy railings. The wiry little woman dragged a broken laundry hamper across to the perimeter fence. She sucked in her lips over her gums as she looked up at the looming barrier. The voices were telling her that she had to climb. She stood on the hamper and prepared to leap upward. Her voluminous nightgown caught firmly on the spike of the rusting railings. The linen was coarse but it was thick; it did not tear. She hung, suspended in the December darkness, still yearning for the sea that she believed would save her. Madness had claimed another victim.

5
Summer 1909

Adulthood was beckoning the four girls, inexorable, inevitable and eagerly anticipated. For now though, they busied themselves stringing daisy chains, still clinging to the last vestiges of childhood. It was obvious that they were dressed in their Sunday best but their workaday bonnets marked out their station in life. Their friendship had endured throughout their schooldays but it had been nearly a year since they last shared a dusty form at the back of the Clovelly classroom. Nowadays, Daisy found it difficult to get together with her friends to gossip. Their little group had split into two pairs. Alice and Mary were close, as both worked for Mary's father at the Red Lion. Bella was living-in as an under housemaid for Mrs Hamlyn at the Court and although Daisy still lived at home, she was working for Mrs Tuke at Gardener's Cottage. The Cottage's proximity to the Court meant that Daisy and Bella had been thrown together as the other pair, even though Daisy felt more affinity with the less opinionated Mary and Alice.

Daisy was barely listening to the girlish chatter of her friends, instead, she was pondering on her own situation. She thought of kindly Mr Tuke, Mrs Hamlyn's head gardener, who was responsible for the impressive Court grounds. She glanced in the direction of the Tuke's cottage and the warm red walls that guarded the secrets of the serene garden; a garden that had gripped Daisy's soul. She had inherited her mother's love of flowers, taking pleasure in the hollyhocks and geraniums that grew round the cottage doors in the village. The neat rows of vegetables and the exotic, delicate blooms waiting to be picked for the Court held a different charm. On her way home from work each day, she lingered within the embrace of the walled garden, inhaling the scents and feeling her step lighten with the sheer joy of being young and alive. It wasn't only the flowers, it was the smell of the newly turned earth, the sight of a robin perched on the handle of an abandoned fork and the sprouting of the unblemished shoots that lifted Daisy's mood; nature's new growth mirrored her own budding maturity.

Mr Tuke had noticed the allure that the garden held for Daisy and the thoughtful gentleman had begun to tell her more about the plants and how to tend them. Sometimes he asked Daisy to take the pennies from the visitors who wanted to tour this part of the grounds. Secretly, Daisy longed to work in the gardens instead of running errands and helping Mrs Tuke in the house but gardens were men's work. The irksome inequalities that separated her from her brothers rankled. Leonard and Bertie would go to sea of course but they could be gardeners if they preferred. She had no choice, no voice; she would be a servant until she married and then an unpaid servant to her husband. How was that fair?

Aside from the garden, there was another attraction of working at Gardener's Cottage and that was Abraham Tuke. A few months younger than Daisy, he had attended Clovelly school with her when they were small. Abraham's ability at his lessons was legendary. He had raced through the standard examinations and two years ago, he'd won that scholarship to a fancy boarding school in Taunton; taking him to a world that was unimaginable to those he had left behind. The social orbit in which he now moved did not touch upon Daisy's. When they were at school together, Daisy had tended to join the crowd who labelled him a swot for his seriousness and left him to his solitude. Now she found that eccentric dedication to studying romantic. Abraham was tall for his age and slender, very different from the other lads of Daisy's acquaintance who were muscled from hauling lobster pots or from farm work. Daisy dreamed of the long summer days when Abraham would be home from school and she might catch glimpses of him, as she had at Easter, immersed in a book, in the corner of the garden. She imagined him turning the pages, his over-long dark hair falling across his eyes. He would push it back impatiently, lost in his studies, unaware of the young girl who surveyed him from the safety of the back kitchen. He was impossibly unattainable for Daisy of course. No one from Daisy's walk of life sent their children away to school. Abraham and Daisy were now on different sides of the abyss that was hewn by society's perceptions of their respective ranks.

On this beautiful, early summer Sunday the conversation of the four girls was superficial and skirted round their deepest feelings. Daisy hadn't even told Bella about Abraham. She supposed Bella was her closest friend now but working at the Court had given Bella a sense of her own importance that made Daisy feel uncomfortable. Bella would remember Abraham from school and would be disparaging about Daisy's dreams, ridiculing Abraham for being a little younger than they were, for not being a man who worked for a living and for, horror of horrors, wearing spectacles. Daisy thought the spectacles made Abraham's dark eyes all the more penetrating but she was aware that her friends would see this as a sign of weakness.

Normally, Daisy was "chapel" but Bella had persuaded her to come to church to see the London fashions worn by the visitors to Clovelly Court. The Prime Minister and his wife were amongst the Whitsun guests. They were elderly of course but they were accompanied by their son. The Honourable Betty Manners, who was heir to the Court and her twin sister were also down for their twentieth birthday celebrations. The besotted Bella peppered her conversation with details of their comings and goings and the elaborate dinner that was planned to mark the occasion. Daisy was intrigued by Bella's infatuation with the younger members of the house-party and was curious to see these paragons.

'Don't know why you're interested in them rich folk,' her mother had muttered, when Daisy had said that she would be going to church this Sunday. 'The likes of us not good enough for you now youm be working?'

But Polly's objections had been cursory and here Daisy was, in her newly-laundered dress, hoping to catch sight of the arrival of those from the Court.

The diminutive figure of Mrs Hamlyn appeared, her ebony cane scratching on the gravel path as she led her guests towards the ivy-clad church. Bella elbowed Daisy sharply in the ribs.

'There's Mr Asquith,' she said, smugly knowledgeable. 'He drove up from Exeter on Friday to avoid the annoying crowds at Bideford station. All those people wanting to catch a glimpse of him were disappointed. It was only Mrs Asquith who took the train as far as Bideford. Oooh look, that's Lord Northcote,' continued Bella, pointing to an elderly gentleman with the most impressive moustache that Daisy had ever seen.

Alice and Mary dutifully made appreciative noises, as Bella went on pointing out Sir this and Lady that. Daisy's attention was wandering; she didn't think that any of the younger gentlemen measured up to Abraham but wisely, she held her tongue. Bella was beginning to irritate her, she seemed to think that her employment at the Court gave her the right to lord it over her friends.

The ladies from the house-party, in their shimmering dresses, looked cool in the flickering sunlight. Swan-like, they floated along the path, their elegant, fitted skirts sweeping out at the back, the feathers and flowers in their hats dipping in the light breeze. Their parasols twirled, ensuring that alabaster complexions were not impaired. Suddenly, Daisy felt conscious of her tanned skin and she pulled the front of her bonnet down over her brow. How could she expect Abraham to look twice at her ruddy face and roughened hands?

The bells rang out, their impatient clamour cutting across the cries of the wheeling gulls and the gossip of the parishioners. All thoughts of daisy chains abandoned, the girls stood and smoothed down their dresses; the service would be starting soon. As she left the bright sunshine and entered the dim church, it took a moment for Daisy to accustom her eyes to the shadowy interior. Mr Tuke, looking strange in his Sunday attire, inclined his head to acknowledge her. Daisy gave a brief, uncertain smile in response. The villagers, ever aware of their place, allowed the Court's visitors to occupy the front pews and ranged themselves behind. Daisy's gaze raked the church, spotting neighbours and friends, their neat but sombre clothing mundane when compared to the finery of the Court ladies. Three young women sitting erect in the first pew, away from the house-party guests, caught Daisy's attention. They seemed to be taking no interest in the congregation that was assembling behind them.

'Who are they?' whispered Daisy to Bella, indicating the unknown ladies. 'I didn't see them come in with the others from the Court, they must have got here very early.'

The women that were the subject of her scrutiny were smartly dressed, one in white, one in purple and one in a fetching shade of green. Although their appearance marked them out from the villagers, they did not turn to acknowledge Mrs Hamlyn and her guests. There was a low hum as acquaintances greeted each other whilst they waited for the service to begin but these ladies sat unspeaking, their eyes fixed firmly on the altar. Reluctantly, Bella admitted that she did not recognise them.

'I'm sure I haven't seen them at the Court,' she said. 'Maybe they are just here for luncheon.'

'They are staying at Mrs Jones' in the village,' volunteered Mary after a pause, disinclined to challenge Bella's authority but eager to contribute her tit-bit of knowledge. 'I saw them leave there and go across to Granny Pengilly's tea-rooms yesterday.'

'Oh, nobody important then,' said Bella dismissively, 'just visitors.' She was clearly put out that she was no longer the provider of all the gossip.

The service began and one of the Court party stood up to read the lesson.

'Lord Hugh Cecil,' hissed Bella under her breath, keen to re-establish her ascendancy.

It was warm in the crowded church and beads of sweat glistened on Lord Cecil's brow. Accustomed to addressing the House, his fruity tones rolled round the church, reaching even those in the congregation whose hearing was no longer sharp. Although she was used to the speech of the gentry, so different from the soft burr of the villagers, Daisy found that Lord Cecil's strangled vowels detracted from the passage he was delivering. She looked again at the three young women in the front pew. There seemed nothing remarkable about them; just visitors, as Bella had said.

As they had been amongst the last the enter the church, Daisy and her friends were seated in the aisle. This made it difficult to see what was going on at the altar but sideways glances gave them a good view of the Asquith family. The service dragged on, the sermon began and Daisy struggled to focus on what Reverend Simkin was saying. She became aware of some scuffling in the Asquiths' pew. Mrs Asquith was scrabbling in the beaded reticule that dangled from her wrist. She appeared to be writing something down. Perhaps she was making notes on Reverend Simkin's rather turgid address, which advocated duty and forbearance. The congregation obeyed the Rector's exhortation to pray and there was a shuffling of bodies and a clearing of throats as they knelt on the stuffed hassocks before them. Daisy could not resist a fleeting look in the Asquiths' direction. Mrs Asquith was shoving a piece of paper into her husband's fist. Instead of closing his eyes in prayer, the Prime Minister was scanning the note. He looked towards the pew a couple of rows in front of him, where the three young women were seated and then to the side door of the church. His jaw-line, with its cleft chin, was set firm and hastily he put the scrap of paper into his pocket. Finally, he bowed his white head and joined in the mumbled intercessions. Guiltily, Daisy did the same, she clenched her hands and screwed her eyes shut, as if this fervency would compensate for her earlier distraction.

The three young women from the front pew got up hastily when the service was over and were the first to leave. Waiting obediently to file out behind the gentry from the Court, Daisy spotted Mr Asquith sidling furtively through the side door. How strange, mused Daisy but thought no more of it. Once outside, Daisy breathed deeply, relishing the warm air, pleased to be free from the formality of Sunday worship. Members of the congregation were huddling in small groups and swapping news, before heading homeward. Mary and Alice set off back towards the village and Daisy was exchanging a final few words with Bella, when the sharp sound of raised voices could be heard.

'Quick', exclaimed Bella pulling Daisy behind her, keen to get near enough to see what was causing the commotion.

A few yards ahead of them, on the path to the Court, the three women from the church had ranged themselves around the Prime Minister. His efforts to sneak away undetected had evidently failed.

'Receive our petition on June the 29th,' the one in green was demanding.

Now Daisy had a better view of the women, she could see that the speaker was not much older than she was, perhaps still in her teens. Her nose was rather too prominent for her to be considered a beauty but her straight dark brows and striking eyes drew attention.

'Will you free Patricia Woodlock?' she was saying.

Asquith was attempting to shake off the restraining hand of the purple-clad young woman, who was impeding his progress.

'Won't you grant us an interview?' asked the woman wearing the white dress. She appeared to be the eldest of the trio and her booming tones carried across to the curious crowd.

'Suffragettes!' exclaimed Bella. 'The cheek of it, disturbing poor Mr Asquith on his holiday.'

'Not for a second,' the disgruntled Prime Minister was saying. 'It's very wrong of you to question me after church.'

By this time, other members of the house-party were ushering Asquith towards the security of the Court. The three women were forced back a little but undeterred, they continued in pursuit of their quarry. The Court guests hustled inside the great doors, which were shut firmly in the faces of the three protestors by Lord Hugh Cecil. The sound of the heavy bolt being drawn could be clearly heard.

Back in the village for her Sunday afternoon off, Daisy listened as the Clovelly gossips dissected the details of the incident after church. It was not necessary to have witnessed it to have an opinion and the story had grown ever more fanciful with each telling. Most shared Bella's view that it was a shame that Mr Asquith could not enjoy the peace and quiet that he deserved. Mrs Jones, who at least was in a position to know, provided the names of the three women and expressed dismay that her guest house was harbouring a vipers' nest.

'Mayhap I should tell them to pack their bags,' she said, keen not to seem to be colluding with the protestors, 'but business be business and they paid for their room in good coin.'

'Elsie Howey, now,' muttered another. 'Baint she the one that was in all the papers last month? Dressed as Joan of Arc on some great white 'orse outside a prison up London way she was.'

The listeners dismissed this as a tall tale but it was clear that the three women had attracted some adverse attention by their past exploits and had targeted poor Mr Asquith before.

'Why did they come after Mrs Hamlyn's guests? How dare they!'

'Well, Lord Cromer now, baint he the leader of some such society that be against all this women's vote nonsense and he be staying there this weekend.'

''Tweren't Lord Cromer they be after though were it, 'twas poor Mr Asquith, after all he's done for us. Shame on them.'

'All three be jail birds,' Mrs Stanbury was saying. 'To think that they be staying right here in the village and have taken tea in Granny Pengilly's tea-rooms!'

Daisy quietly kept her sympathies for the three women to herself. She didn't know much about the fight for women's suffrage, that kind of thing usually passed Clovelly by. Surely though, this was a worthy cause and how thrilling to be one of those women, travelling the country together and making a difference.

The next day, Daisy was on an errand for Mr Tuke, taking some early strawberries up to the Court. As she approached the square white building and swerved to one side, heading for the servants' entrance, she was aware of three women heading towards the front steps. They were instantly recognisable as the suffragettes who had caused all the fuss the previous day. Daisy shrunk back into the hedge and held her breath. She watched as they marched up to the steps and the one who Daisy now knew to be Elsie Howey, wielded the heavy brass knocker with gusto. After a few moments, Mr Caird, the agent, answered the door. This in itself was unusual. Responding to visitors' summons was not his role. Daisy was transfixed, not daring to move for fear of being spotted. She need not have worried, Mr Caird had all his attention taken up by the women, who were demanding to see Mr Asquith. Their strident voices reached Daisy's ears.

'Votes for Women,' cried the youngest of the trio, whom Mrs Jones had named as Vera Wentworth.

Mr Caird shut the door firmly. Undeterred, Elsie knocked again. The door swung open.

'Be off with you,' blustered Mr Caird, shaking his fist before closing the door a second time.

Once more the women tried to gain entrance. Daisy, silently cheering, admired their persistence. She was amazed to see Mr Caird come to the door for a third time. At that moment she spotted Mr Asquith and Lord Northcote, accompanied by two policemen, emerge from the side of the house, laden with golfing bags. Presumably, Mr Caird was trying to divert the women's attention, allowing the Prime Minister to make his way to Mrs Hamlyn's private links.

Wary of loitering, Daisy delivered the strawberries. Her task completed, she could not resist a glance towards Mrs Hamlyn's golf course. A flash of colour, as if a bird had landed on a branch, caught her eye. Moving closer, she peered into the hedgerow and spotted the suffragettes hiding, not far from where the Court party were gathered to watch the golfers. Two policemen stood a respectful distance from the guests, presumably intent on protecting the Prime Minister. Risking the wrath of Mrs Tuke, if she were to be too long delayed, Daisy crept nearer. Suddenly the sharp-eyed police constable noticed the three women. Blowing his whistle and calling to his colleague, he made his way towards the suffragettes at a trot. The young ladies leapt up. With hats falling and hair flying, they headed for the cliffs. As the constable set off in pursuit, the women wisely dispersed in different directions. Daisy saw George Reilly, the local photographer, carrying his cumbersome camera, scurrying after the runaways. The possibility of a shot of three leading suffragettes would be a greater scoop than puffed up politicians at their golf.

Within minutes, the policeman returned, breathless and thwarted.

'They're too fleet of foot sir,' the constable was saying to his sergeant.

The next moment, Daisy saw that Vera Wentworth was getting closer to the policemen. Too scared to cry a warning, Daisy wordlessly willed the young woman to get safely away. The policemen caught sight of the suffragette and it became clear that this was exactly what she wanted. Whilst the officers were occupied apprehending Vera, her colleagues had pushed their way through the crowds and were once again haranguing Mr Asquith.

'Receive our deputation on June the 29th. There's no back door here,' one was shouting. From Mrs Jones' gossip, Daisy knew her to be Jessie Kenney.

'You're a beast and a coward,' boomed Elsie.

'Remember Sheffield.'

Asquith looked discomforted but some of the guests, ranged on the picnic rugs, were attempting to disguise smiles of amusement. Realising that she dared not postpone her return any longer, reluctantly, Daisy set off for Gardener's Cottage, casting longing looks over her shoulder as she did so. Thrills such as this were extraordinary. The villagers were used to visitors, even important visitors such as those who came to the Court but today Daisy felt that she had been granted glimpses of an exhilarating and unfamiliar new world, full of exciting possibilities.

Daisy slipped through the back door. As she entered, Mrs Tuke looked up but thankfully, did not pass comment on the length of time that Daisy had taken. Instead, she asked her to fetch some boot laces from Ellis' shop.

'I'm afraid it can't wait for you to bring them in with you tomorrow,' she said. 'Mr Tuke's lace has snapped right through and he can't go up to the Court this afternoon with string in his boots!'

Daisy welcomed the opportunity to run down the cobbles as she had as a carefree child. She was no longer barefoot of course but it meant that she could escape the isolation of Gardener's Cottage and be part of daytime village life for a short while.

It was clear that, by a process of instant osmosis, accounts of the latest deeds of the suffragettes had already reached the village. The local women were out in force, brimming with indignation.

'You heard about the palaver up at the Court?'

''Tis a dreadful thing. I hear they was arrested.'

'Well Mrs Jones has given them their marching orders, told them to pack their bags and go, she has.'

'Quite right too. We don't want the likes of them round here with their London ways and newfangled ideas.'

'Well they be goin' at any rate. Booked Eli's cart they have, for the 10.59 London train from Bideford tonight. Good riddance I say.'

'Votes for Women, indeed. Whoever heard the like?'

'Stuffing young girls' heads full of a load o' old nonsense they be.'

As she passed the gossiping women by the fountain, Daisy saw the cause of their consternation. The suffragettes, their boots muddied and their hems torn, were walking up the street. To Daisy's surprise, the youngest woman, approached her and proffered a hand. Daisy shook it hesitantly, wary in case she was spotted by the baying crowd of Clovelly wives but at the same time, delighted to be caught up in the day's events.

'Good day. My name is Vera and you are?'

'Daisy miss,' Daisy whispered, hardly daring to breathe. This would be something to tell Bella, not that she would be believed. Or maybe it would be better to keep this a special secret, to hold in her memory and to tell her children.

'You don't have to call me "miss",' Vera smiled. 'You seem to be local. We just want to know where we can buy some artists' materials.'

'Ellis' shop is just down there on the left,' Daisy said, more confident now. No one could be angry at her politely giving directions to trippers. 'Mr Ellis is a bit of an artist himself, I am sure he would have what you need.'

'Thank you,' said Vera, as the three women began to retrace their steps down the street.

Pausing for a moment, Vera turned and thrust a newspaper into Daisy's hand.

'This is what we do,' she said, 'and why.'

A quick glance showed Daisy that the publication, *Votes for Women*, was not one of which her mother, her employer, or indeed most of the village would approve. She tucked it in the bottom of her wicker basket and ensured that it was hidden.

Daisy's working day was over before she had a chance to look at the newspaper. Instead of going straight home, she went up to the woods, where she would not be disturbed and began to read. The paper was not new, it was a February edition but to Daisy it was a revelation.

"I say to you young women... come and give one year of your life to bringing the message of deliverance to thousands of your sisters... this noble girl has undergone two periods of imprisonment for the sake of women less privileged and happily placed than herself. She is one of our most able and successful organisers and takes on all the duties and responsibilities of our chief officers."

Daisy was enthralled. Yes. This was what life should be. She skipped involuntarily as she set off for home. Somehow she needed to be involved. The sheer impossibility of this engulfed her. There was no hurry. She would bide her time but her time would surely come.

The following day, Daisy was up at dawn. Tuesday was market day and Mrs Tuke was leaving early with produce to sell. Daisy was needed to help pack the baskets. Even at this hour, with daylight barely breaking, most cottages in the street were showing a dim light. The morning mist swirled and dew was thick on the ferns by the side of the path as Daisy left the village street for the woodland lane to the walled garden. Unexpectedly, she found Bella waiting for her.

'I hoped I would catch you. You won't believe what's happened,' exclaimed her friend excitedly. 'I just had to slip out and tell you. There's such a to-do, I will never be missed.'

Daisy knew that her role was to listen quietly and then provide intermittent gasps of admiration at the appropriate points in Bella's narrative.

'Well, yesterday there was such a banging on the door. I was proper scared and Mr Caird was there and he said I wasn't to answer. He marched to the door and do you know, it was those awful suffragettes! Bold as brass on the doorstep, demanding to see Mr Asquith. I never heard the like. What cheek! Mr Caird gave them a piece of his mind I can tell you,' Bella wrinkled her nose and giggled at the recollection. 'Told them they needed a nurse to look after them he did. Do you know, they had the cheek to say that they had paid to see the grounds. Well Mr Caird soon put them straight. Said it was private property and they weren't in the part of the grounds that were open to the public at all. Threatened to set the police on them. They soon left after that. It would take something to ignore Mr Caird when his dander is up. I'm surprised you didn't see them Daisy, if they were in the walled garden.'

Daisy smiled enigmatically.

'I didn't see them in the walled garden,' she said, truthfully. 'Is this going to take long? I mustn't be late.'

'But you've not heard the last of it,' Bella gabbled. 'Everyone thought they'd gone back to London. They took Eli's cart yesterday evening for the train. It seems they walked back, all the way from Bideford in the dark. They were seen at Bucks Cross.'

Daisy was genuinely shocked. What had these women done now?

'When we got up to light the fires for the hot water we spotted it. All over the lawn. It was dreadful. Ribbons and leaflets all over the place. It's going to take the staff all morning to clear up and there are hand bills blowing everywhere.'

'What do they say?' enquired Daisy.

'Oh, you know, all that political nonsense. "Votes for Women", "Dare to be free", "No Surrender", that sort of thing.'

'Have you got one?' asked Daisy, hopefully.

'No. Of course not. Scurrilous things. Why would I want one?' replied Bella. 'Anyway, I must go. It is going to be a busy day. We've police guarding the doors and all. I am sure Mr Tuke will be furious, so you will hear all about it.'

Daisy did indeed hear more. It seemed the three women that she so admired had painted slogans on banners that lay across the hedges that surrounded the Court's lawns. Purple, white and green rosettes were strewn amongst the ribbons and leaflets that were scattered across the manicured turf. Daisy marvelled at the tenacity of the women who had trudged eleven miles by starlight, carrying all the handbills and other items that now met the view of the Court's visitors, as they flung back the shutters to greet the day. She supposed that the suffragettes had then had to walk all the way back to Bideford to make their escape on the milk train.

Daisy was sent to gather up the leaflets that had blown into the walled garden. A disk of paper, emblazoned with the words, "Down with Asquith. Death to Tyrants," in suffragette colours of green and purple, indicated that the young women had put their artists' materials to good use. She spotted a handbill that gave an address for the WSPU office in Torquay. Torquay was hardly next door but it was at least in Devon. Daisy slipped the paper in the pocket of her apron. Not now. Not yet but one day, maybe she really could be part of this wonderful new world. Merely the thought that she would be able to tuck that address away in the back of a drawer, hidden under her bonnets, was comforting, enthralling, luring her towards the unknown.

This was not the last that Clovelly would hear of the suffragettes. Rumours of their escapades were on everyone's lips. When Daisy and Bella met again that evening, Bella had another incident to report.

'And then this afternoon,' she said importantly, 'there was a lady at the door of the Court, all dressed in black she was, claiming to be a Mrs Pond from Ilfracombe and saying she wanted to play the church organ. It was all most peculiar. Surely, if you wanted to play the organ you'd ask the vicar or the churchwarden. Why would you come disturbing Mrs Hamlyn? They say,' went on Bella, without elaborating on who "they" were, 'Mrs Pankhurst is supposed to be in Ilfracombe just now, you don't suppose it could have been her do you, pretending to be Mrs Pond? How fearfully thrilling.'

Daisy's fingers felt for the stiff yellow paper that still lay crumpled in her apron pocket and she smiled.

6
May 1914

P & A Campbell's steamer disgorged its latest load of passengers into the waiting fishing boats. As the holidaymakers were rowed ashore, Clovelly's drab quayside was rejuvenated by their bright colours and excited hum. Although the piercing blue skies were cloudless and the air was still, a brassy sheen over the sea threatened thunder. The old fishermen, ruminating in the shade of the Red Lion's archway, nodded sagely and muttered that the dry spell would break before the week was out. For days now, the weather had been more like August than May, with an oppressive heat and sluggish tides. Seaweed and debris lay strewn on the beach instead of being drawn back out to sea and streams had dwindled to a trickle. In the soaring temperatures, villagers had become too lazy to lug the contents of their full privies up to the gardens to be buried and had taken to using the stream. Instead of being dispersed by the tide, effluent lingered on the beach. As the mercury rose, an unpleasant odour hovered menacingly over the village and the water from the wells was thick with sludge. The tangled mess of old nets, discarded hooks and flotsam on the shoreline was hardly attractive to the visitors but the local lads had seized the opportunity to scavenge for riches in the rubbish cast up by the half-hearted waves. The stench made noses wrinkle and eyes sting but day-trippers rarely ventured far from the quay, giving the boys a territory that they could call their own.

Bertie, with his younger brothers Mark and Nelson, had spent the long, light evenings after school scrabbling for rusty buttons or broken bits of plate and bickering with friends over who had spotted a particular treasure first. As they ranged across the beach, using old branches to make dens above the water's reach, their unbroken voices mingled with the raucous cries of the gulls and echoed back. Young, carefree, oblivious of the gathering storms, their thoughts were of the moment. Who had the best den? Who had cadged an illicit Woodbine from the older boys? Who had found a tanner that could be exchanged for humbugs in Ellis' shop? None looked further than the horizon of their immediate concerns.

It was Friday morning. Albert, accompanied by Leonard, had long since gone down to the harbour to put out to sea, grumbling that the lack of wind would leave sails limp and that they would need to row out to empty their lobster pots. Polly called the younger boys to get ready for school. The girls needed no such chiding. Violet had already helped to get her sisters dressed and was munching a slice of bread and scrape when Bertie and Nelson came downstairs, collars awry and boots unlaced.

'Where's Mark?' asked Polly. Mark was usually the one of the three who needed no chiding.

'Says he baint feeling right,' Bertie commented as he reached for the mug of tea that Polly was proffering.

'Baint feeling right?' echoed Polly. 'Too many of Ellis' sweets no doubt.'

At eight years old, Mark was growing fast, his hair was darkening and he had left the attractive stage of chubby childhood behind. The times when the female holidaymakers gushed over his fair good looks and endearing smile were waning. The visitors were still lavish with their tips if he ran errands and any pennies he was given were usually converted into a twist of sherbert or a bag of toffees. Soon though, he would be beyond the age of appeal and would have to bequeath the task of charming the tourists to five year old Nelson.

'Says his head hurts and he feels hot,' said Bertie.

'We'm all hot,' remarked Polly. 'I've never known it this hot so early in the year.'

'Well, he says he bain't going to school,' said Bertie.

Polly began to feel concerned. Her children rarely missed school. They had all won medals for good attendance. Rosie was banging her spoon on the wooden table, adding her own marks to those made by her siblings in earlier years. Absently, Polly tested the warmth of the porridge in the bowl that was just out of Rosie's reach. Satisfied that it had cooled sufficiently she pushed the enamel dish closer and instructed Violet to oversee Rosie's inexpert efforts at feeding herself. The infant was fractious from a night's teething. It really was not the weather for porridge but it was gentle on sore gums.

Polly sighed, the day was already uncomfortably warm and lately she was finding the heat more difficult to cope with. Maybe she was starting the change she thought, breathing heavily as she climbed the stairs to the room that the four boys shared. Space was a little easier now Daisy was living-in at Gardener's Cottage but Violet's box room, squashed under the eaves, would not accommodate Lily and Rosie when they were too big to share a room with their parents. Perhaps they should ask Mr Caird, the agent, if there was a larger house coming vacant. It was a shame they had had to leave Chapel Street. Their old home was now part of the New Inn, providing extra rooms for visitors.

Polly pushed open the door to the bedroom where the boys slept. It always smelled musty, as only a boys' room can. The clothes Mark had discarded the previous night were pooled on the floor next to the bed that he shared with Nelson. Polly passed her hand across the lad's forehead. It felt clammy to the touch.

'How be ee boy?' she asked.

'I'm so cold ma,' he said, 'and my throat hurts something cruel.'

'Cold?' queried Polly, 'Bertie said you was hot.' She paused as Mark began to shiver violently. 'I'll get you some honey for your throat,' she said, 'and maybe a lemon later if Ellis' have any in.'

Already Polly was calculating the likely cost of lemons. The boy pulled the coverlet up to his ears as he huddled on the sagging mattress.

Mark would normally make the most of schoolless summer days, rushing down to the quay to be with his friends but as Saturday passed into Sunday, he remained in bed. Nelson had moved across to share the larger bed with his older brothers but Mark still could not rest. Polly tried to tempt him with beef tea and fish stew but he did not want to eat, saying he could not swallow. Then the coughing began, racking his thin body and echoing through the cottage.

'He's a bit old for croup,' Polly remarked to Albert. 'But I think that's what 'tis.'

Despite his lack of food, Mark complained of feeling sick. Polly stayed home from chapel to tend the boy, in case the chamber pot needed emptying. All through Sunday afternoon Polly remained indoors whilst Violet chanted rhymes to keep the younger girls occupied and the boys went down to the quay, where Albert pottered stoically.

Leonard popped into the kitchen to exchange a few words, enquiring after Mark's welfare, before setting off on a jaunt of his own. Her eldest son was becoming a man, thought Polly. Soon, like Daisy, he'd be gone. Alone with her thoughts, Polly's children came to mind one by one. Her eldest daughter was a real young lady now. Since she'd moved out, Daisy had taken to going to church with her employers, so they rarely saw her in chapel but she usually called in when she had a day off. About time she was walking out with someone, thought Polly, remembering the fondness that Daisy had had for their married neighbour, Samuel Harris. There had been no hint of a grown-up romance for Daisy. Was she perhaps holding a candle for someone? If so, she was keeping her secret well.

Then Leonard, who was so much like his dad but with more of a sense of adventure about him. Bertie was, well, just Bertie. Happy in his own way but he would always need a bit of looking after. Violet was so much better now, though the rheumatic fever she had had would always leave her frail. She was such a help with the little ones. Lily and Rosie were tiny yet; their personalities still unformed.

She looked down at Mark, wondering if perhaps the fever was dropping and the coughing less frequent. Mark, wiry, determined, desperate to be like his older brothers and to disassociate himself from Nelson, whom he viewed as a baby. Mothers shouldn't have favourites of course but Nelson was her golden boy. Polly's brand of motherhood was gruff and practical, not demonstrative but there was something special about Nelson. He was still young enough to climb on to her lap for an embrace, his moist hand finding its way to the back of her neck in a gesture that he found comforting. Even the births of the two youngest girls had not usurped Nelson's position in Polly's mind as her baby.

Monday dawned. The air was still thick and oppressive, crushing the breath from the villagers' lungs. Wearily, Polly rose from her bed at first light to check on Mark. He hadn't seemed to cough so much in the night. Was this because he was getting better, or a sign of something more sinister? The bottom of the bedroom door scraped on the uneven boards as Polly opened it. She resolved to get Alb to see to the hinges. Mark's head turned on the bolster at the sound of his mother's entrance. The light from the hallway brightened the stuffy room and Polly could see Mark's eyelids flicker. His forehead seemed cooler and the coughing had certainly abated, could he be improving? Polly retreated quietly, not wanting to disturb the other three boys. She looked fondly at Nelson, lying crossways at the bottom of the large bed, trying to avoid his brothers' feet. As she did so the young boy's breathing rattled.

Then the coughing began.

Tuesday afternoon and Polly sat in silence with her youngest son. She could focus on nothing and no one else. It was only the two of them, she and Nelson, suspended in this stifling space. The deep, rhythmic clicking of the clock on the mantleshelf was audible throughout the house, as all the doors were open in a vain effort to cool the air. Its tones denoted the passing of time, yet this moment seemed as if it was forever. The house was uncannily quiet without the babbling of the two youngest girls. That morning, Polly had approached her neighbour, Mrs Abbott, seeking her help.

'Could you take care of Lily and Rosie for me?' Polly had asked. 'Only I've had to tie Rosie to the bedstead, Lily's not up to minding her. I can't have her wandering into the boys' room while they be sick and now she's up on her feet, she could tumble down them stairs.'

Mrs Abbott had agreed to look after the girls for a few days. Polly was thankful that Rosie was recently weaned. Only the week before, Rosie had seemed irritable when Polly proffered the breast for her evening feed. The close proximity of her mother's flesh was uncomfortable in the sticky heat and Rosie had grizzled and struggled. Polly had wanted to persevere, aware that this was a sensation that she would probably never again experience. After all, the older children had been fed until they were close on two years old. Rosie though had shown no further interest, turning her head sharply, newly emerging teeth clenched. Then, with Mark being ill, Polly hadn't had the strength to persist. Now it was a blessing that she did not have to worry about the baby girls.

With Violet ensconced with her sisters at Mrs Abbott's, they moved Nelson to the smallest bedroom, so the other boys would not disturb him. Mark was still weak but had today gone with the others to sit on Mrs Abbott's bumpy chair in the window and play with the wooden boats that Mr Abbott had carved for his boys when they were small. Mark was keen to get back to school and was adamant that tomorrow he could manage the walk up to Wrinkleberry to join his friends. Polly thought this was unlikely but maybe by next week he'd be strong enough.

Nelson stirred and a fit of coughing convulsed his body. His blond curls were dark with sweat and foul smelling, blood-stained mucus escaped from his nostrils. Polly held a tin mug to his lips. He managed only few sips of the brackish, warm well water before his head dropped back on his pillow.

'Can you manage some broth do you think, lad?' she asked.

Nelson moaned softly and raised his head, attempting to sup the thick liquid from the spoon. He leant back on the pillow.

'Can't swallow nothing, ma,' he whispered. His voice was so quiet that Polly had to bend her head to catch what he said. 'It's me neck. 'Tis so sore, ma. Stop it hurting ma.' Tears squeezed from the child's reddened eyelids.

Fear constricted Polly's chest in an ever-tightening band; an appalling echo of her time of anguish when Violet was so very sick. Mark had recovered in a few days. Surely, tomorrow, Nelson would begin to brighten up too. Through the night Polly dozed by her son's bedside, wiping his face, flinching every time he wheezed and struggled for air. Again and again Polly jerked awake in panic at the sound of his coughing. More terrifying still, were the occasions when she roused to the night's silence and had to put her ear to Nelson's chest, to seek a reassuring beat. The boy's heart seemed to race and to Polly, it's thudding threatened to drown the inexorable sound of the clock, ticking away each moment.

Next morning, Nelson's symptoms intensified and it was as if every breath required an insurmountable effort.

'Alb, do we have enough money for the doctor?' Polly asked. 'Him's getting real bad. Could we ask the chapel, or maybe the Rechabites, or even Mrs Hamlyn for help?'

Albert could tell Polly was desperate. Not since Violet's illness had she suggested calling in a doctor.

'There's not many lobsters about but the mackerel's run well this week, Pol. There's enough in the pot if the chile needs a doctor.'

Doctor Crew had only established his practice covering Hartland and Clovelly a year or so ago. His arrival had caused quite a stir, as he had brought with him a young wife. To the astonishment of the neighbourhood, it seemed that she too was a doctor. Folk had gradually overcome their initial reluctance to call upon their services, although, truth be told, they still hoped it would be Mr Dr Crew and not his wife who arrived on their doorstep in response to a summons.

Dr Crew was a man in his twenties with a hearty manner and a neat moustache. Only the previous month Polly had had occasion to speak to him when he came to help Will Oke who'd gone over the cliffs when they were cutting down the trees behind the New Inn. The old man, who was not too steady on his feet, had been keen to help throw the rubbish away over the cliffside, to save it being taken up or down the street. Best thing would have been to burn it, thought Polly but they hadn't and Will had paid the price. She'd watched as he was carried back to his home on the square and Dr Crew had approached Polly, asking her to keep an eye on Mrs Oke, who seemed bewildered. Polly had gone along to the Oke's cottage whilst Dr Crew was still there. She had found him chatting to Mrs Oke in an amicable manner, not like a doctor at all. He was asking the old lady about the chickens that she kept in the back yard. Polly had heard the gossip that spoke of the doctor's eccentric interest in chickens. It was said he kept dozens of them at his home in Hartland. Lots of fancy breeds and such. That seemed strange too for a doctor. Will Oke had died, despite the ministrations of Dr Crew. Sending for the doctor didn't always mean that people recovered. Polly pushed that thought aside.

It was mid-afternoon when Dr Crew breezed into Polly's cottage after a perfunctory knock.

'Where's the patient then?' he asked.

Polly resisted the temptation to curtsey. Despite working for the Pine-Coffins and then the Powells, she really wasn't comfortable with posh folk, not when they encroached on her own domain. Whatever they said about Dr Crew being friendly, he was still not one of them. He belonged to a different world, like the minister, like Mrs Hamlyn and even Mr Caird. Polly wished she'd had time to give the tiles another mop but

Dr Crew didn't seem to be taking any notice of the state of the floor.

'Will you take a cup of tea doctor?' Polly enquired. They so rarely sent for the doctor that she wasn't sure what was expected of her.

'Perhaps later,' he replied, 'first I will see the youngster.'

Although she was usually taciturn, something about the doctor's manner made Polly feel obliged to keep the conversation going.

'Is your horse being looked after at the top?' she asked.

The doctor smiled. 'No,' he said gently, as he ascended the narrow stairs behind Polly, 'I have a motor and I have parked it where the cobbles begin.'

Despite the hot and humid day, Polly had drawn the heavy curtain and closed the tiny window. She had even stuffed the gaps round the frame with old rags, in the belief that Nelson needed to sweat out his fever and that the air would be bad for him. The child moaned and rolled to turn his head away from the door, as if the light hurt his eyes. The room smelt stale and Polly hastily stooped to remove the chamber pot, as she had not emptied it since Nelson vomited last.

''Tis the morbid sore throat doctor, isn't it,' said Polly, hardly daring to voice her deepest fears. 'I don't know what to do. I thought he'd get well like his brother but he just gets worse. How'd he get it doctor? Was it something I've done?'

'Don't you worry about that now,' said the doctor kindly. 'I'll just take a look at the lad.' His smile at the anxious mother belied the doctor's grim thoughts. It was not for nothing that diphtheria was known as the strangling angel.

Dr Crew examined the boy gently and competently, then suggested letting light and air into the room. Polly pulled back the curtain and struggled with the catch. It was so close outside in the afternoon sun that opening the window made little difference to the temperature inside.

'He must keep his fluids up,' advised the doctor as they descended the stairs. 'If he will take broth then so much the better. Maybe a bread poultice on the chest to ease his breathing and I'll give you some capsules to burn that may help. The next twenty four hours will be crucial.'

Polly felt confused. Mark had got better. Surely, Nelson would recover as his brother had done. She could not think beyond this.

The doctor seemed quite at ease, as he accepted her invitation to sit and he lowered himself on to a kitchen chair. Polly reached for the cake tin. What a good job she'd managed to make that fruit cake, even though Mark had been ill. She put the cake on a knife-scarred board and cut an uneven wedge. Thinking that this might not be right for a gentleman like the doctor, she tried again, severing a smaller portion this time. As the kettle came to the boil on the Bodley, the back door opened and Bertie and Violet came in from school.

'Oh, Vi,' said Polly. 'I'm mighty glad youm back. Can you get the others from Mrs Abbott? She's been baking, there may be a biscuit for you.'

Violet headed out to do her mother's bidding whilst Bertie shuffled his feet awkwardly, seemingly unsure of what he should do. He saw his mother frowning at him and hastily he removed his cap. The doctor looked at Bertie appraisingly.

'Hello young man,' he said. 'You look just the age for my Scout Patrol. Have you heard of the Boy Scouts? I am sure you would enjoy the jolly times we have. We are off to camp in a week or two. What do you think of that?'

Bertie looked desperately at his mother for guidance. How on earth should he respond to this gentleman? He might have been speaking a foreign language for all Bertie understood of the words.

'Oh no, sir,' exclaimed Polly in horror. 'Not Bertie sir, he's well…. He's not the sort for being away from home, camps and the like, no, no, no it would never do for Bertie.'

Dr Crew looked from Bertie to his mother and back again.

'All lads are welcome,' he said, 'be they church or chapel, rich or poor. It sets the boys up for life, teaches them useful skills and fits them to serve their country should war come.'

'I don't mean to be disrespectful sir,' Polly countered, 'but you'd not make a soldier out of our Bertie. He leaves school soon and will help his da a bit but he was never one for schooling and such.' She coloured as she realised that she had dared to contradict someone so learned as a doctor.

The need for tact was slowly dawning on Dr Crew. He stood up and surreptitiously brushed the cake crumbs from his moustache with his pristine lawn handkerchief.

'Thank you kindly for the tea and cake,' he said. 'Don't forget to send for me again if there is any change.'

'I'll settle with you now doctor,' said Polly reaching for the old brown jug with the broken handle that sat on the mantelshelf and held the family's emergency fund.

'There's no need,' replied the doctor firmly. 'Let's wait and see if I need to come again. I can send you a bill.'

Polly maintained her vigil by Nelson's bedside as the burning afternoon was eclipsed by evening shadows. Mrs Abbott had sent the girls back with a pie for the family's meal. Albert occupied his usual chair at the head of the table and faced the six children who sat before him. He wished Polly had come down, she needed to eat. To eat and to help him decide what to say to the family. Outwardly, Polly had seemingly cheered after the visit of the doctor. It was as if she had closed her mind to any possibility but Nelson's full recovery. Mark, with the resilience of childhood, was regaining his strength rapidly and eagerly looking forward to playing with his friends again. Polly was focussing on this and seemed to assume that Nelson's illness would follow the same course. Albert felt he should somehow prepare the children in case ...... But how to do this? More to the point, how could he get Polly to see that their youngest son was rapidly losing ground? Bertie, chomping rhythmically, seemed unaware of his father's concerns but Leonard caught Albert's eye and read the tension in his face.

'What's to do lad?' Albert said desperately. He really shouldn't be loading adult worries on to the shoulders of his sixteen-year-old son but there was no reasoning with Polly.

'Shall I take the young 'uns back to Mrs Abbott, da?' Leonard asked. The girls had all spent the last two nights with their neighbour.

'Yes. Yes, I think so boy and Mark too. Violet, get what your brother needs and I'll see if Mrs Abbott can find room for him as well tonight.'

As the children readied themselves to leave the cottage, Albert wondered if they should be allowed to say good-bye to Nelson; if this would be their last chance. Not the little girls of course, the danger of infection was too great but Violet and Mark perhaps. Compared to other villages, the inhabitants of Clovelly seemed to be fortunate when it came to sickness. It was rare that their children fell mortally ill, that school desks were left empty and names were no longer called when the register was taken at the beginning of the day. Within reach of the healthy sea air, it was unusual for a child to die; leaving as their only legacy a fresh mound of churchyard earth and maybe later a cold granite memorial, if the parents could afford it. There was a time when Albert and Polly had feared for Violet but she was nearly eleven now and no longer a worry. Had they been lucky to rear all their eight youngsters? Was their time of good fortune over? In the end, Albert decided to send the children straight to Mrs Abbott's. Nelson looked so fearfully ill now, in a permanent doze, his skin a translucent bluish colour. If the worst happened, best they remembered him as a rosy child with a winning smile.

There was no room for a chair beside the bed in Violet's cramped room where Nelson lay. Polly was wedged on a rickety wooden stool between the bedstead and the door. When Albert approached, she sat up, straightening her shoulders as if bracing herself for confrontation. Albert had offered to sit with their son. He wanted to sit with their son but Polly was resistant. Albert and his feelings were superfluous. It was as if Nelson was all hers. Her responsibility. Hers to nurse. Hers to fret over. Her son.

Albert wanted to clasp his son in his arms, in an attempt to transfer some of his own strength into that limp body but Polly was defensive, protective of her child and brooking no interference. Albert felt he could not go near. The boy was too weak to raise his head to cough now. A trickle of saliva escaped from the corner of his mouth as the terrible, terrifying sound of his attempts to draw breath rent the air. Tears prickled under Albert's eyelids, surely there was no way back from this. Polly remained upright on her stool, staring straight ahead of her, as if she was concentrating on something distant and not on her child.

'Shall I stay Pol?' asked Albert. He ached to say, 'I'd like to stay,' but Polly's demeanour was far from welcoming.

'No need,' said Polly abruptly. 'You've to be fishing at first light.'

Excluded, saddened, confused, Albert sighed and with a last glance at Nelson, he descended the narrow steps.

Alone with her child, her baby, Polly sat as the sky darkened outside. She had taken the doctor's advice and left the window open. The evening sounds of the street gradually gave way to silence. Still Nelson's breathing rasped and rattled. Still the downstairs clock ticked on, a sonorous metronome marking the days, the hours and now the minutes left to Polly and her son. Polly dozed fitfully. As the first gold and pink of day tinged the sky and the dawn birdsong began, Polly was aware of a strange silence. Then she realised.

The coughing had stopped.

Overlaying the early morning stirrings of the villagers, came an eerie and penetrating wail. A sound that was barely human. Fleetingly, Polly wondered where the noise was coming from. Then she recognised the scream as her own. In the kitchen, Leonard, comprehending, gripped Bertie's arm and stopped him from climbing the stairs. Albert went to his wife and held out his arms but Polly, silent now, remained rigid, unmoving. Then, as if a shutter had descended, cutting off all the emotions of the past few days, she became practical, bustling.

'There's all to do Alb,' she said. 'We must tell the doctor. The authorities have to know if 'tis morbid sore throat. Then there's the vicar and the undertaker. Can we afford a stone do you think? He needs a stone. We'll have to send word to Daisy and to my parents and your ma. I need to get the others from Mrs Abbott. Do you think they will be allowed in school today, or will folk think we are infectious?'

Albert let his wife run on, defeated. She seemed to need no comfort, nor be aware that comfort needed to be given. Her way of coping was to concentrate on the necessities of everyday living. It was as if, for Polly, the chasm left by the loss of Nelson was being covered, as the holes that the boys had dug on the beach were obliterated by the tide.

Two days later, Albert prepared to lead the sombre cortège that wound its way up the cobbled street. This was his chance to take charge, to perform a final service for his son. Polly was at home, it was not done for women to be seen at a funeral. Funerals were the responsibility of the menfolk. The neighbours had drawn their curtains as a mark of respect and the donkeys had their hooves muffled, so no unseemly clatter would intrude on the solemnity of the occasion.

The villagers stood on their doorsteps, heads bowed, as the tiny coffin, carried between Albert and Leonard, passed. They made their way to the churchyard. The sun was still relentless and the trees by the church cast a welcome shade. The sexton had done his job and the coffin was slowly lowered. Such a small hole it seemed, such a short, unblemished life, such an insignificant impression this little child had made on the world. Albert and Leonard stepped back, the black armbands that they wore marking them out as the chief mourners. Hats clasped in hands and eyes downcast, the men waited for Reverend Simkin to begin the brief burial service.

Having declined offers of company from her neighbours, Polly sat with only her thoughts to occupy her. The younger children were again being cared for by Mrs Abbott. She knelt on the floor by the bed where Nelson had died, clutching the child's nightshirt in her hand. She buried her nose in the rough linen fabric and inhaled, trying, somehow, to recapture the essence of her son. The unthinkable nightmare of the past week kept surfacing in her mind, however hard she tried to put it aside. Mrs Powell's dire warnings haunted her. Why had she allowed herself to love him? Why had she loved him the best? Was this her punishment for not loving them all the same? She had nothing left of him. The only reminder would be the cross in the churchyard that Albert promised they could have. They would need to save of course but if the mackerel continued to run well, as they had in the past few weeks, that would go a good way towards it. Already, Polly was struggling to bring a picture of a healthy Nelson to her mind. All she could visualise was that poor convulsed body as he struggled for breath and always she would hear that awful, aweful breathing.

Why hadn't she agreed when that portrait photographer had offered to take the family's likenesses? There were always photographers touting for business in Clovelly, hoping to find visitors in a generous mood, wanting to capture their brief holiday happinesses, so that they had something to linger over in the cold winter months. The villagers would be asked to pose whilst cameras captured scenes of the street and its inhabitants. There were several photographs of Daisy and even one of a blond baby Mark but of Nelson, nothing. The thought grew in Polly's mind until it reached the proportions of an obsession. Yes, a portrait and soon, before anything could happen to the others.

She closed her heart. The pain was too great, never again must she allow herself to love a child as she had loved Nelson. She pulled herself together. From now on she would be a mother. She would feed and clothe her children, she would see they were safe but love, love had died with Nelson.

Outside, the clouds gathered. The thunder barked and the storm broke.

7
1915

Leonard pulled his cap down over his thick hair, wishing that his mother was handier with the scissors when she decided that he needed a haircut. The stirring street showed its early morning face, cobbles damp and mist rising. He trudged down the hill, boot-nails striking and sparking against the stone. The village was starting to wake, cats returning from nocturnal prowling, acrid wood-smoke curling from the chimneys, milk-filled buckets squeaking as they swung on the expertly carried yoke. Fishermen were on their way to the harbour, eager to be the first to see if the recent gales had abated sufficiently for them to catch the tide. The older men, joints stiff with years at sea and the daily climb up the slope, were slower. Touching his temple and grunting a greeting to those he overtook on his downward path, Leonard's journey progressed as usual; his daily routine circumscribed. His father and brother had gone on ahead, leaving Leonard to chop the last few logs for his ma before hurrying to join them.

The rain of recent weeks had halted its onslaught but as daybreak gripped the bay, scudding dark clouds could be seen pitching across the pinkening sky. It was warm for January but the wicked south-westerly still swirled and stabbed through the street. There would be no fishing again today, thought Leonard. The sea, its vagaries, its beauty and its menace was the counterpoint to his life; an all pervading rhythm to which his body and his soul must respond. The idleness, the frustrations and the privations of days ashore made tempers short and bellies rumble. He did not relish another day of mending nets, repairing pots and tidying the cellar; tasks that had already been repeated and completed as the insidious storms, that had come in with the new year, persisted.

Leonard lingered outside Granny Smale's, inhaling deeply as the aroma of baking brought a halt to his purposeful gait. Short, sturdy and energetic but elderly now, Granny Smale hadn't been Granny Pengilly for twenty years or more but the sign outside the shop, that swayed and creaked in the salt-laden gusts, still read "Pengilly's Tea-Rooms". Harry Smale had succumbed to a sudden attack of influenza just last week and there had been speculation as to how Granny Smale would manage the business alone.

Hushed tones as they whispered, 'She's rising seventy you know.'

'Harry was the one who did all the heavy work, what with her rheumatics.'

'If she can't get help she won't cope when the season starts.'

As Leonard drew level with the small panes of blemished glass his eye was drawn by a sudden movement within. Enveloped in a large, wrap-round apron, a slender girl was in the window, dusting the deep sill and readying it for the day's display of cakes. Leonard flushed and looked away, embarrassed that the girl had caught him staring. Studiously concentrating on her dusting, the girl did not look up again but he knew that she was aware of his presence outside the window. He hadn't paid much attention when his ma and Mrs Stanbury had spoken of a granddaughter coming out from Bideford but the sight of this unsmiling scrap brought the conversation back to mind. Surely she wasn't old enough to have left school? Her long dark plait swung errantly forward as she reached into the far corner of the sill and the girl flicked it back behind her, exasperated.

Now seventeen, Leonard had recently begun to view girls as an intriguing, rather than mildly irritating, segment of humanity. The girl in the shop window awakened his curiosity but there was no glimmer of romantic interest; she was a child, as his eleven year old sister, Violet, was a child, unformed and unremarkable. Leonard considered himself to be a man; he'd been working these past three years and more, helping his father with his fishing boat, *The Flowers*, named for Leonard's sisters. When Bertie had finished school last summer, he had joined them. Such a small boat did not warrant three men but Leonard knew that his brother was unlikely to find a job elsewhere. Bertie could be trusted to do simple tasks under supervision but he really wasn't the crew that anyone apart from family would choose. Leonard was vaguely aware that his father was expecting him to find other regular employment, leaving Bertie to work *The Flowers* with Albert.

Leonard was not immune to the patriotic hysteria that had sent his unheeding contemporaries into the jaws of this pernicious war. His mother's reaction to his tentative suggestion that he might form one of their number had rocked the cottage for days. She'd screamed, she'd wept, she'd begged, citing the ominous casualty lists in the newspapers. Inevitably, the loss of Nelson was brought up; it always was the lever that Polly used to promote her cause. The months since his death had done nothing to assuage the raw emotion, the devastation and the guilt.

Quietly, his da had said, "Taint worth the bother lad.'

As the impetuous haste to sign up subsided, Leonard thought more cautiously about his future. Maybe it was best he bided at home for now. The adventure was already palling for those of his mates who had gone at the beginning.

'Over by Christmas,' they'd grinned, boasting of getting one over on the Hun and joking about bringing a wife back from France.

Eager to kill, to do their bit but seemingly oblivious to the fact that to kill meant the likelihood of they themselves being killed. Christmas had come and gone but the war showed no sign of doing the same. Leonard's da, who laboriously read the *North Devon Journal* each week, saving it smooth and virginal for a Sunday afternoon, said it wouldn't be long before everyone had to go, like it or not. They said some jobs would make you safe, some of the boys on the farms maybe but the third man on a two-man boat could be spared. Joining the merchant service could save him. His mother clung to this thought with all the desperation of a woman whose family were slipping from her grasp, whose future was beyond her control.

As more village lads left their boats to answer Kitchener's call, Leonard was getting casual work filling in for absent crewmen but he knew that the day was coming when he would need to think seriously about finding a full-time job. For years he had sat on the quayside, listening to the old men yarning about their younger days. He had envied their memories, stories of travel and exploits that became more far-fetched with every telling but which awed the small boys whose lives had yet to unfold. Now the old men pontificated about the war, what so-and-so should or shouldn't have done, how our brave boys would win through and wasn't it a pity about Postman Branch, who'd been taken prisoner. Periodically, as Leonard pondered his future, the tales that he had absorbed in childhood rose up to tempt him to journey beyond the bay. He knew that his destiny lay on the intractable ocean but would it be on a merchant ship, a naval frigate, or one of the large trawlers? It was not a matter for today but soon he would need to decide. Then his experiences would form part of the warp and weft of Clovelly tradition, exclaimed over outside the Red Lion and preserved for future generations. For the present, he was reasonably content with his lot, thinking no further ahead than returning home for his lunchtime soused herring, after a morning in the cellar.

It was Sunday before Leonard saw the girl again. Leonard's attendance at chapel was borne out of habit rather than conviction. His parents went, many of his neighbours went, except, of course, the Anglicans who plodded up the hill to All Saints or crammed into the tiny, village chapelry that was St Peter's. It was what you did. This particular week, Leonard's family arrived later than usual, Lily's hair ribbon had not passed muster and the hunt for an acceptable replacement had delayed them. As they hustled in, Leonard caught sight of Granny Smale, sat as usual in the back right hand corner of the crowded Methodist chapel. Her Sunday-black shawl was not so much an acknowledgement of her husband Harry's recent passing, more a practical garment for an elderly woman. The girl was next to her, squeezing against the wall, as her grandmother's ample frame settled on the hard, narrow pew. She was, as he remembered, small and slight, sitting rigidly upright, her tightly plaited hair secured with a dark bow. Her face was shaded by a voluminous bonnet and she did not look round as the late arrivals entered at the back of the chapel. Newcomers were always a source of whispered interest in a community such as Clovelly and sidelong glances were cast in the girl's direction but the service was beginning and all attention was focussed on the minister as he bade them welcome, uttered a prayer and announced the opening hymn.

After the service, the ladies assumed concern for Granny Smale's recently widowed state, using this as an excuse to appraise the new arrival. Leonard wasn't particularly interested but the gossip swirled round him, whilst he waited impatiently for his mother to indicate that it was time for them to leave.

'Yes, this was Annie.'

'You remember, she's Mabel's girl. You'll mind Mabel, her who married at seventeen to Ben Stoneman over to Bideford and only just in time that was too.'

'Well, they say Mabel's eldest 'tweren't Ben's, you've only got to look at young Susan to know that.'

'Susan's married herself now of course and gone to live down Newton Abbot way.'

'This one's the youngest, well the youngest that's survived of course.'

'No, not the youngest, Mabel's last babe survived, born last year she was.'

'Well, Mabel's not had a lot of luck with her chiles.'

The chattering rattled on.

'Left school at Christmas young Annie did, so just handy to come and help her Gran.'

At this point, Leonard raised his estimate of the girl's age by about three years but his ability to assess girl's ages, based largely on his sisters and girls he had known at school, was rudimentary. When was his mother going to be ready to leave? He'd promised to go up to the woods with the lads. They would ignore the drizzle, share cigarettes and companionship, enjoy an afternoon that was free from chores. As soon as he'd left school, Leonard had assumed that he could now join the queue in Ellis' shop for an occasional packet of ten

Woodbines without being gainsaid. His parents were broadly accepting of this habit, which in turn had extended to Bertie when he too reached fourteen, as long as they didn't smoke in the house or on a Sunday. The one exception was Christmas Day, when the men of the family might light up after tucking in to whatever Mrs Hamlyn's generous seasonal gift to her tenants had been. This year, each household had received a haunch of venison from the estate; it had been a good shooting season.

Granny Smale had positioned herself near the chapel door, with Annie, once again eclipsed by the sheer bulk of her grandmother, trying to appear inconspicuous. Granny Smale obviously thought that, as near neighbours and possessing children of a similar age to Annie, Leonard's was a family that should be especially introduced.

He joined the queue to leave the chapel and muttered, 'Good day,' as he and his siblings were named by Granny Smale in turn, in strict order of their age.

Annie looked at her polished button boots and twisted her fingers awkwardly.

As the war took 1915 in its grasp and played with people's lives as a cat will with a hapless mouse, Leonard's routine remained largely unchanged. Sometimes he caught sight of Annie, hanging dishcloths on the line, wiping down the tea-room tables, or struggling down the street, burdened with shopping bags. In half-forgotten pre-war holiday seasons P & A Campbell's steamers had brought hundreds of day-trippers from Ilfracombe, or even South Wales. Tourists were tolerated. They spoiled the solitude, the silence and the regular rhythm of the fishing year. Yet with them came colour, diversion, bustle, excitement. Moreover, their pennies, their shillings, their florins, were secreted in the pockets of boarding house owners and dropped in the wooden drawers of tea-room tills. The sight of the white funnels on the horizon sent the fishermen scurrying to their boats. Passengers in their finery had to be ferried from steamer to land and many a coin could be earned rowing a boat that was acting as a tender. A day's fishing might yield a bumper sea-harvest or it could bring nothing more than hands calloused from the oars but P & A Campbell landed a certain catch. The war, of course, meant fewer visitors to Clovelly. It was said that White Line steamers would soon be required for use as troop-ships and now Clovelly's harbour no longer thronged and hummed with jostling sightseers.

Even in peacetime, the winter was never busy for tea-rooms and boarding houses but there were always those who travelled to the balmy south-west for their health and the occasional artist or writer who found inspiration in the sea air, the crashing waves and the quaint cobbles. True, the lodging houses more often than not displayed cards in their windows that read "Vacancies" but the businesses had limped through the early months of the hostilities. This was testament to the tenacity of Clovelly's residents, who were able to adjust to changing circumstances and to turn their hands to finding different ways of putting food on the table. So the tea-rooms stayed open and as the year stretched towards Easter, the girl remained with her grandmother, smiling shyly now whenever she saw Leonard.

Spring beckoned, mufflers were left off and Clovelly stirred from its winter slumbers. The gales abated, rain and mist retired gracefully to their lair and the weather turned unseasonably warm. Hibernation was over, boarding house rugs were beaten and tea-room silver shone. Leonard, with the restless energy of youth, found inactivity irksome. When no one needed an extra hand on a boat he was reduced to running errands for his mother. Anything to get out of the house, where his two small sisters squealed and Nelson's absence echoed. He had been up to the woods to collect branches to split for next winter's kindling when he spotted Annie on a similar mission. Cheeks besmirched with earth and her hair uncharacteristically untidy, she was attempting to drag a large branch behind her.

'Baint no good for firings 'til it be seasoned,' he remarked, conversationally. The past weeks of Granny Smale's home cooking had filled Annie out and although she was still not much taller than Violet, she no longer looked like a child. She was, Leonard noticed for the first time, even quite pretty. Undaunted by her lack of response, Leonard tried again.

'Can I help you carry that down?' he asked.

'If you like,' she shrugged. Then, more graciously, 'Thank you.'

It wasn't a very auspicious start and their journey back down the street was accompanied by long silences that were none the less companionable. As Leonard and Annie reached the tea-rooms Granny Smale came out.

'Youm busy boy?' She asked Leonard.

'No,' he replied. 'Not 'til father comes back to shore.'

'Could you help Annie here move the tables out into the yard so she can spring clean?' she asked. ''Tis too much for me with me rheumatics.'

There were three solid pine tables, scrubbed and scarred, in the tea-room. Lacking their starched, white tablecloths they looked vulnerable and unloved. Leonard glanced from the large tables to Annie's slim frame and lifted his eyebrows slightly.

'Us can give it a try,' he said.

Annie took hold of the edge of the first table and with a strength that belied her stature, began dragging it backwards towards the door. Sunlight streamed in from the yard and aura-like, specks of dust flickered round her. Leonard grabbed the other end of the table and began to lift, trying to take the greater share of the weight as Annie, silhouetted against the brightness of the late March day, deftly manoeuvred herself through the doorway.

Once the tables were outside, the pair returned for the chairs and upended them, placing their wooden seats on the table tops. As they went back and forth to the yard, they could hear Granny Smale banging pans and slamming shut the door of the Bodley.

'Pasty boy?' she asked gruffly as the room, empty now, echoed to the sound of their footsteps.

She waved Leonard into the back kitchen and he sat at the small table. He took his first bite of the savoury pasty, pastry flaking on to his plate as his teeth sunk through the crust and the flavoursome, hot gravy oozed into his mouth, scalding his tongue. He was aware of the silence and Granny Smale's disapproving stare. Her pasty, like Annie's, still lay intact and unblemished in front of her.

'Grace,' she barked.

Leonard hastily returned his pasty to his plate and was glad that Annie's bowed head meant that she could not see his scarlet cheeks. Grace muttered, Granny Smale poured strong tea from a large brown pot into the waiting enamel mugs and spooned in generous amounts of sugar. She was eyeing him speculatively as he thanked her and resumed his feast.

'Could you wait tables boy?' she asked.

Wait tables? That wasn't work for a lad. Did she really want him to take dainty plates of scones to expectant visitors?

Seeing his hesitancy, Granny Smale elaborated, 'Annie does the serving but could you take the heavy trays from the kitchen to the dresser, help stoke the Bodley, fetch and carry some? Just on a weekend mind, when it is too much for one to manage. I be in the kitchen brewing up and I can't lift the trays no more.'

Leonard thought swiftly. It didn't sound like much of a job. The lads would rib him and say he'd turned into a maid. He caught sight of Annie's eager expression, she seemed to be holding her breath. She really was very pretty. Perhaps that would go down well with his chums, that he was spending time with a girl, even one as young as this. Jerked back from his musings, Leonard was aware that Granny Smale was talking.

'I can't pay you more than a shillin' a day but there's a good dinner and tea in it for you and mayhap a pick of any left-over cakes that won't keep 'til Monday.'

'I'll do it,' said Leonard; Annie exhaled visibly.

Easter was early that year and those whose incomes depended on the annual influx of rich folk from up-country were confident that, despite the war, there would still be visitors. Surely those who wanted cheering up, as the international news worsened, would make their usual westward journey. Others, who were eager to escape the food shortages of the towns, would travel to enjoy the countryside's plenty. At Granny Smale's there were gradual adjustments being made. The once brisk, bustling wife of Harry Smale, was, in widowhood, diminished. No longer vigorous and stout, she had lost the appetite for life. As Annie settled in, she shouldered more and more of the work of the tea-rooms. The baking still needed Granny Smale's own light touch but the old lady's hands would not always obey her and she was becoming unsteady on her feet, making carrying pots of hot tea hazardous. Annie undertook her increasing responsibilities with equanimity. As the season got underway, Leonard hauled lobster pots during the week and heaved trays at the weekends. Once their initial shyness had worn off, he and Annie drifted into a comfortable friendship.

One morning, when the village was painted bright with early May sunshine, Leonard found Annie unusually downcast.

'What's the matter maid?' he asked.

''Tis me ma,' she said. 'She's in the family way, she's old to have another baby and she's lost four. Hettie's a year old now and she's fine so far but I'm worried.'

With six younger siblings, Leonard was not ignorant of the risks associated with child bearing. He was acutely aware of the impact that the loss of a child could have. Thinking of his mother's failure to cope with Nelson's death, he wondered how on earth she would be if she'd lost four. Annie was explaining that her brothers and sister had all been infants when they'd died. Leonard supposed the fact that Nelson had been older, with a proper personality all of his own, might make a difference but he didn't know.

'It was so awful,' Annie was saying, 'she didn't have another baby for seven years after we lost Norman and then there was Hettie. Who knows what will happen this time?'

'I'm sure 'twill be fine,' said Leonard, knowing full well that this was a platitude and that all might be far from fine. Then a thought struck him.

'Will you have to go back to help?' he asked.

'No,' she replied. 'Granny can't manage without me and Fanny will cope back home with ma.'

A sense of relief seeped into Leonard's consciousness and surprised him with its force. He was used to his new weekend routine in the tea-rooms and it dawned on him that he would miss this quicksilver girl, if she had to disappear back to the town. They sat unspeaking, waiting for the heavy kettles, hissing and sizzling on the Bodley, to come to the boil. Leonard broke the silence.

'How do you think Granny Smale's managing without Mr Smale?' he asked. 'She seems to have got... I don't know, old I suppose.'

'At least he had been ill,' said Annie, 'and he was old. So it wasn't a shock, not like when my granfer died young and she was left with children to look after. That's why the tea-rooms were so important, when she hadn't got his wage.'

'He was lost at sea wasn't he?' said Leonard, trying to recall the tales he'd heard about the demise of Annie's grandfather, Granny Smale's first husband, Captain William Pengilly.

'Well,' said Annie, huddling closer and lowering her voice. 'In a way. It was all years before I was born of course but I've heard my mother gossiping about it. I don't think I am supposed to know the details.'

'What happened?' asked Leonard, enjoying this moment of intimacy.

'He had an accident,' went on Annie, conspiratorially. 'His ship docked somewhere called the Isle of Wight. He went in to town on the train and then missed the last connection home to the ship. He was walking back along the railway line when he fell through the viaduct.'

She paused, obviously hoping for a reaction. Leonard managed to assume a suitably surprised expression, although, now she mentioned it, he did recall having heard something of the sort.

'He had to be buried there of course. Granny sometimes talks about how she went all the way there for the funeral. She told me he's buried in the middle of the island. It worries her that she can't visit the grave. I always said I'd like to go and pay my respects one day but I don't see how I could ever make the journey.'

'How did he manage to fall?' queried Leonard.

Annie dropped her voice even further, so that Leonard had to strain to hear her.

'They say he was *drunk*,' she whispered. Now, Leonard was genuinely astonished, surely Captain Pengilly had been a Methodist.

'Is that really true?' he asked.

'I don't know,' said Annie. 'Ma never talks about it. She was living with *her* grandparents when it happened.'

Granny Smale's footsteps could be heard coming in from the tea-room, where she had been inspecting Annie's table-laying efforts. Leonard hurriedly changed the subject.

''Tis going to be a fine day,' he said, 'we should be busy.'

'Yes,' the old lady agreed. 'There's dozens of scones baked and plenty of cream in the cold safe. They'll all be wanting cream teas.'

Leonard and Annie exchanged a glance and Leonard felt that somehow their relationship had moved on a stage, in the light of the confidences and concerns that they had shared. Annie had shrugged off her despondency and his attempts to distract her from her worries about her mother seemed to have succeeded.

The tourists emerged in the sparkling spring sunlight, eager to relax and forget the enormity of the news from the front. Leonard and Annie were kept busy serving the iconic cream teas for which Devon was famous. Normally, Granny Smale would help in the kitchen but deflated, she dozed in the worn, wicker chair by the Bodley and did not stir as the two young people rushed in and out to fulfil all the orders. As the afternoon wore on, the last few visitors straggled down the street, replete from pasties and scones and Annie turned the sign on the tea-room door to "Closed". Leonard had barely kept pace with washing the dishes in the scullery and a tottering mound of crumb-filled plates and tea-stained cups awaited attention.

'Let's sup some tea,' said Annie. 'We deserve it.'

She poured Leonard a cup of well stewed tea and knowing his preference, added three teaspoons of sugar. As they sipped the steaming liquid, they were alerted to sounds of Granny Smale moving about in the kitchen. They heard the banging of a door, followed by a loud exclamation.

'Where's the cream? I left it in the cold safe this morning. Someone has pinched me cream. Annie!' she called, agitated now, 'have you not been keeping watch? Who's been in and took me cream?'

Annie smiled and opened the wooden drawer of the till. 'Look Gran,' she said, revealing the mound of shining half-crowns and sixpences in the drawer. 'We've been that busy that we sold it all.'

Granny Smale muttered and grumbled but was clearly pleased with the day's takings. For Leonard there was contentment and peace, his worries about the war, about the direction his life should take, pushed to one side. He knew that this tranquillity was a fleeting interlude and that soon decisions would have to be made. Should he ignore his mother's protests and join up? Should he opt for the adventure of the merchant service? That would comfort his ma, although he knew that her belief that this would somehow keep him safe was a delusion. He glanced at Annie. Suddenly, he felt optimistic about the future, whatever shape it might take and somehow, he knew that the girl who sat smiling at him could be an important part of what was to come.

8
Summer 1916

Abraham Tuke peered through the dust-smeared train window, apprehension vying with anticipation. As the train idled, soldiers lowered the windows and unmindful of the smuts, leaned out into the steam clouds, eager to catch a final glimpse of familiar scenes. Abraham studied his comrades. Full of nervous laughter and bravado, with kitbags bulging and gaspers lit; carefree masks concealed their innermost anxieties. Family men rubbed fingers over sepia images of chubby infants. Scared boys scribbled hasty notes to their mothers. The flashy young townies, the poodle fakers, slicked back their macassared hair, as they blew kisses to girls on the platform and boasted of imagined conquests, past and future.

It was a few minutes after 9.30am when the clattering troop-train steamed out of Tidworth station, bound for Southampton, taking its reluctant passengers on the first stage of their journey to Armageddon. Abraham cast his mind back to the unreality of his training on Salisbury Plain and before that at Chelmsford. Unending lectures by medal-laden officers and the shock of fixing the cold-steeled bayonet for the first time. Major Shilland shouting, fashioning half-competent soldiers from inexperienced recruits. It was only three years since Abraham had left King's College but already his schooldays had faded into pre-war oblivion; consigned to the soft, safe space that was the past, along with his Clovelly childhood and his aspirations of becoming a teacher. The train's rhythm beat into Abraham's brain like a brand, its thudding tattoo helped to block out his fears. He could only focus on the here, on the now; to look further ahead was the sure route to Bedlam.

The men from Abraham's battalion gradually adjusted to life on the Western Front. For the first week, billeted near Les Lobes, training continued much as it had at home. Some of the men attempted to maintain the fiction that this was all a bit of a jaunt, a chance to show the Boche what for. They walked in the ruins of the town, where resilient locals sold gingerbread and cognac-filled sweets, in a mocking parody of Christmas. They were jerked back to reality by the battle-scarred landscape and the sounds of shellfire; a constant reminder that they had taken a step nearer to death. Far removed from the security of Salisbury Plain, they continued to learn how to kill.

It was the last day of May when the order came to move on from the trenches at Les Lobes. In the eerie pre-dawn light, Abraham, still not fully at ease with his rank, supervised the evacuation of the trench.

'Come on man, we must leave no litter,' he chided a lazy Tommy.

The man resentfully picked up the cigarette packet that he had discarded. He crumpled the maroon-coloured carton in his fist and grunted.

'It's only a pack of smokes guv,' was the mumbled response.

Abraham thought it wise to pretend that he had not heard. The chap was some years his senior and was obviously finding it as hard to be disciplined as Abraham was to discipline. With the vestiges of sleep still slowing them, the men began the arduous task of filling in the latrines. Abraham cast around for flat stones on which he painted an "L" to mark the spot. That way no unsuspecting future inhabitant of the trench would get an unpleasant surprise. Abraham gathered up the maps and order sheets and put a lucifer to them. As they smouldered and crumbled, he ground the ashes into the mud with his heel. The men breakfasted at daybreak and then moved off to the new dangers of the Festubert sector.

Frenzied days were interspersed with periods of inactivity. In a stolen moment of quiet, Abraham unbuttoned his breast pocket and extracted a small notebook. His dreams and his plans for the future might have been fractured but his love of literature remained untarnished. At school he had risked the ridicule of his classmates with his fascination for the poets of the romantic era. Only his ability on the cricket field and later on, in the debating society, had earned him a grudging respect and saved him from the savage bullying that is a schoolboy's second nature. He had gone willingly from senior prefect at King's to the more congenial atmosphere of St. Luke's College.

As his body began to behave itself and he left boyhood behind, he found that he too could play rugby and succeed as a corporal in the Officers' Training Corps. During his time with the Territorials at Tavistock, he'd risen to the rank of sergeant. It was this experience that now made him, in his ignorance and ineptitude, a leader of men. Words still fascinated him; he used them to soothe his spirit, to distract his mind from the devastation and the utter futility of what was evolving around him. At St. Luke's, his literary ambitions had found an outlet but the superficialities he had written, in his role as the editor of his college magazine, were far removed from the gritty reality he now sought to immortalise in verse.

Abraham re-read his attempts at setting down his emotions. Scattered throughout the notebook were fragments, ideas, impressions. He turned the pages with a muddy thumb to find the poem he had finished the previous day. Perhaps he would submit it to one of the trench news-sheets that enterprising men were producing to raise morale. It needed work still but the words he had penned between the ruled pages' faded lines, gently pleased him.

From Playing Field to Battlefield

He fought reluctant but he fought as bid
By masters uttering sonorous banalities
In dusty school room halls. And thus they did
With no more thought than they would give
To cries of 'play up lad, score for the team,'
Urge young men on the brink of life to finalities,
To deaths on battlefields where none can dream.

He fought reluctant but he fought as bid
Wondering why his life was subject to the idle whim
Of the unheeding, faceless men who hid
Behind red-taped officialdom.
But an idle stroke of their pen would mean
His lifeblood left on Flanders soil, where none would name him.
Memories fading as if he'd never been.

He fought reluctant but he fought as bid
One of many schoolboys who believed their masters' lies
Quelling the fears of which he must be rid.
Fleeting dreams of classroom days as
The sniper's bullet finds its mark
Searchlight's beam rakes over sightless eyes
It was all going to be such a lark.

Encamped by the little market town of Laventie, the officers sighed over dog-eared plans that appeared to show an intricate web of trenches; trenches that were, in reality, no more than useless, waterlogged drainage ditches. Trenches were a lifeline, enabling equipment to be moved but they were also a deathline; all too frequently required to evacuate a man who'd copped it or gone west. The euphemisms helped to shield them from the true horror of a comrade wounded or killed. So Abraham's unit resigned themselves to days digging vital trenches. Shovel and pick were employed with relentless monotony. To Abraham, it seemed that their exertions were fruitless. The water seeped, unerringly, into the newly dug trenches, reclaiming its own and making the dark journeys with fallen pals harder to endure. Abraham dug alongside his men. He paused in his labours to ease his aching shoulders and to wonder how the locals had lived before the heedless troops wreaked destruction on the countryside that now surrounded him.

There were hints of peacetime prettiness, here a rose, there a cobbled path, a tangled lawn, still visible to the discerning eye. Amidst the ravaged terrain, fruit hung heavy on the boughs, unpicked. Replete wasps fed on fallen plums and bees droned. The River Lys flowed with summer sluggishness. On its banks, stark stumps now stood where willows once grew. With a flash of iridescent wing, a pheasant started up from the nearby wood, its raw cry echoing. Barbed wire coiled across the long grass, self-seeded crops from happier years dared to grow and poppies painted the fields. Abandoned and broken, ploughs rusted where they lay. Then there were the agonising reminders of war. The wooden crosses, roughly hewn, inscribed only with a date; the names of the soldiers who fell on that spot forever forgotten. The skeleton of the derelict church pierced the clouds in poignant beauty. The convent school was deserted now; nun's soft voices no longer nurtured eager pupils. Fat pigeons scavenged at the field's edge and protected from the carnage by the hedgerows, jewelled cornflowers bravely bloomed.

The road stretched from Fauquissant to Trivelet, below the northern slopes of the Aubers Ridge. There was nearly four miles of enemy front line to capture and the Sugar Loaf bastion to take. No Man's Land receded into the distance, a far wider stretch to cross than the men had been led to expect. Next to Abraham's unit were the Anzacs, some were untried recruits like his own men but others were bluff and battle-hardened from the campaign at Gallipoli. In the boredom of the mud, cocooned in sodden sandbags, Abraham perched on a broken crate. Waiting. It was all about waiting and trying not to start at every sound. The Tommy next to him scratched desultorily.

'Bleddy chats,' he said ruefully.

Abraham had long since renounced the battle with the lice, accepting them as an unavoidable accompaniment to war, like the rats, the bleeding blisters and the saturated socks. He shrugged companionably. Nearby, a soldier clenched his hands in prayer. The God that Abraham had known in the shelter of Clovelly church, the deity who had uplifted him in the lofty chapel at King's, was absent now. He remembered the scarlet and gold shards that fell on the floor of the school chapel, as the sunlight permeated the stained glass of the oriel window. Here the scarlet shards were bloodstains left by fallen men and blessed assurance no longer came from sunlit skies.

Some men carried snapshots to remind them of a girl back home. Already, Abraham had had to write letters of regret to those smiling young women; women who had waited eagerly and anxiously, women who would smile no more. No photograph accompanied Abraham on to bloody battlefields. Instead, in the back of his pocket book, he had pressed Clovelly flowers: fragrant rose petals, forget-me-nots and starry daisies. When he wanted to wish himself back in the embrace of the walled garden of home, he would hold the drying blooms flat in the palm of his hand. Sometimes, there would be a young girl flitting gracefully across the garden of his dreams. He was comforted by the belief that she was not waiting for him in fretfulness and fear. He had not wanted to make his nascent feelings known. That way, he reasoned, he had at least spared her from the worry and the mourning. He balanced his now tatty notebook on his knee and began to write.

> *By day I gaze at daisies kissed by dew*
> *By night, the twinkle of the lingering star*
> *The fearsome sound of guns is muted through*
> *My dreams of beauteous gardens afar.*

It had rained for the past week, with an intensity characteristic of thundery squalls. Nothing had prepared them for the realities of the storm-soaked fields of France. Rain dripped on corroded corrugated iron. Mud-laden boots grew ever heavier. Even the sharpest shower could not wash away the scent of slaughter. Without discrimination, wet earth clung to the rough wooden breastwork, sandbags and broken men. When the rain ceased, a dank miasma lingered above the low-lying plain. The men were preparing for an inspection by a major from HQ. The whisper in the dugouts was that this was a fact-finding visit, prior to an attack. Abraham hoped that the top brass would see how thinly spread the men were and that this would halt the plans for an advance across the aching expanse of No Man's Land. Some four hundred yards separated them from the Boche at this point. Four hundred yards without cover, four hundred agonising yards where every man was offered up as a sacrifice for an enemy sniper.

Above the drenched ground, the soldier manning the periscope spotted an insidious, prowling enemy, more deadly than machine gun or mortar shell. It crept up in a cloud of yellow and green. It rolled above the ground, gaining momentum on the stiff breeze.

'Gas!'

If they did not act swiftly it would capture their lungs. Within seconds, men would be clutching at their throats, their breath rasping as they fought for air.

'Respirators on!'

Abraham shouted to alert those under his command, reaching for the bag slung over his shoulder as he did so. He pulled the chemical-soaked canvas over his head. The smell of the rubber made him retch as he hurried to push the tube into his mouth. A new recruit, barely more than a boy, looked helplessly at Abraham with terror-struck eyes. Reading the silent plea, Abraham realised that the youngster had flouted the command to wear the regulation issue bag at all times. The bag that would contain two gas-masks, the bag that might spare him from an agonising end. Knowing that he had only a few moments to save the lad, Abraham reached for his spare gas mask and helped the trembling boy to secure it; his gauntlet-clad fingers fumbling on fastenings that were slippery with mud.

The men sat silently, watching each other through alien eyes, heads pounding from the gas masks' pressure. The lethal fog snaked through the trenches, felling rats and the ill-prepared in its path. The soldiers called this silent killer "pear drops", as if, by giving it a name that was reminiscent of childhood sweet shop visits, they could diminish its power. In the aftermath of the horror of the attack, the rumours circulated, as sinister in their own way as the gas itself.

'Wasn't even the Boche. It was our bally gas. Men from 61 division didn't check the wind direction.'

'Bad enough being killed by the Hun but when ruddy incompetence…..'

Abraham sighed and felt the need to isolate himself from the indignation and the recriminations of his fellows. He was finding it more difficult now to compose meaningful verses but he withdrew his notebook and tried to put his feelings into words.

Men wounded, dying needless
Sharp order bellowed, heedless.
Scars within and scars without
Above the gunfire a shout
Is heard. 'Need a stretcher here'
You must go on, show no fear.

The carrier pigeons wheeled above the carnage, conveying the latest instructions to prepare for action. It seemed that there was a big show further south. The troops on the Aubers Ridge were to be assigned the job of keeping the enemy occupied, to prevent them from marching to the aid of the German battalions elsewhere. Orders went out to conserve ammunition. Abraham and his men were amongst those charged with moving fifteen hundred gas cylinders before the planned attack. Monotony and exhaustion gripped the troops in equal measure. After three days, Abraham doubted that they had shifted a third of their load. Fatigued and frightened, the men took refuge in grumbling about the perceived senselessness of their task. Officers, themselves ignorant of the overarching strategy, made vain attempts to chivvy those under their command.

With a sense of foreboding, they readied themselves. The more experienced Australians had got things organised, establishing signal posts and installing jamming sets. Each man carried a pick or a spade and several sandbags. They toiled through the crumbling trenches as the duck-boarding failed to do its job. Gas masks inspected and water bottles filled, they watched and they waited; fear-knotted, overwrought, with every nerve tightly strung. Reports that the Hun were sat safely in concrete block houses with electricity, beds and pumps, spread resentment. When men are bored tales grow taller. In the British trenches, stories circulated of the locals colluding with the Germans, sending signals by the use of different coloured farm horses, or by ploughing in different directions. There were orders to shell the German batteries in advance of the main attack. The flying boys would be putting up flares and flashing mirrors at hourly intervals, so the officers knew the extent of the troops' advance.

Across the plain where the purple clover once bloomed and the swallows used to dive, men prepared for death in a blood-stained ditch. The lurking mist that accompanied the persistent drizzle obscured the view but the deathly crumps of falling shells resounded as the wire-cutting party were sent into the abyss. From the vantage point of the higher ground, the Germans were set to defend the salient without thought for the cost in human pain. Abraham knew that he needed to be an example to his men, to ignore his own quickening pulse and hammering heart. He had been indoctrinated by his schoolmasters to play up and play the game, to do his bit for king and country. Patriotic fervour soon lost its lustre in the realities of the Western Front. Abraham remembered the excitement as recruiting posters were pasted on town hall walls; no one then regarded Kitchener's accusatory finger as a harbinger of death. As the playing fields of England had once echoed with the crowds cheering a winning try, now the battlefields resounded with the shrieks of the horses and the cries of damaged men. Abraham had grown up with the gentle shires who pulled the ploughs on neighbouring farms. The Clovelly donkeys were known to him by name. Here, the screaming suffering of the terrified horses and mules was a descant to the appalling symphony that assailed him.

Desperate men tried to tear themselves from menacing wire. Others struggled to keep their footing as they fought their way through the chest-high water of the ditches that had failed to drain; the swirling water dyed crimson by their comrades' blood. Then came the disheartening news that the first attack had failed. No time to mourn for departed friends, no time for that last letter to an anxious sweetheart. Stores were stocked and ammunition was delivered from further up the line. The men had a hasty meal and snatched sleep. Somewhere in the darkness of Abraham's trench a lucifer flared and the peaty smell of pipe smoke drifted on the night air.

In the early hours of Wednesday morning they regrouped once more, in anticipation of the infantry assault that was planned for 9am. By summer's early daybreak the rain had eased but heavy mist still haunted the flat plain. Shorn tree stumps loomed ghost-like above the haze. The order echoed down the line, warning of further delay. There could be no bombardment until the visibility improved. The men's spirits were low and they felt ill-equipped. Some of the heavy artillery batteries had not fired before and the infantry were poorly trained. There were rumours that one of the Australian Lewis guns had been captured by the enemy.

The attack, when it came, dislocated time. Minutes crawled like hours yet suddenly it was dusk. Men fought like automatons, consciousness suspended, their senses temporarily divorced from reality, no thoughts beyond survival. Inexperience took its deathly toll as the British shells fell short and landed on their Australian allies. Unaware, the Tommies fought on. Some failed to keep the horrors at bay and crept further from the line of fire, where they hugged their knees and hid under blood-stained blankets, shaking, shuddering, unable to forget. Or, hallucinating in blissful oblivion, others fancied themselves at home. Still others copped it; wrong place, wrong time. Oh, more than anything, was this the wrong time. Shattered, sobbing men, with blood pouring in a damnable, undammable tide.

Darkness was lapping at daylight's fringes before the firing ceased. Shrouded by the shadows the search for the fallen began. Moonlight rarely penetrated the thick, rushing clouds. The search party blundered across the endless expanse of No Man's Land, guided only by the unearthly moans of wounded men. In scarlet ditches they crawled over bodies, bodies of those who had been friends for a season. The corpses of those whose anguish and hardships they'd shared. A soldier clutched a grimy, creased photograph of his sweetheart. As his eyes glazed, his grasp weakened and the image of Gladys, or of Betty, or of Joan, fluttered away in the breeze.

Abraham struggled back across the aching vastness of No Man's Land, the feet of the wounded man that he carried, dragging on the clinging mud. It was three hundred yards to the relative safety of the British trenches. Abraham felt every step as if it was a marathon. The ground was as slippery as an abattoir's slab but here the carcasses were men. He hoist his burden higher and took a firmer grip on the arm that was draped across his shoulders. He strained his eyes to avoid the craters that pitted his route. Bitter smoke rose from isolated fires on the ravaged plain. Remnants of what had once been men carpeted the ground, scarcely human. A soldier, naked to the waist, lay in Abraham's path, the hole in the back of his shoulder was wider than a man's fist. He was still alive, still groaning but already encumbered, Abraham had to leave him. It was hard to believe that this morning these men had been his comrades, living, breathing, loving, hoping.

The gunfire was spasmodic now but still lethal. A single, ominous shot divided survival from death.

Through dreamlike haze, Abraham fought to focus on the face above his own, ghostlike in the muted moonlight.

'Sergeant Tuke, Sergeant Tuke, bear up man. The stretcher boys will be here soon. We will have you back to the medics in two ticks. Now it's dark we can bring in anyone who's copped it.'

'Squance?' he whispered, almost beyond speech but recognising at last the corporal who had already once that day braved enemy fire to repair the telephone cable between HQ and the firing line.

Frustratingly, Squance's earlier efforts had been rendered ineffective by continued shellfire.

'The ruddy line's gone again,' the corporal replied. 'We'll not let the square heads get the better of us but I need to mend it pal.'

Corporal Squance looked fearfully over his shoulder, unwilling to leave a comrade to die alone but well aware that here was a man who would soon be past all aid. Reluctantly he moved away, knowing that the wire needed to be mended.

A white-feathered owl swooped on silent wing. Abraham heard the gentle hiss of the wave song, sensed the scent of the sea on an errant breeze. Somewhere in the depths of remembrance a seabird cried and he crushed the daisy that he held in his hand.

9
1917

A well-dressed couple in their thirties alighted from a chauffeur driven hired motor at Head the Hill and stood surrounded by three large portmanteaux, two hat boxes and a picnic hamper. Clovelly was no stranger to posh folk visiting. True, they had been fewer in number since the hostilities started but they came, they went, leaving little of themselves behind. There was no reason to think that this particular pair would make a lasting impression on the fishing village or its inhabitants, no suggestion that their actions would bring trauma and anguish, fear and pain. The past experiences of these holidaymakers and the burdens that they carried, were still concealed behind a veneer of bland normality.

There was a desolate air about the couple. The man, tall, lean and pale, stood uncertainly as the woman arranged the cases at their feet and paid their fare. Their luggage showed little sign of wear. Embedded in the shiny leather were clues to their identity; tooled gold initials glistened in the sunlight. The car's driver cranked the starting handle on the Model T Ford and the engine burst noisily into life. Putting his foot on the running board, he swung himself behind the wheel. The vehicle set off on its return journey, the exhaust exploding vociferously. The man that had been jettisoned at the top of the cobbled path twitched and began to tremble, an indication perhaps that the pair were not merely ordinary visitors. The woman put a steadying hand on her husband's arm. His shuddering gradually subsided and he looked round apprehensively, to see if anyone had witnessed his anxiety. The motor rattled on up the road, emitting clouds of smoke, its driver oblivious to the distress he had caused.

Once the sounds of the combustion engine had died away, the street was silent once more, unusually quiet for the time of year. If there had been any observers, a cursory glance might perhaps have led them to wonder if the couple were honeymooners but closer scrutiny would reveal no newly-wed nervousness about the woman. Several minutes passed as they remained unspeaking and watchful, in the dappled shade; they appeared to be waiting for someone. The man began to pace back and forth, he fingered his necktie repeatedly and wrung his hands, then he withdrew a pocket watch from his waistcoat.

'It's three fifteen,' he remarked irritably. 'We were to be met at three fifteen.'

'Someone will come soon Edward dear, I'm sure,' replied his wife, soothingly.

She transferred her weight from one foot to another, trying to ease the pressure of her side buttoned boots. Some children clattered past and the lady watched their retreating figures with a wistful smile. At that moment, a weather-beaten man appeared, leading a recalcitrant donkey. He cleared his throat to attract the couple's attention.

'Mr and Mrs Collins?' he enquired. 'Jack Foley.' His fingers waved in the region of his cap in a gesture of respect. 'I'm to take your things down to Mrs Stanbury's and show you the way. She be expecting ee.'

He deftly removed packages from the wooden frame that spanned the back of the donkey and gave the animal's nose an encouraging scratch, as it pawed the greying stones beneath its feet. Judiciously, Mr and Mrs Collins maintained a safe distance from hooves and teeth. Foley tied the donkey to the white-painted railings and abandoned the boxes for collection by their owners, who were labouring up the street. Donkeys carried luggage up the hill but they could not manage laden downward journeys, so the Collins' belongings were heaped on to a waiting sledge. Amelia wished that Edward had not been so insistent that they travelled with their cases. He had vetoed her suggestion that they send a trunk on in advance. She exhaled deeply, with what might have been mistaken for a sigh, took her husband's arm and followed Jack Foley as he began the descent to the village.

'Your first visit to Clovelly ma'am?' asked their escort, seemingly aware that Mr Collins was a man of few words.

'Yes, indeed,' she replied. 'We are here for my husband's health.'

That was true enough, she thought, hoping fervently that the complete contrast to their life in Liverpool and respite from the traumas of wartime, would restore Edward to the man she had married two years previously. It was fortunate that the family engineering business was prospering due to the demands of the military machine. It meant that they could fund a lengthy stay in a haven where sea air and solitude might be balm to her troubled spouse. The Collins trailed a few paces behind their luggage as the lurching sledge negotiated the cobbles under the adept guidance of Jack Foley.

'They're looking at me Amelia,' hissed Edward Collins to his wife in an undertone. The passing villagers were in fact indifferent to the Collins' arrival. Visitors were two a penny at this time of year, despite the war. This couple were unremarkable, arousing no especial interest.

'I am sure they aren't dear,' she said, reassuringly but she knew that her words would make little impression.

Edward was convinced that he was being watched. The army doctor had explained that this was part of his affliction and that it would pass, like the other worrying symptoms but Amelia was finding his uncharacteristically suspicious nature wearing.

As they placed their feet gingerly on the unfamiliar cobbles, Amelia wondered how suited she and Edward really were to married life. She did not delude herself that theirs was a grand passion. Perhaps it was better that their relationship was not complicated by strong emotions. They had been casual acquaintances since childhood, their fathers being business associates. Edward was an only son and with the passing of the years, his father had become increasingly worried about the future of the family firm. As an engineer, Edward's work was considered to be essential in wartime but when he had told his father that he was considering volunteering for the front, the pressure to produce an heir became more acute. It was decided that Edward, already in his thirties, should marry. Amelia often questioned why she, regarded by her friends as a confirmed spinster, had been deemed a suitable brood mare. True, she represented a connection with her father's engineering concern but her brother would inherit this, so there could be no economic motive behind the union. If providing a son to secure the future of the business had been so important, surely it would have been better for Edward to marry someone younger? Her husband had never given an explanation but Amelia suspected that she had been selected because Edward would have been intolerant of a bright, young woman, who might prove to be superficial or flighty. Amelia represented someone with gravitas; perhaps her appeal was that she was familiar, less demanding and more willing to fit into Edward's rigid routines. The drawback was that here they were, two years into the marriage and no sign of the anticipated heir. Edward had of course been away on active service for some of that time but even before he went to war, his approach to procreation had, at best, been lacklustre. With his illness, his enthusiasm had dwindled still further and Amelia acknowledged that they were now unlikely to become parents.

Was Clovelly going to provide the tranquillity that Edward needed and solve their difficulties? Amelia was pinning her hopes on the healing effects of this little community on the dramatic North Devon coast. Edward had expressed a desire to recuperate further west still, in the Cornish fishing village of Newlyn, where his parents had grown up. Amelia had feared that a place Edward had visited as a child and where the family was known, might not provide the complete break with the past that he sought. On the recommendation of a friend, who had visited from South Wales before the war, Amelia had proposed Clovelly as a compromise. Already, the tangy sea air was invigorating and she took comfort from the fact that, on the train from Liverpool, Edward had spoken positively of getting a small boat to relive the fishing expeditions of his youth. Perhaps this extended stay would be the new start that they both required.

The path divided; Jack and his sledge swung to the right. Amelia was roused from her musings as they drew up at the far end of a row of cottages. Bright hollyhocks framed the newly painted door and the brass knocker shone.

'You there Mrs Stanbury?' bellowed Jack, rapping vigorously with the knocker. 'Your guests be 'ere.'

As Jack raised his hand to knock a second time, a brisk, older woman opened the door and greeted them with a smile.

'Thank you, Jack,' she said, 'no need to break the door down.'

She turned to the couple in front of her as Jack began to unload the luggage from the sledge. A fleeting look was enough to give her the impression of an affluent couple. Mrs Collins was stylishly dressed but in an understated manner, befitting the fact that the bloom of youth was now a memory. Emma Stanbury's glance took in the expensive-looking cases and Mr Collins' highly polished shoes, visible beneath the hems of his carefully tailored suit. It wasn't Emma's place to question her guests' motives but she did wonder why they had chosen a small, inconspicuous guest house in Clovelly, when everything about them indicated that they were more accustomed to staying in better class hotels.

'Welcome to Clovelly,' she said, shepherding the couple into the kitchen, leaving Jack to stack the cases inside the door. 'Your room is ready for you. I have reserved it for the whole season, so you can stay as long as you like.'

For the first time since they left the safety of the motor, Mr Collins seemed aware of his surroundings, rather than being concerned about the accusatory eyes of his imagination. He took in the cosy kitchen's rough, whitewashed walls, adorned with a black-bordered portrait of the late Queen, torn from a magazine and an inexpertly worked sampler, which was hanging askew. Edward paused to straighten it, taking several seconds before he deemed it to be at the desired angle. The stove was emitting an unwelcome heat; the kettle on its hot plate was beginning to rock and sing. Amelia hoped they would be out of the room before its hissing gained momentum. It seemed that even something as simple as a cottage kitchen contained hazards that she hadn't anticipated.

'Your evening meal will be served here at six,' said Mrs Stanbury, gesturing toward the oil-cloth covered table.

Much to Amelia's relief, Mrs Stanbury led her guests swiftly up the narrow stairs to the largest bedroom at the front of the house. The establishment might be lacking in grandeur but it was scrupulously clean. The crisp coverlet was stretched tautly across the highly polished, brass-framed bed. An elaborately flowered jug and bowl stood on the wash-stand in front of the window. There was a bright rug on the rough floorboards, an oversized wardrobe and two bentwood chairs, flanking an oak chest of drawers. Edward Collins adjusted the position of one of the chairs that was protruding slightly further forward than its fellow. Amelia tried to suppress a grimace as she looked at the print above the bed, which depicted a fox gorily devouring a game bird. Dejected, Edward sat on one of the chairs, kept his eyes firmly on the floor and began pulling at his cuffs.

'I hope this will suit,' Mrs Stanbury was saying. 'Three guineas a week all found, as we discussed. You will find the food plain but wholesome. You passed the Post Office on your way down; you'll be wanting to send a card or telegram to say you've arrived. Oh and it's two pence a week to use the Reading Rooms at the top of the street, should Mr Collins wish to look at the newspaper.'

As Mrs Stanbury rattled on, Amelia could see Edward's fists clenching on his knees and she knew that he was resisting the temptation to put his hands over his ears.

'I think we would just like to change into fresh clothes now, thank you Mrs Stanbury,' Amelia said, firmly.

'There's always hot water on the stove,' Mrs Stanbury went on, failing to take the hint.

Amelia attempted to place herself between Edward and their hostess and to steer her towards the door.

'There will be tea and cut-rounds when you're ready.'

With these words, Mrs Stanbury finally left the Collins to survey what was to be their home for several months, or as long as it took for Edward to recover. The doctor had been firm; complete rest and freedom from anxiety was essential. When Amelia had questioned the doctor further, he had admitted that there was no knowing how long it might be before there were any signs of improvement. Well, they had made a start, now it was up to her to see that Edward was restored to health.

As the summer blended into golden days with hints of autumn and the vibrant fuchsias and hydrangeas, that bravely shone in the cottage gardens, began to fade, Amelia and Edward established a routine. Mr Collins' desire for solitude soon became apparent and Emma Stanbury left the pair alone as much as she was able. Mrs Stanbury was a widow, so there was no husband to be seen off to work but her day started long before the Collins took their breakfast at nine. Edward would then walk up to the Reading Rooms to peruse the daily newspaper, whilst Amelia wrote letters or did embroidery in the small parlour. They sometimes took a short excursion in the afternoon, perhaps having cakes in a tea-room at Hartland. When Edward felt up to a day trip, they went further afield, to Bude or Ilfracombe. Clovelly villagers were not the sort of people who would have been included in the Collins' circle of acquaintances at home and genuine friendships would have been inappropriate. Nonetheless, being long-term paying guests, rather than casual holidaymakers, they soon began to recognise some of the neighbours and Amelia would exchange pleasantries when she saw them in the street. She participated in sewing circles and knitted socks for servicemen, gradually getting to know the women of the village.

Even when he was well, Edward had been retiring, standoffish even, inept in social situations and reluctant to form friendships. Since his illness, the strangeness of his behaviour had placed him even more firmly on the side-lines. He had managed to acquire a small rowing boat, which he kept in the harbour. The local fishermen resented his ineptitude but Edward seemed unaware of their derision. He was insensible to the fact that they viewed him as someone from up-country, an outsider, a toff, not one of them. He would return from a morning spent rowing aimlessly round the bay, perhaps with a couple of mackerel to show for his efforts. These he would solemnly present to Mrs Stanbury who would dutifully prepare them for their tea. In his lighter moods, Edward spoke eagerly to Amelia of the camaraderie he shared with the other fishermen but she was astute enough to realise that he was deluding himself and that he would always remain on the periphery. Alone. Unreachable. Broken.

Night time was the worst. By day, Amelia could sometimes imagine that this was simply an extended holiday, taken purely for pleasure but the hours of darkness held unseen terrors for Edward. Each evening they would prepare themselves for bed but Edward would use every excuse to postpone the moment when he must join Amelia under the coverlet. It wasn't that the proximity to his wife was distasteful, he was fearful of sleep and the horrors that it might bring. Obsessively, he fiddled with the items on top of the chest of drawers, assuring that cuff-links, brushes and pomade jars were neatly aligned. He would pace the small room restlessly, as the pearlescent moon cast liquid shadows over the bay below the cottage. When he did eventually lie down, at Amelia's insistence, sleep eluded him. It was often the early hours before he drifted into fitful slumber. For Amelia, undisturbed nights were a distant memory, something that belonged to her single days, to days before Edward had come back from the war, a hollow, damaged, barely recognisable version of his former self. She had learned to cope with the cards that life had dealt them. She had had little choice. So now Amelia too approached the coming of darkness with trepidation. Would this night be one when Edward had one of his turns? Would he wake, screaming, sweating, writhing, rejecting all her overtures of comfort?

Mrs Stanbury's cottage, situated as it was at the end of one of Clovelly's few side streets, was comparatively peaceful for the Collins. Two things served to mar their quietude. Firstly, that autumn, Mrs Stanbury's married daughter came from Swansea to take up residence in the third bedroom at the back of the house, for the duration of the hostilities. If that was not bad enough, with her came her infant son, Stanley, who was given to raucous night-time wails. These nocturnal disturbances, left Edward trauma-struck, undoing the benefits of their first months in the serenity of Clovelly; months that had soothed and nurtured, as Amelia had hoped they might.

Then there was the family in the adjoining cottage. The husband and a son, who seemed a little simple, worked a fishing boat. Apparently, the eldest son was away at sea but there were several younger children and an older daughter who was in service elsewhere in the village; she visited occasionally, when she had a half day. Edward had tried to claim some sort of ownership of the family, dogging the footsteps of the father, Albert, badgering him with questions about fishing, expressing opinions on matters of the sea about which he knew little and about which the canny fisherman knew everything.

Watching from the upstairs window, Amelia's stomach knotted as she witnessed Edward being rejected ignored and ridiculed by the villagers. She flinched as Albert and his son hurried down the street with their heads bowed, as if they were trying to avoid Edward's importunities. It wasn't that they meant to be cruel, they had a living to earn and could find no common ground with a "blow-in" from up country. Edward even attempted to engage the oldest daughter, Daisy, in conversation when he spotted her visiting the family. He couldn't seem to grasp that it might be inappropriate to accost a young, unmarried woman in this way. Edward spoke fondly of Daisy to Amelia, describing her as 'the flower of the flock' and 'his Marguerite'. Amelia knew better than to be jealous. She understood that the feelings that Edward had for the young woman were not sexual; he would have been mortified if anyone had suggested that this was the case. Daisy was enigmatic, earthy, far removed from the porcelain, middle class women with whom Edward had come in to contact in his previous life. His regard for Daisy was a chivalric respect for the unattainable, the other-worldly and not that of a married man looking for a diversion.

The mother, Polly, was a prickly, unpredictable woman. In an unusually gossipy mood, Mrs Stanbury volunteered some information about her neighbour.

'Well, you'll find her a little odd,' she said, adding, 'she's got worse since her lad died back along and she frets about their Leonard being at sea. His ship was torpedoed you know.'

Amelia did not know but Polly was not alone in having a family that was being moulded and defined by the impact of the war. It was a few days after this conversation that Amelia was accosted by Polly as she walked up to Ellis' shop. Without preamble, Polly had waved an admonishing finger in Amelia's face.

'What's that husband of yours sniffing round our Daisy for?' she'd demanded.

Before Amelia could gather her thoughts to respond, Polly had continued her diatribe.

'She's a good, respectable girl, brought up in a chapel-going family. She don't want naught to do with the likes of an old man like him and him married too.'

The angry woman had paused to draw breath before issuing her final gibe.

'What's to do with him anyway?' she'd asked, rhetorically. 'Is he mazed or summat? All that shaking about and don't think we've not heard 'im hollering and screaming in the night, fit to wake the dead. Should be up the asylum if you ask me.'

With that, Polly had turned on her heel and entered the shop, leaving Amelia gazing after her, dumbfounded. She was thankful that this exchange had not been witnessed by Edward. It also made her acutely aware that her husband's tentative recovery was constructed on decidedly flimsy foundations.

Amelia was always punctiliously polite when she saw Polly but she resented the threat that the family posed to Edward's gradual but fragile, journey back to normality. The mackerel season finished and Edward lost interest in fishing, although he muttered about perhaps going out for winter herring later in the year. Ever more confined as he was by the four walls of their room, he became increasingly distressed by the goings on in the neighbouring cottage. Polly's incessant cries of, 'Alb, where youm too?' or 'Have you chopped the kindling yet Mark?' and her continual noisy bustling round the small girls at the tail end of the family grated on Edward.

Schooldays gave daytime respite but one tea time, the commotion from next door made it clear that the youngest child, Rosie, had failed to return home. Amelia cringed and looked anxiously at Edward, as the sound of Polly berating the other children for not keeping an eye on their youngest sister could be heard through the walls of the cottage. Doors slammed as the older boys set off in search of the missing child.

'There's a child lost Edward,' said Amelia, 'we should offer to help search.'

'She can't have gone far,' replied Edward, who was cowering in the chair.

He no longer felt the need to cover his ears at every loud noise but the din from next door had clearly unsettled him.

'We need to help dear, folk will think it odd if we don't.'

Even as she uttered it, the irony of this statement was brought home to Amelia. Despite all her efforts to conceal her husband's most acute eccentricities, Polly wasn't the only villager to have remarked on Edward's strange behaviour.

'Will they take lanterns Amelia? I can't stomach the lanterns.'

Amelia knew that Edward was always reluctant to go out after dark and that the swaying lights disturbed him.

'Hardly, dear. It is several hours before dark and surely we will find her by then.'

Edward seemed reassured by this. He removed his carpet slippers and placed them precisely under the bed, equidistant between two other pairs of shoes that were there. He put on a thin coat and stout footwear, clearly resolving to join in the search. Amelia donned hat and gloves, even in Clovelly she maintained certain standards. Firmly securing her hatpin, she followed Edward down the stairs to offer their assistance.

'I don't want to speak to that woman,' said Edward, referring to Polly. 'I'll look for the girl but don't make me speak to her.'

'We need to know where's best to search,' said Amelia, gently. 'There's no point everyone looking in the same place.'

'I'll go up the top by the Court Gardens,' said Edward.

Amelia sighed. Edward spent all too much time in this part of the estate. She suspected that it was because he hoped to catch a glimpse of Daisy, as she went about her work in Gardener's Cottage.

'Surely the child wouldn't go right up there,' said Amelia.

Defying all logic, Edward was fixated on the likelihood of Rosie being in the Court Gardens. Realising that he would not be dissuaded, Amelia let him go and he strode off up the street. Clovelly families never locked their doors but Amelia did not feel that she was on friendly enough terms with Polly to enter the cottage unheralded, so she knocked, timidly.

A girl of about six opened the door. She had clearly been crying and Amelia correctly guessed that she had borne the brunt of the blame for her sister's absence.

'I hear your sister's missing,' Amelia said, kindly, 'I wondered if I could help.'

'There's folk out looking all over,' said the child, 'I thought she was behind me as we ran down from Wrinkleberry but then I looked and she weren't there no more. I'm to stay here now in case she comes back by herself. She's only started school this few weeks since. She will be all right, won't she?'

The child was obviously looking to Amelia for reassurance, reassurance that Amelia felt ill-equipped to offer. A wooden cross on the outskirts of the village was a potent reminder that missing children were not always restored safely to their families. Amelia knew that the child in front of her would be well aware of this. The tragic tale of the two young girls who had gone missing some fifty years earlier was woven into Clovelly folklore. Accounts of their fate reverberated down the cobbles of the present, an ominous echo, a reminder of life's vulnerabilities. As Amelia was wondering how she could comfort the young girl, who plainly felt responsible for the loss of her sister, the child's father, Albert, returned home. Dressed in his fishing gear, it seemed that he had been called from his work to search for his daughter. Anxiety etched in his face, he looked at Amelia uncertainly.

'Can I help?' she asked. 'My husband has gone to look up in the Court Gardens. Where would it be best for me to search?'

Albert hesitated, incapable of coherent thought and unable to make a decision.

'We have to find the maid,' he said, almost as if Amelia hadn't spoken. 'We have to. I don't know how Polly will cope if she were to lose another child. Rosie is our baby, she's only a little mite.' He repeated the mantra, as if by that very repetition he would make it so, 'We have to find her.'

They searched frenetically, fruitlessly, looking in places where no child could possibly lurk. Dusk claimed the cobbles and weariness sent searchers back to their homes. As Amelia reluctantly retraced her steps back to Mrs Stanbury's, a shout went up from the end of the street.

'We've got her, she's found!'

Mrs Abbott, who Amelia recognised from the sewing circle, was in full flight down the road, dragging a dishevelled small girl behind her.

'Daft maid came back to your old house after school,' said Mrs Abbott to Albert. 'Seems odd when you've been moved this year since but I suppose she found herself alone and just turned up on the doorstep. She's been sat in my kitchen with a nice bit o' bread and jam. I'd no idea folk were worried until Mrs Stanbury knocked and said you was all frantic.'

Rosie ran indoors, oblivious of the commotion that she had caused. The good news rushed down the street faster than a flood tide. Villagers came to express their relief, or to check if the rumours of Rosie's safe return were true. Rosie's brothers and sister arrived home and joined in the excited chatter. Time passed. There was no sign of Polly, or of Edward. Amelia felt out of place amongst the family and close friends who were fussing round Rosie and enjoying strong tea from thick china mugs. She left quietly.

In the melancholy of the darkening churchyard a swift shadow moved across a gravestone. The intertwined roses carved on the top of the cross were thrown into sharp relief by the deepening dusk. The shadow took form. A weeping woman clung to the base of the cross. Forsaken, bereft, she sobbed alone. Edward, having hunted somewhat cursorily for Rosie in the region of the Court's walled garden, heard the sounds and approached, thinking that it might be the young girl. The clouds scudded across the moon, giving him sufficient light to see that this was no child before him. Empathy was not an emotion that was familiar to Edward but he knew that, if Amelia were there, she would have approached this distraught woman, who was prostrate on the dampening grass. He hesitated, recognising that here was Polly, his bête noire.

From somewhere in the horrors of his past, two lines of poetry rose up to hammer at Edward's consciousness. "In an obscure night, Fevered with love's anxiety". When Edward was at the depths of his own despair, the chaplain had given him a copy of a poem, explaining that the words spoke of man's struggles, struggles that were a prelude to salvation. For this woman there was no salvation, nor, he thought ruefully, had he been saved. As Edward gazed helplessly at the scene before him, the words whispered and settled like a sigh. He racked his brains for the poem's title. *The Dark Night of the Soul*, that was it. Chillingly apt. As Edward witnessed the woman before him, wrestling with her own demons, he acknowledged that here truly was a fellow human being, who was fevered with anxiety borne of love. Before Edward could decide how to approach Polly in her suffering, she became aware of his presence and hastened to her feet, brushing grass and leaves from her skirt as she did so.

'Time to go home,' said Edward in an unexpectedly compassionate tone. 'Let's see if she has been found.'

✴

In the November night time, Edward joined the watchful fishermen on the Look-out; he stood with the group, yet he was apart. Damp Woodbines gripped in their gums, the Clovelly men exchanged a few words in undertones. No one addressed Edward and he was unsure how to initiate a conversation with these men who, despite all his efforts to fit in, led lives that were so different to his own. Edward had braved the terrors of the swinging lanterns to come to the Look-out because it was what the men did. No one had asked him to accompany them in their boats and Edward lacked the confidence to drift for herring on his own. Fishing was far from his mind. A conversation he had had with Daisy earlier in the day was tormenting him. She had been unusually forthcoming when he had encountered her on her way back from a first aid lecture at the New Inn. She had been animated, full of all that she had learned. Yet Daisy had seemed unsettled and had spoken of changes that the New Year would bring. She'd asked him about the places he'd been.

'There's so much more than Clovelly,' she'd said. 'Look at my brother, travelling all over, getting away.'

'But you are happy here aren't you?' he'd replied.

'Maybe, just for now,' she'd said, after a pause.

Was she thinking of leaving the village? Edward was unsure of his reaction. He reasoned she would probably marry soon. Not that he had heard her name linked to any of the village lads. Perhaps she had a sweetheart who was away at the war. Yes, surely she would marry but on the rare occasions when he had thought about this mythical future husband, he'd envisaged someone local. Since he had arrived in Clovelly, Edward had enjoyed seeing Daisy about the village now and again, admiring her confidence, her vitality, her difference. Her very presence was energising. It had not occurred to him that she might leave and that she would no longer touch his life.

It was past midnight and all eyes were trained on the molten sea, seeking the gleam of oil that heralded the arrival of the herring.

'There they be!', was the sudden cry.

Galvanised, the fishermen pushed past Edward and rushed towards the harbour. Ignored and alone Edward hesitated. Should he follow them? Dispirited, he wearily turned for the cottage that he could not bring himself to call home. The worst of his terrors were abating but he knew that he was not yet better. Would he ever be better? He dragged himself up the stairs at Mrs Stanbury's and faced Amelia who was sitting up in bed waiting for him. He shied away from looking directly at the flickering candle.

'I've been thinking about getting away,' he said, 'applying for engineering jobs overseas. There are plenty of openings in South America.'

Amelia raised her eyebrows. She was not sure whether to encourage him in these unrealistic ambitions or to point out that there were days when he could barely cross the street.

'Yes,' he was saying, 'when this is over we will go abroad.'

Over, thought Amelia, would it ever be over? A twisting worm of apprehension made her wonder if the horror was only just beginning.

10
1918

Daisy alighted from the train at Torre Station, a worn carpet-bag in her hand. She looked around her and breathed deeply, taking comfort from the familiar sea air. Gulls wheeled above her, as they did at home but the cobbled streets of Clovelly were distant now. This was to be her adventure, her new beginning. She had finally broken free, discarded the sad associations that had oppressed her. Here at last was an opportunity to strike out on her own, to leave behind the places that reminded her of Abraham.

It was hard to believe that it was eighteen months since that dreaded telegram had arrived at Gardener's Cottage, devastating her dreams. On that stifling August afternoon, she had known that one day she would need to escape but it had not been easy. In the months that followed Abraham's death, there had been several occasions when Daisy had heard news of a place elsewhere. Some had been too close to home, in Bideford, Appledore or Westward Ho!. If she went there, weekly visits to Clovelly would still be expected of her. It wasn't that she wanted to cut herself off from her family completely but she knew that her mother would cope better without constant reminders of Daisy's desertion.

She had been right to bide her time and now here she was in Torquay, with the glorious opportunities of the south coast beckoning. In Daisy's imagination, Torquay was the gateway to liberation. She wanted, no, she needed, to surround herself with the harshness of war and not remain shut off in the seclusion and safety of Clovelly. Of course, her home village had been wracked by the last four years of turmoil and she had suffered alongside her neighbours. Somehow though, Daisy thought, in Clovelly, the war all seemed rather remote, as if she were looking on from behind a thick pane of tarnished glass, instead of taking part. Here the platform was crowded with convalescent soldiers. Abraham was beyond her aid but there were other men, faceless and in need, whom she could tend. In Torquay, Daisy resolved, it would be different. Now she could expose herself to the conflict's raw realities and bury the guilt that she felt. They had died. She had not.

Daisy glanced at the letter in her hand, which gave the information that she needed in order to find her new home. Obeying the detailed directions, she set off up Newton Road. There, on the right, was a large cream-painted house with its name affixed to the wrought iron gates. Aylwood. Daisy's heart gave a lurch of excitement. That was a name she recognised. She owed this thrilling opportunity to the house's mistress, Mrs Gilley.

Her thoughts turned to the October day last year when this great venture had first seemed possible. Mrs

Gilley had been visiting Clovelly with her husband, as part of a large shooting party at the Court. They had arrived for the start of the grouse season and stayed for several weeks. The Gilleys had been taking a stroll in the Court Gardens when Daisy was cutting the last of the pale yellow dahlias. Mary Gilley was small and solidly built. Despite her greying hair and a slight stoop, she was impeccably and fashionably dressed; her speech underlining that she was a woman of some refinement. Mr Gilley, brusque and tweedy in his plus-fours, had exclaimed over the beauty of the late roses and expressed an interest in the hothouses. Daisy had fetched Mr Tuke, who was pleased to find someone who appreciated his work and was gratified when Mr Gilley engaged him in a lengthy discussion about the possibilities of growing grapes. Meanwhile, Daisy was required to serve tea to Mrs Gilley, in the rarely used parlour of Gardener's Cottage. The afternoon stretched on, daylight began to fade. Daisy lit the oil lamps and offered yet more tea. She was at a loss to know how Mrs Gilley might be entertained. Mrs Tuke had died three years earlier, so it was not as if there was a lady of the house, who might have magazines their visitor could peruse whilst she waited. Mrs Gilley however had seemed unperturbed. She'd even asked an embarrassed Daisy a few questions about herself and her life in Clovelly.

The autumn day was unseasonably chilly and Daisy was glad that she had lit the parlour fire when Mrs Gilley first arrived. The men came back indoors, stamping their feet and rubbing their palms to warm them. Daisy noticed that Mr Gilley's hand was bleeding steadily from a deep scratch.

'Oh sir,' she exclaimed, 'I believe you have hurt yourself.'

'Must have been those damned thorns,' Mr Gilley replied, examining his wound, 'Pity they don't make thornless roses, eh Tuke!'

Mr Tuke looked concerned, as if he could somehow be held responsible for the misbehaviour of his roses. He sent Daisy to find a bandage and she neatly dressed Mr Gilley's hand, pleased to be able to put the first aid that she had learned into practice.

Mrs Gilley had remarked on Daisy's efficiency and explained that she was involved in overseeing volunteer work in a military hospital in South Devon, where more than two hundred wounded men were cared for.

'I wish more of our girls were as proficient as you,' she had said.

Respect for Mr Tuke stilled Daisy's tongue but she had longed to blurt out that she was desperate to nurse, to be useful, to contribute in some meaningful way. If only she could help other soldiers, it would be in some measure an atonement for Abraham, for missed opportunities, for the relationship they had never had.

As if he could read her thoughts, Mr Tuke responded, 'Daisy's needed here for the time being,' he said, 'but I am getting too long in the tooth for this. I shall be stepping aside for a younger man afore long.

Time enough then for her to go gallivanting about the county nursing and what not.'

Daisy could not conceal her disappointment. Mrs Gilley, sensing this, addressed her directly, 'I'll give you my card,' she said, withdrawing a gilt card case from the bag that hung over her arm.

She passed the embossed scrap of board to Daisy, who looked at it reverently, as if it were the key to untold treasures. Daisy read the elaborate script. "Mrs T Gilley, Aylwood, Newton Road, Torquay". Aware that Mrs Gilley was looking at her appraisingly, Daisy bobbed hurriedly in acknowledgement and scarcely containing her bubbling excitement, she put the precious address in her apron pocket.

To Daisy's amazement, Mrs Gilley had said, 'Mrs Hamlyn and Mr Tuke both speak highly of you.'

Goodness, when had Mrs Hamlyn, or Mr Tuke for that matter, discussed her worth with this eminent lady? Daisy wondered. She could only think it must have been on one of the occasions, during the last few weeks, when she had been delegated to help out with the guests at the Court.

'There are a number of convalescent homes in Torquay that would welcome your help,' Mrs Gilley was saying. 'You would need a position of course. I've many contacts. If I hear of a suitable vacancy, I will send word and if the time suits Mr Tuke, I am sure he would give you a good character.'

Shortly before Christmas, an envelope had arrived at Gardener's Cottage, bearing Daisy's name, inscribed in florid purple ink. The letter explained that Mrs Gilley's former servant, Mrs Cornelius, had done well for herself. She had married a local butcher and established a small household in Torquay. There was now a vacancy for a general servant with the Cornelius family. If Daisy could secure a satisfactory recommendation from Mr Tuke, she could take up the post in the New Year, if she wished.

Daisy's spirits had soared. This was her moment. It was as if providence was finally on her side, especially as Violet had recently left school and was looking for work. The duties in the Tuke household had diminished with only Mr Tuke to do for. Violet, even with her poor health, would be capable of managing a little light housework and preparing the meals. Surely, thought Daisy, she could persuade Mr Tuke that her younger sister would make an adequate substitute, thus freeing Daisy for this position in Torquay. So it transpired and in the few weeks since the letter arrived, Daisy had been able to show Violet how Mr Tuke liked things done.

Breaking the news to her mother had been more difficult. Polly had been terse and dismissive when Daisy had announced that she was moving to take up a post in the south of the county. It had been Daisy's half-day and she was helping her mother with the weekly wash. The two women were alone; it had seemed as good a time as any to broach the subject.

'What do you want to be off down there for?' Polly had said, as she wrung out Lily's newly laundered pinafore. 'The likes of us too dull for you now? Suppose that'll be the last we see of you then.'

Polly had turned her back, mangling the clothes with a renewed ferocity. The subject was closed. Daisy knew that Polly would not do, or say, anything that would betray her true feelings; her emotions were too deeply hidden for that. Nonetheless, the girl sensed that the barrier of indifference, that her mother had constructed to keep out her grief, was remarkably fragile. Nelson had been Polly's hardest blow of course but it was not only the loss of Nelson. Since then there had been all the worry with Leonard joining the merchant service and being torpedoed not once but on three occasions. Awful though the past few years had been, Daisy resolved to harden her heart. She deserved to have this chance to make her own way, as Polly herself had done in her time. She could not be held back by her mother's pain.

Daisy's box had been sent on ahead, so she was unencumbered by heavy luggage as she wound her way up the street above Torre Station. The steepness of Upton Hill caught many a visitor unawares but Daisy was accustomed to the Clovelly cobbles, so she was barely conscious of the gradient. Another glance at her instructions informed her that she would find number 48 on the left hand side of the road, three doors up from Bertram's grocers' shop. The air was cold and she tightened the belt of her serviceable woollen coat. Her dark blue hat was pulled on firmly against the wind.

Here was a small shop, on the end of a terrace and here, as expected, was number 48. Daisy was surprised that it was so small, a typical Victorian house, like many she'd seen in Bideford. There was no sign of a basement, nor an attic and Daisy wondered how it could accommodate the household that she had been led to expect. She could not help noticing that the privet hedge was overgrown and that a few weeds were forcing their way between the cracks in the paved front garden. There was no obvious rear entrance, so Daisy climbed the two steps to the blue painted front door and raised the brass knocker tentatively. A lady, approaching forty, opened the door. She was well turned out but her roughened hands told their own testimony, branding their owner as a former servant. This must be Mrs Cornelius. She greeted Daisy stiffly and began by showing her to a tiny upstairs room at the front of the house. Daisy's trunk stood forlornly in a corner, the tattered labels bearing evidence of its lonely journey across the county. Laid on the narrow, iron-framed bed were two uniforms, one of coarse blue linen for the rougher work, the other of finer material, in black, for the afternoons, when Daisy might be called upon to serve visitors. Mrs Cornelius studied Daisy closely.

'You are a good deal more slender than I was expecting,' she criticized. 'I am afraid the uniforms might be a little large for you. I had to guess the size. I hope you will be up to the heavier work.'

Daisy was aware that she had lost weight over the past months. Somehow, since Abraham's death, eating had seemed such an indulgence. Nonetheless, she replied firmly, 'Oh yes, I am really quite strong. I did everything for Mr Tuke.'

'He writes in your character of you doing some of the garden work,' said Mrs Cornelius. 'There is the vegetable garden to tend. I don't suppose it affected you in the countryside but we've had trouble obtaining foodstuffs here. Of course, there's never a problem with meat, Mr Cornelius being a butcher but we'd like to have a few more vegetables for the table. It will soon be the time of year for getting seeds in. My brother Francis used to see to it but now he's too busy up at the market garden to be spending his time on our little plot.'

Daisy's eyes lit up, 'Oh, I loved to help Mr Tuke in the garden,' she enthused. This job was going to be better than she'd expected.

Left alone to change into her uniform, Daisy began to unpack her few belongings, laying her clothes neatly in the two drawers beneath the oak wardrobe. A strong smell of mothballs caught her throat as she opened the wardrobe doors and hung her coat on the wooden hanger. The room was no more than nine feet by six but it was her own. The advantage of being the sole servant in a household was that she did not have to share. As it was well past midday, Daisy opted for the black uniform and looked out her tortoiseshell comb, so she could tidy her hair. She peered in the speckled mirror that formed the panel of one of the wardrobe doors. With difficulty, Daisy secured the lace cap on her head with hairpins and sighed. She longed to have her hair styled in a fashionable short cut. Her mother would be horrified but maybe, when she had saved enough from her wages, this was something that she could do. Satisfied that she had made every effort to look presentable, given the over-large uniform, she went downstairs to begin her new life.

Daisy listened patiently as Mrs Cornelius explained what was expected of her. It all seemed quite straightforward. She was stood in the back room, whilst her employer sat in a high-backed chair on one side of the fire. The room was gloomy, with only a small window, looking out on to the long garden; a thick net curtain blotted out much of the light. A door in the corner led to the narrow kitchen and beyond that, the scullery. Daisy took in the large table that was pushed to one side of the room. Eight wheel-backed chairs were tucked tightly underneath it. The cushioned seats by the fire were upholstered in deep red velvet, which was showing signs of wear. Embroidered antimacassars protected the backs of the armchairs and matching doilies adorned every surface.

Mrs Cornelius was talking of the inhabitants of 48 Upton Hill.

'There's myself and Mr Cornelius and our daughter Kathleen. She has just started school and I shall have to fetch her shortly. I will show you where the school is, then it will be your job to collect her.'

Daisy nodded. Little Kathleen must be about the same age as Rosie. Accompanying the small girl on her way to and from school would be a pleasure.

'Then there's my father, Mr Meyers and my brother Francis, you'll address him as Mr Francis of course. They have the downstairs front room.'

Mrs Cornelius gabbled on, 'My brother is out all day, gardening but you will have to be careful what time you do their room, as my father is elderly and has had to give up work, so he spends most of the day in there. It's best that you clean that room in the mornings, when he walks down for his newspaper. Then there's my widowed sister-in-law, Mrs Alice Meyers, who shares the back bedroom with Kathleen.

Daisy, who had already had the composition of the household described to her by Mrs Gilley, found her attention wandering. Her gaze alighted on a black-framed photograph on the mantlepiece. The soldier whose likeness had caught her eye was not a young man, much older than Abraham but his image was a harsh reminder of her loss. Mrs Cornelius noticed Daisy's lingering glance.

'That's my brother Owen,' she said, for once forgetting herself and taking tentative steps across the divide that social convention had created between them.

'He died on the Somme, that's when his wife, Alice, came up from Plymouth to live here.'

With a start, Daisy realised that Mrs Cornelius' brother had been lost at the same time as Abraham. Mistress and servant were united in a silent moment of reflection.

Alice Meyers appeared to have come to terms with widowhood but Mrs Cornelius found it difficult not to dwell on her brother's death. She stole quiet moments to mourn. Daisy often glimpsed her, sat in the chair, with Owen's picture on her lap and a damp handkerchief balled in her hand. How thankful Mrs Cornelius must be to have her surviving brother, Mr Francis, living with her, Daisy thought. Daisy usually only encountered Mr Francis at meal times and then he seldom addressed her directly. However, an incident that occurred shortly after her arrival aroused Daisy's sympathy for the uncommunicative man. Aware that old Mr Meyers had gone for his daily walk, Daisy went to clean their room. It was mid-morning, so she was surprised to find Mr Francis at home. He looked up guiltily as Daisy entered and she backed out of the room, with an apology. As she did so, she couldn't help noticing that Mr Francis' eye was blackened and his lip was bleeding, as if he had been in a fight.

Although she had not been at Upton Hill for long, Daisy had already overheard dining table conversations about the mistreatment that the Meyers family had suffered because of their Germanic sounding surname. In truth, the Meyers had been Devonshire folk for generations. They'd chosen not to Anglicise their name when war broke out, relying instead on being well known in the neighbourhood. There had been incidents though, name calling and those who snubbed them in the street. Could it have been something of this kind? Daisy wondered.

She had just begun sweeping the hall when Mr Francis came out of his room.

'You won't say 'aught about this, will you miss?' he'd said, looking around nervously, making sure that no one else was within earshot.

Daisy smiled to herself, thinking that it was a good job Mrs Cornelius couldn't hear her brother addressing the maid of all work as "miss".

She guessed correctly that Mr Francis, who had only joined his sister's household the previous year, was unused to dealing with servants.

'Of course not sir,' she reassured, wondering how he was going to explain away his visible injuries.

Francis Meyers banged the front door as he left the house, presumably on his way back to work. Daisy finished her tasks in the hall and re-entered the front room that Mr Francis shared with his father. Their belongings were sparse and there was little to tidy away. Daisy ran the feather cobweb brush round the coving and then began to dust. The bottom drawer of the chest by Francis Meyers' bed was not shut properly. Daisy pushed it firmly. It appeared be stuck, so she went to remove the drawer from its carcass, intending to rub the runners with a candle, a sure way to free a sticking drawer. Aghast, she looked at the four seagull's feathers, waxy white and condemning. They lay, a symbol of reproof, poorly concealed under a pile of undergarments. Hastily, Daisy replaced the drawer, attempting to leave it exactly as she had found it.

Although she grieved for a lost soldier, all Daisy's sympathies were with Mr Francis. Had he been fighting with someone who had branded him a coward? She supposed whoever had done this, saw a fit and healthy man and resented the fact that he was not at the front. His unthinking accusers did not consider that he might be doing vital work at home. Daisy saw him set off each day, heading for the market garden that had been carved from the allotments by the reservoir. She knew that he came home late each evening, exhausted from the extra hours that he did without pay. There was no shame in his contribution. At least he was doing something useful, providing much-needed food. The sense of her own worthlessness burdened her.

Daisy sat self-consciously on a hard, wooden chair at one end of the large polished table, in the summer drawing room of Aylwood House. Outside, the early spring sunlight flickered as it filtered through the newly greened foliage. She was here because Mrs Cornelius had pronounced that this afternoon would not be given over to the next stage of the spring clean but that Daisy should accompany her to Aylwood instead. Mrs Cornelius, intent on clinging to the periphery of Torquay society, had eagerly accepted an invitation to the home of her former employer. A score of ladies of Mrs Gilley's acquaintance were gathering to roll bandages for the convalescent home that had been set up in the Grand Hotel for the duration of the hostilities. The Grand Hotel, one of the largest in Torquay, dominated the seafront at the station end of the bay. In happier times, under the proprietorship of Mrs Gilley's brother-in-law, it had been the destination of choice for the gentry, who flocked to partake of the soft Torquay air. Now it was hoped that same balmy climate would aid the recuperation of men appallingly damaged by the war.

Mrs Cornelius had been informed that some of the ladies would be bringing maids to add to the workforce and she had resolved to be one of that number. So, after the luncheon crockery was cleared away, Daisy obediently trotted down Newton Road, in her employer's wake. When they arrived at Aylwood, Mrs Cornelius had hesitantly gone to the front door. Daisy knew that it was only a few years since Kate Cornelius had been required to use the servants' entrance. Will I ever knock on the front door of a grand house, with a servant behind me? wondered Daisy. Tantalising possibilities teased the corners of her mind.

A maid showed them into the drawing room where Mrs Cornelius greeted Mrs Gilley deferentially, before retreating to sit with another woman, who also seemed out of her depth in these opulent surroundings. The furnishings were in the latest style and Daisy had glimpsed a telephone on the wall in the hall. She gasped as Mrs Gilley flicked a bakelite switch, illuminating the central chandelier. Even the Court did not yet have electric lighting. The room was already bathed in sunlight but Daisy sensed that turning on the light unnecessarily was Mrs Gilley's way of drawing attention to this indicator of prosperity.

Daisy heard her employer explain to the other early arrival that she, Daisy, was her parlourmaid. Parlourmaid? thought a shocked Daisy. Yes and every other kind of maid as well and gardener for good measure. Daisy reasoned that being dubbed a parlourmaid, implied that she was one of a number of servants in the Cornelius household, thus enhancing her employer's status. How ridiculous, she thought. One servant or one hundred, won't change the fact that Mrs Cornelius had once been Kate Meyers, housemaid to the Gilley family.

Upright on her designated chair, Daisy quietly watched each lady make her entrance. You could not grow up near to Clovelly Court without becoming aware of the subtleties of rank and Daisy soon realised that this was far from being a gathering of equals. At the head of the table, furthest from Daisy, sat Mrs Gilley, imperious and more intimidating here, in her own setting, than she had seemed in the parlour of Gardener's Cottage. Their hostess was flanked by the cream of Torquay society; affluent women who had arrived by carriage from the mansions on Warberry Hill, or who lived in the large houses closer by. Mrs Cornelius might pretend that she was attending on the same footing as these grand ladies but it was clearly not the case. In the short time that Daisy had been at Upton Hill, she had come to realise that Mrs Cornelius exhibited all the snobbery of the social climber. Kate Cornelius would be horrified if these securely middle-class matrons realised that she, Kate, was formerly one of Aylwood's servants.

Daisy knew that it was not her place to engage these ladies in conversation. To them, she was of no more significance than the seat on which she perched. There was Mrs Cornelius, in the middle of the table, along with the other acolytes, the hangers-on, who aped their social superiors and aspired to acceptance. It was noticeable that the conversation was monopolised by those closest to Mrs Gilley. Mrs Cornelius and her ilk were permitted the odd word or two, especially if it consisted of sycophantic agreement with the comments of the real ladies but heaven forefend that they should express an opinion of their own. Daisy and the two other girls who had been brought along as essential accessories, to be paraded as badges of rank, sat in silence by the window.

Bandages were distributed and the women set to work. Pieces of lint flecked dark skirts and gradually, waiting cardboard boxes were filled with neat cylinders. Daisy, her fingers deftly rolling, relieved the boredom of the activity with thoughts of Abraham. Despite the monotony and the absence of someone to converse with, she was deriving a sense of satisfaction from the afternoon. She could not fight to avenge Abraham's loss but here was something she could do. The fact that it was not a particularly congenial task helped. It would not seem right for her efforts to be enjoyable. Each strip of cloth she tamed, she tallied as her contribution. This was not nursing, which was her dream but she was getting closer; she was doing something more meaningful than black-leading stoves or mopping tiles.

Daisy worked conscientiously, without pausing. Snippets of conversation eddied to her end of the room. Mrs Miller, stationed on Mrs Gilley's left, was holding forth in the strident tones of the hard of hearing. She was talking of her daughters, whose lives seemed impossibly glamorous when compared to Daisy's own. One, it appeared, had gone to Girton College in Cambridge. The other, Agatha, had been a VAD nurse right here in Torquay but had studied for examinations and was now working as a dispenser in the town. Torquay was certainly more exciting than Clovelly but Daisy still felt restless; there was a whole world of opportunity that was passing her by.

Daisy's thoughts continued to wander, as she applied herself to the repetitive task. The talk of Mrs Gilley and the other ladies turned to recent news and the fact that they had finally been granted the right to vote. Only a few weeks ago, Daisy had heard the newsboys crying out that the Representation of the People Act had been passed. It did not apply to Daisy herself of course, it would only be older women but she felt a sense of pride nonetheless. It was as if her encounter with the suffragettes in Clovelly, all those years ago, had made her part of the campaign, able to take some credit for the victory. She still had the scrap of yellow paper, with the suffragettes' slogan emblazoned on it. It lay in the bottom of a box of treasures that she had left behind in Clovelly, together with the handbill and the precious newspaper that Vera Wentworth had given her. There wasn't much chance to fight for women's rights in Clovelly but Daisy secretly regarded the cause as her own, always believing that she should have the same opportunities as her brothers. Coming to Torquay was somehow part of her personal struggle to take control of her own life, to do something different, to escape. Not that she had accomplished that, Daisy thought, regretfully. Working for Mrs Cornelius wasn't much different to working for Mr Tuke, although she was looking forward to making the vegetable garden flourish. Still, Torquay was a beginning, it was not Clovelly and that was what mattered.

A cheerful maid entered the room, pushing a rattling trolley. She began to serve tea in dainty, gold-rimmed cups. Her starched cap and pristine apron made Daisy conscious of her own ill-fitting uniform.

'Well of course,' their hostess was saying to those closest to her, 'our class are obligated. We should set an example by freeing our servants for war work. I am so pleased to see that some of you have done just that by bringing your maids here today.'

Mrs Cornelius failed to disguise a triumphant smile.

'I pride myself in knowing a good servant,' Mrs Gilley went on. 'Indeed, some of you have benefited from my recommendations.' At this juncture she looked intently at Kate Cornelius, who reddened under the scrutiny.

'Take Winnie here,' she said, indicating the girl who was now handing round cucumber sandwiches.

Despite the food shortages, the Gilley household had obtained both white bread and butter.

'She has given the greatest satisfaction,' Mrs Gilley went on, 'but I know that I must spare her for patriotic tasks. She spends two afternoons a week nursing at the Town Hall infirmary. Those poor boys up there need to see a kindly smile.'

An unfathomable look crossed Winnie's face but Daisy's attention was on Mrs Cornelius. If Mrs Gilley allowed her maids to nurse, might Mrs Cornelius, not wishing to be outdone, grant Daisy a similar opportunity?

Daisy was not hungry, so she shook her head as the maid reached her with a near empty plate of sandwiches. One of the girls next to her had also refused, so it seemed that it was not considered rude to decline. Refreshments distributed, Winnie was now required to be a living example of Mrs Gilley's beneficence. She drew up a dining chair next to Daisy and pulled a bundle of unrolled bandages towards her. The two girls smiled at each other, shyly. The other maids, sat on Daisy's right, were whispering to each other. It appeared that it was acceptable for those exiled to the bottom of the room to speak, if only amongst themselves.

As the resident servant, it was fitting that Winnie should open the conversation and the girls exchanged conventional introductions. For the first time, Daisy allowed her pace to slacken and she snatched stealthy looks at her neighbour. Daisy judged that Winnie was the younger by several years, probably not much older than Violet. Although not a hair was out of place, there was a light dusting of freckles across Winnie's pert nose, which somehow made her seem more approachable. They continued with their task and chatted inconsequentially, making the time pass quickly.

After half an hour, emboldened by Winnie's friendliness, Daisy found the courage to ask the question that had been burning in her mind since Winnie had arrived, 'Do you really work at the hospital? Oh, I do so wish I could do that. It must be wonderful. Do tell me all about it.'

Winnie looked at her inquisitor appraisingly, as if weighing up whether her response should be a mere platitude or the unvarnished truth. She decided on the latter.

'I hate it,' she said. 'Oh, it's all very well, folk think all it involves is holding the hands of handsome soldiers and giving them tea and reading to them but it's not like that at all.'

Daisy looked incredulous but Winnie, having unleashed her confession, resolved not to hold back. 'There's some of that of course but the men, they're so, so, oh, I don't know, so dreadfully hurt. You must have seen them coming off the troop trains, awfully injured. And then there's the ones that look fine but aren't right in the head. They're the worst. They rant and shout and jabber all manner of nonsense.'

Daisy could see unshed tears gleaming in Winnie's eyes. She didn't know what to say. Winnie blinked several times and reached for another bandage.

'Just hope your mistress doesn't get ideas about sending you up there,' warned Winnie. 'Do you think she's likely to?'

'I don't know,' said Daisy, thoughtfully. 'I hoped she would let me go. I thought that's what I'd do when I came here. I'd heard about the big hospital and all. I suppose I somehow felt that, if I were closer, I could get to work there. I'm not sure if Mrs Cornelius can spare me, there's only me to tend to the family.'

Daisy cast a guilty look in her employer's direction, wondering if she should have been so forthright. Had she now revealed Mrs Cornelius as a pretender to the rank of gentry?

'If you really want to help,' continued Winnie, 'see if you can get in at one of the convalescent homes, like the one at the Clarence Hotel, or even the Grand, though that would be further away for you. The men there are in some state but it's not like down at the hospital,' Winnie shuddered.

'What's so bad at the hospital?' asked Daisy. 'I mean, I know that the men are fearfully wounded and that …. and that some of them … well, some of them don't get better. But surely it is wonderful to be part of it all? I feel so useless. There's all the men risking their lives, off to war and all I can do is polish the brass and empty chamber pots.'

Winnie continued to unburden herself, 'It's the operations that are the worst,' she said, her voice trembling as she articulated her innermost traumas. 'If they can't save a leg or an arm, well, then they amputate it.'

'I know,' said Daisy, hoping to give comfort but wondering why Winnie was stating the obvious. 'Sometimes that's the best they can do.'

'No,' said Winnie. 'You don't understand. It's not the operations, or even bandaging the stumps, I can do that,' her voice dropped to a whisper, 'It's, it's what happens to the, to the, err, to the bits they cut off.'

Daisy looked at her, mesmerised. Here was something that she had not considered. She had thought about men with arms and legs missing, of course. She'd seen plenty of them, especially since she had come to Torquay and they no longer aroused her morbid curiosity; she accepted them as part of her surroundings, her war-torn world. It had never once occurred to her to wonder what happened to the mangled limbs that the surgeons severed.

'They make us take them to the furnace,' Winnie went on. 'It's awful. Last Saturday there was a little maid helping out, she can't have been more than about eleven, she just broke down when they said that's what she'd to do and I, I couldn't help her.'

Daisy looked around but the other women were lost in their own conversations and Winnie's distress went unremarked.

'I don't know what to say,' Daisy responded, horrified. 'That must have been terrible and that poor little girl. Try not to think about it.'

Winnie swallowed, surreptitiously wiped her eyes with the back of her hand and stood up to take the full box of bandages to the small table by the door. When she returned, she seemed keen to change the subject and began to tell Daisy of the delights of Torquay. By the end of the afternoon, the two young women had resolved to meet up when their half days next coincided. Despite Winnie's revelations about her work at the hospital, Daisy left Aylwood feeling more content than she had for months. She had made a friend, she was being useful and spring was on its way.

Daisy and Winnie's friendship thrived. Although Winnie was barely seventeen, her air of sophistication, borne from an upbringing in the town, eroded the disparity in their ages. As the weather grew warmer, they abandoned the shopping streets in favour of listening to bands in the park, or strolling along the pier. As they rested on the wrought iron seats, they caught glimpses of eager visitors taking to the water from the bathing huts on the promenade. Men in striped woollen swimsuits, hauled the straps over their shoulders and struck out from the shore. Young women shrieked in their frilly, knee-length costumes and mob caps. Although her brothers swam naked in the sea at home and Daisy loved to wet her feet in the Clovelly waves, she knew that she would never dare to don such an outfit and immerse herself totally in the sea. Sometimes, Daisy and Winnie would linger by the Punch and Judy show, pretending that they were too old for the puppets' antics but secretly enjoying Mr Punch's foibles. Or they would watch the donkeys giving bouncing children rides across the sand. The uncomplaining animals reminded Daisy of home but she had no regrets.

The holiday season reached its height and visitors outnumbered the soldiers on the streets of Torquay. The girls walked down to the busy town, dodging hurtling trams and struggling through thronging tourists, who were intent on enjoying the Devon sunshine. An animated group, heading in the opposite direction, strung across the street. Like bookends, two men in white trousers, striped blazers and straw boaters, flanked their parasol-twirling female companions. Winnie and Daisy had to side-step into the road to avoid them. Daisy was used to Clovelly's tourist hum but here, even in wartime, the atmosphere was more intense; everything was on a much larger scale.

Winnie had suggested a visit to the recently opened picture palace at the Pavilion. The cinema had been a revelation for Daisy and she eagerly awaited the announcement of the new programme each week. On this particular day, Winnie was impatient to see her idol, Eugene O'Brien, in the next episode of *Rebecca of Sunnybrook Farm*. She hurried Daisy along, anxious that the crowds had made them late. Daisy was daydreaming of having wonderful curls, like the film's heroine, Mary Pickford. She patted her own straight hair that was caught in a loose bun at the nape of her neck. She still hadn't plucked up the courage to have it cut short. Daisy had bravely taken Winnie's advice when buying her new summer dress though and she was proudly wearing it for the first time. She was pleased with the effect, even though it showed rather more calf than she was accustomed to.

The girls rushed along Fleet Street, keen to catch the two o'clock screening. When they reached the Pavilion, they were breathless and uncomfortably warm from their exertions. A young lad, in a brass buttoned jacket, his pill box hat set at the approved angle, stood on guard by the door. The girls hastened into the gold-painted entrance hall and paid for their tickets. The uniformed usherette showed them to a pair of plush seats on the end of a row. The lights dimmed in anticipation. Daisy never tired of the unworldliness of a visit to a picture palace. The organ gradually rose from the floor and the fulsome notes echoed around the auditorium, drowning the whirr of the projector. The pictures flickered and crackled into life and the opening feature began. Within minutes Charlie Chaplin was waddling across the screen and Daisy was mesmerised. The laughter died down as *A Dog's Life* came to an end and the crowing rooster announced a Pathé Newsreel. Winnie's attention was distracted but Daisy, keen to savour every moment of the outing, even the news, was looking intently in front of her. She was astonished to see that the film depicted an elegantly dressed woman in a wedding gown climbing into a carriage.

'I know her,' she squeaked, elbowing Winnie violently, 'That's the Honourable Betty Manners. I knew she was going to marry Mr Asquith's son but I never thought to see her on the screen down here in Torquay.'

The short film showed crowds lining the street, as the Prime Minister's son, resplendent in his army uniform, accompanied his bride. Daisy's two worlds collided, leaving her drained and a little homesick. Even Mary Pickford's dramatic performance and the accompanying swirls of the Pavilion's proficient organist, could not drag her thoughts away from the cobbles.

As usual, the girls ended their afternoon in a tea-shop. Rationing meant that there was rarely sugar available for their tea and today both butter and milk were in short supply but despite this, the girls enjoyed the ritual. Daisy purchased a cake because that was what was expected. She cut it neatly in two with the dainty silver knife and then sat sipping her tea, still unsettled by memories of Clovelly. The Victoria sponge lay untouched on her plate.

Much to Daisy's relief, Winnie reached across and helped herself to a portion of the sponge with the comment, 'I say, aren't you going to eat that? Let's not waste it, I am fearfully hungry.'

Daisy reduced the remaining half to crumbs. Her once hearty appetite had dwindled of late. Foregoing the food she once loved was part of her penance for survival.

Winnie, teased her with a plump-cheeked smile. 'There's naught left of you,' she said, biting into her own hefty slice of fruit cake.

Daisy glanced at her wrists, poking out from under the sleeves of the new summer frock. She turned her hands over. Yes, perhaps she was thinner than she used to be.

Mrs Gilley's devotion to patriotic duty had the desired effect and before the summer was over, Mrs Cornelius, eager to emulate her social superiors, announced that she had arranged for Daisy to spend an afternoon a week working at the billeting centre, that was housed in the forbidding Baptist Chapel at Upton Vale. To Daisy's delight, Mrs Gilley had decided that Winnie too could devote her Wednesdays to this cause. Daisy revelled in the work and Winnie was grateful for the respite from the Town Hospital. Many of the men at the centre were convalescing New Zealanders, who professed not to understand the Devon accents of those who attended them.

The girls were employed cleaning the long high room that had once resounded to the preacher's ringing tones. They emptied chamber pots, washed endless plates and cups and folded recalcitrant sheets to the satisfaction of the sister in charge. There were lighter tasks too, writing letters for men whose damaged eyes or hands prevented them from sending messages home. On several occasions, Daisy found herself weeping, as a soldier dictated sentences that begged his sweetheart to forget him, in favour of a man whose body was still whole. Sadder still, when the lines she was asked to pen were a desperate plea to a girl whose affections were already engaged elsewhere. It wasn't nursing exactly, unlike Winnie, who was an official Red Cross volunteer, Daisy was not permitted to dress wounds but she did wash the broken shells of damaged men and sought to comfort the distressed.

It was October and darkness was already falling as the girls readied to leave at the end of a particularly tiring shift. One of the senior nursing staff rushed up to them, waving a piece of paper.

'Could either of you just fetch these medicines?' she asked, 'Your legs are younger than mine.'

Winnie and Daisy exchanged a glance and decided that they would both walk round to the dispensary, then they could gossip on the way. They hurried along the road and pushed open the dispensary door, glad to be out of the wind. A pleasant looking young woman, with heavy features, bustled up in response to the bell. She looked at the prescription.

'I can make that up for you,' she said. 'I will only be five or ten minutes, if you'd like to wait.'

With that, she disappeared into a back room.

'That's Miss Miller,' said Winnie. 'She often comes to see Mrs Gilley with her mother. Mrs Miller is always talking about her wonderful daughter who works at the dispensary. You'd think such a paragon would be a dreadful bore but actually she seems perfectly pleasant when she visits.'

'Do you think she recognised you?' asked Daisy.

'They live in Barton Road,' Winnie replied.

It didn't seem like an answer but Daisy understood. Even if Miss Miller had realised that Winnie was the maid who served her tea at Mrs Gilley's, she would not break the unwritten social rules and acknowledge her.

Medicine delivered, the girls set off wearily up Union Street. Usually, Daisy strode on ahead, with Winnie struggling to keep up but today it was Daisy who trailed a few steps behind. They paused on the corner of Upton Road, where their ways divided.

Winnie looked at her friend, 'Surely you aren't wearing rouge?' she asked, astonished. 'You do look dreadfully flushed.'

'Of course not,' replied Daisy, reaching in her bag for an enamel-backed mirror.

A gaunt girl stared back. Her dad's family had eyes that sparkled blue but she had inherited her ma's tawny eyes, flecked with gold and green; "gypsy eyes", her schoolfellows had called them, when they wanted to taunt. The eyes in the glass were burning coal black and certainly, her cheeks did seem to have a heightened colour.

'Are you sure you are alright?' Winnie persisted, 'It was a hard shift today and then the trip to the dispensary but you do look jolly queer.'

Daisy became aware of a tightening pressure across her forehead and the hill did somehow seem steeper than usual; it was as if her limbs were slow to respond to the instructions from her brain.

'Now you come to mention it,' Daisy said. 'I don't feel quite myself. I've probably overdone it a bit with the extra hours I've done at the billeting centre this week. I'll go back and lie down before I have to get the supper.'

Daisy crawled back up the hill, focussing on the blissful prospect of slipping between the rough sheets on her lumpy bed and closing her eyes.

11
October 1918

The autumn dusk fell swiftly, leaden clouds and unrelenting rain hastening its approach. The room was infused with an ominous chill. Despite the invading night, no curtains shut out the shadows and no guttering candles alleviated the gloom. Outside, the lamplighter ambled along. Mindful of his years, he had slowed his pace in response to the steepness of the street. The gaslights flared in turn, denoting his progress and a thick yellow glow shafted across Daisy's coverlet. She stirred; her eyelids fluttered as she was drawn slowly into wakefulness. Disorientated by the darkness, unable to tell how long she had been dozing, she remained motionless and confused. The hall clock marked the hour, giving shape to Daisy's day. She had slept the afternoon away but still she felt wretched. Wearily, she scrabbled to strike a lucifer and light the candle that stood on the narrow shelf by the door. This small amount of exertion expended all her energy and she slumped on to the bed. Bile rose in her throat. Teeth chattering and legs weak, she struggled back to her feet. The embarrassing prospect of vomiting in the chamber pot brought a flush to her already hectic cheeks. She knew that she had to drag herself across the landing to the lavatory.

Kneeling in front of the floral, porcelain toilet bowl, Daisy blessed the superior plumbing arrangements at Upton Hill. The nausea gradually passed and she rested her head against the cool, green tiles. Why did she feel so unwell? She had been ailing ever since her trip to the cinema. Then, on Thursday, a dizzy spell had beset her, as she attempted to serve the dinner. Mrs Cornelius, her exasperation barely veiled, had sent Daisy to her bed, making it clear that her wages would be docked accordingly.

During Daisy's illness, life in the Cornelius' household had gone on without her, after a fashion. She felt cut off, isolated from the daily routine and ignorant of what was happening beyond the four walls of her room. She did not see Mrs Cornelius, it was the sister-in-law, Mrs Meyers, who periodically brought damp flannels to cool Daisy's forehead, or light meals that Daisy pushed round the plate out of politeness. Until the last few days, Alice Meyers had been a dim figure, on the periphery of Daisy's world, the archetypal dependent relative, submissive and retiring. Now, Daisy was learning that Alice was something more than merely a timid little widow. Emerging from the eclipsing shadow of Mrs Cornelius, Alice Meyers appeared resolute, confident; no awkwardness accompanied her ministrations. She seemed to derive satisfaction from tending to Daisy. The responsibility suited her, gave her a purpose that had been lacking since her husband, Owen, had died.

Mrs Meyers pushed open Daisy's door and rested a tray precariously on the corner of the washstand. She uncovered a dish containing steamed fish. Daisy hauled herself into a sitting position and meekly took the spoon that was offered to her. At Alice Meyers' insistence, Daisy ate a mouthful or two before rejecting the bowl and turning her head to the wall. The older woman removed the stone hot-water bottle for refilling and fussed over pillows and bedcovers. Friendly conversation would not have been appropriate, nor had Daisy the strength for more than a few words, however, as she tucked in the sheets, Mrs Meyers did intimate that Mr Cornelius had returned from the butcher's shop that evening complaining of a headache.

'It is not just Mr Cornelius, Mrs Cornelius took to her bed this morning,' she said, 'and I have some concerns for little Kathleen too. She is decidedly seedy.'

This was news of a sort, thought Daisy, herself worried about Kathleen, of whom she had grown fond. She sighed. Her malady was stealing through the household with a sinister vengeance.

Listlessly, Daisy watched the candle sputter and burn low. The alternating fevers and chills of her illness had stretched into another day. She'd not seen a soul for several hours. Voices rumbled downstairs in the hall, Mr Meyers and Mr Francis were talking but Daisy could not distinguish their words. She loved to listen to the Meyers men; their fruity Devon accents reminded her of her da.

Daisy flushed guiltily, aware that she had made efforts to moderate her own accent, studiously copying the inflections that she absorbed at the cinema. In many ways she was rejecting her origins, leaving Clovelly behind. Did that make her as bad as Mrs Cornelius, trying to be better than she ought? With her aching head, such thoughts were beyond contemplation and she closed her eyes. Then Mr Meyers' foot was on the stair. He only ever came to the upper floor to use the bathroom. This time though, he knocked on Daisy's door but remained discreetly outside.

'Them's all falling sick now,' he called, with a lapse of grammar that would have earned a reprimand from his daughter. 'I hopes you can shift for yoursen a bit. Francis has just taken hisself off to bed and Mrs Meyers started with it this afternoon. There's only me left standin'. What's that they say about creaking gates eh?' The old man chuckled to himself.

'Anyroad,' he went on, 'I shall do me best and bring up some nammit for you now'n ag'in, so's you'll not go 'ungry. I've hopes that someone will be up and about to cook proper in a day or so. You be able to manage for now then? I be leavin' the tray out here for ee. 'Tis the broth Alice made this morning, afore she took bad.'

Daisy croaked her thanks and as the old man went back downstairs, she was seized with a fit of unrelenting coughing. The broth remained untouched in its bowl.

Polly lay in bed, listening to the gale, as it teased at the windows and set roof tiles rattling. Her mind whirled, racing alongside the windblown leaves, wakefulness an unwelcome ally. Little things loomed large and assumed a disproportionate significance. She was acutely aware that the sheet was becoming threadbare, the striped ticking mattress underneath was beginning to show through. A job for Lily, turning sides to middle, not that Lily was the keenest seamstress. The patchwork quilt was made from scraps of worn out clothing, its hexagons reflecting the past like diamonds, recalling days of contentment when she had worn this blouse, or Daisy had proudly shown off that new smock.

Hot, stiflingly hot, heart racing, why was her body betraying her? Unbearable sweating swept unerringly over her, despite the season. Polly threw back the covers in anguish and flung her body over on to her right side, sighing resoundingly as she did so. Albert stirred sleepily and reached out a hand to rest on her shoulder. Polly shrugged him off, his touch a brand on her already heated body. That was something else that troubled her. It wasn't that she didn't want him, love him she supposed. Since the change, she'd come over proper queer, especially at night. His caress was like a blow and his presence beside her no longer a welcome source of warmth but another weight on the scales of her disquietude. Sleep, intangible, out of reach, yet its oblivion so desired, so needed. The worries of the past weeks oppressed her.

There had been that business with Mr Caird, then the longed-for letter from Leonard had not arrived and now, the ultimate burden, this news of Daisy's sickness. Her daughter's move to Torquay had been another bereavement for Polly, an abandonment, a betrayal. She dreaded the thought of having to visit Daisy tomorrow. It was not just that she was reluctant to reawaken her relationship with her daughter, the prospect of the unaccustomed journey terrified her. She was not one to go gallivanting, she scarcely left Clovelly now and it was years since she'd been on a train. She must overcome her misgivings. Like it or not, go she must, folk would talk else.

Her mind turned to Leonard. Polly weighed up this particular concern. She had been glad when he'd finally made a decision and signed on for the merchant service, more than a year ago now. He had sailed with Captain Bate on the *Hillhouse*, escaping from conscription's rapacious maw just before he turned eighteen. Then, after only a few short weeks, the telegram had arrived, shattering her complacency. Naïvely, she'd thought that the merchant service would be safer than the navy; she had been so wrong. Leonard and Charlie Bate had been lucky to escape with their lives when the German torpedo had struck. That wasn't the only time. Twice more since then he had been on ships that had been hit. Receiving the unspeakable news did not get any easier; repetition did not bring immunity. When Leonard was away from her, she had to force herself not to think of him, or the anxiety consumed her. It was a joy to have him home between voyages but each visit brought with it the inevitable leave-taking. Every departure struck Polly like a death. She coped by locking the worries away, by renouncing the children who were lost to her, closing her heart to them as if they had never been.

Next, she fretted about the exchange she had had with Mr Caird a few weeks ago. He'd wanted to talk about Bertie. She didn't have to worry about Bertie going to war; it was the one good thing about him being the way he was. Besides, Bertie was needed here to help Alb with the boat. Then Mr Caird had come along and upset her. It wasn't as if the agent had just stopped her in the street, he had called, purposely come to the house, making the whole thing seem more serious. He'd said someone had complained that she'd been too harsh with Bertie. Well you had to tell Bertie what was what, be firm with him, or he'd no idea. Always been the same, ever since he was a little tacker and they'd realised he was a bit on the slow side. Maybe she had raised her voice to him a time or two but what of it? It was naught to do with Mr Caird, nor anyone else. Mr Caird wouldn't say who'd gone tattling to him but she had her suspicions. That interfering Collins next door for a start. He wasn't right in the head himself that one and look how he'd been with Daisy when she'd been home. There was a man who was leading his wife a merry dance, she'd be bound.

Polly's thoughts turned back to her eldest daughter and the intricacies of the journey that she must make come the morning. She worried about finding the right platform, about missing her connections, about getting lost in Torquay, which seemed impossibly distant. And all for what? She wouldn't have much time with Daisy before she had to up and leave to catch the train back home. And what was she to do when she got there? Bring Daisy back with her? No, the girl was better off down south. How could she, Polly, who had unquestionably failed to keep her other children safe, be expected to protect Daisy from whatever ailed her?

Polly was ill-served by the pre-dawn start and the arduous journey. She arrived in Torquay physically exhausted and emotionally drained. After Eli had dropped her in Bideford, she had, with some effort, managed to find her way on and off the four trains, becoming increasingly flustered with each stage. The busyness of Exeter had overwhelmed her. She was bewildered by the number of platforms and the swarming crowds. Was it only she who was at a loss? In the end, Polly had been obliged to ask a porter where she should get the train to Newton Abbot. She loathed having to seek advice, conscious that it exposed her as an outsider. She sat in the dingy carriages, squashed between strangers, with nothing to occupy her mind but thoughts of her destination, of Daisy, of her feelings for her eldest child. She had allowed distance to create a comforting barrier between her and the daughter she had tried to forget. This visit would rip open old wounds and expose her to impossible hurts.

In comparison to Exeter, Torre Station was small, more like Barnstaple but it still pulsed with hectic life, hypnotising Polly into inaction. Reminders of the war were ever-present. Each person carried with them the scars of the past four years; the age had marked them all. Anonymous, khaki-clad Tommies, with their old men's unfathomable eyes staring from the bodies of boys. Bold young women, their shorter hem-lines and bobbed hair, reflecting a new freedom. They were more confident than Polly's generation and yet more lost. She shuddered against the hubbub. People pushed past, unseeing, indifferent. Newsboys screamed the latest headlines about German concessions as they thrust the mid-day editions under her nose. It seemed that the Hun were nearing defeat. Steeling herself to cope with her own immediate concerns, Polly took no comfort from the prospect of peace. Head down, trembling, she took a few tentative steps towards the house that held her eldest child.

It was chilly in the unheated bedroom. Polly stood in her worn woollen coat and her Sunday hat, staring at her sleeping daughter. In the months since they had last been together, Daisy had left all traces of girlhood behind. Dark, smudging bruises lay under her eyes, her cheeks were hollowed, her laboured breathing heart-rending. Not again, Polly thought. Her past years had been an incessant sequence of sickrooms, of sitting in fear, watching over her children. Violet, Mark, Nelson and now Daisy. Too many bedsides. Too much pain.

Mr Meyers knocked politely to offer Polly tea. She accepted gratefully; she had not eaten since her early breakfast.

'I'll be bringing up some beef tea for the girl dreckly,' he said. 'Mrs Cornelius' cousin popped in with it from up along. I just have to set it on the stove. I be glad to see 'e here, iffen only for an hour or two. I've a mite to do, there's others in the household who be taken sick now.'

Polly mumbled her thanks. She sat heavily on the chair clasping her hands round the cup to warm them. Daisy stirred, her eyes were dull and a cough ripped at her frail body, making Polly recoil. She had dreaded the moment when she would need to speak to her daughter. She found herself uttering inanities. She had no meaningful words, yet the silences were unnerving.

Daisy wrapped her sickness around her, a safeguard against the need to respond to her mother's terse comments. There was no common ground. Polly was unused to inaction; being confined in a room, with nothing to do but talk, made her uneasy. Mr Meyers knocked with the beef tea. Polly made a half-hearted attempt to get Daisy to swallow it, at least that gave her something to do. It had been a wasted effort though; the girl had steadfastly refused to take any nourishment. It was with relief that Polly got up to go, little more than an hour after her arrival. She needed to leave, she told herself. If she waited any longer, she would miss the last train to Bideford. There were no expressions of affection, there was no embrace. Mother and daughter parted as strangers.

Polly's brief visit had disturbed Daisy's equilibrium. The girl dwelt on her mother's coldness and fuelled by her fever, rising resentment severed filial feeling. All reason left her as her sickness nurtured imagined threats. In the days that followed, Mr Meyers continued to offer Daisy rudimentary care but food was an anathema, tasty morsels and precious milk were abruptly refused. What was the point of eating, thought Daisy, why bother striving for recovery? How much easier it would be to release the flimsy thread and to sink simply into nothingness. As her body weakened, Daisy became increasingly uncooperative and irritable. Tending to her was no easy task for Mr Meyers and the elderly man was distressed when Daisy rebuked him. Alice Meyers struggled from her sick-bed to try to assist her father-in-law but her efforts were unappreciated.

Wearily, Alice entered the kitchen, carrying a full bowl of soup. Mr Meyers glanced at her.

'That Daisy still not eating then?' he remarked. 'Young girl like that. I can't understand why she's took it so bad.'

'Nothing again today,' replied Mrs Meyers. 'Everyone else seems to be turning the corner but she's no better at all. I don't know how much longer we can care for her, especially now she's become so wilful. I am surprised the mother didn't take her back with her.'

'She was a proper rum 'un,' observed Mr Meyers. 'She weren't the slightest bothered about the maid. No sooner had she got here than she was saying she'd need to be off to catch the 2.57 home. Still,' he added charitably, "tis a rare old journey and she'd youngsters to see to.'

'It is awkward,' said Alice. 'Maybe we should send for Doctor Cook. It was all right at first but now she seems to be failing. I can't be doing with her stubbornness when I'm so tired and I've the others to see to.'

It was resolved that the doctor should be sent for. Alice Meyers answered his knock and directed him to Daisy's room. On the way upstairs, she explained that Daisy had become intractable and that they were finding it difficult to cope with her excitable moods.

'It isn't just that, Doctor,' she said, 'she's refusing to eat and we've all been unwell ourselves. We've not the energy to sit with her for hours on end, badgering her to take food. We can't expect Mrs Cornelius' cousin to keep coming round from Ellacombe Road to help.'

'Let me examine her first,' replied Doctor Cook, 'and then we will see what's to be done.'

The examination over, Doctor Cook gave his pronouncement.

'The girl has taken this influenza particularly badly. She is also suffering from gastritis, which explains the aversion to food. As you are unable to care for her here, the best thing is for her to go to the infirmary at the workhouse. I will arrange for transport. I am happy to sign a certificate to say that she is fit to be moved.'

'Oh, Doctor,' said Mrs Meyers, 'that is such a relief. We managed in the beginning but then there was only my elderly father-in-law who wasn't sick and we just can't handle her since she became so headstrong. I'll send a telegram to her family to say that you felt it was best that she went to the workhouse.'

A skipping rope thudded on the pavement outside, beating its regular tattoo, as a group of small girls chanted in time.

'I had a little bird, its name was Enza, I opened the window and in flew Enza.'

Periodically, the rhythm was interrupted, as one of the less proficient children stumbled on the rope, to the derision of her playmates. The incessant repetition of the ridiculous words tortured Polly and she pulled the thick curtain across, in a vain attempt to deaden the pervading sound.

There was a knock and Mrs Howard was on the doorstep, waving a telegram aloft. It was rare that the postmistress delivered telegrams herself. This would not be good news.

''Tis another telegram about your maid,' she said kindly. 'Seems she's no better and they've taken her to the workhouse. Weren't you down there just a few days since?'

The workhouse. The very name was a portent of misfortune. Polly grabbed the telegram and slammed the door without a word. For a few moments she remained motionless, leaning back against the door, the telegram crushed in her clenched fist. Gradually, her breathing calmed and she braced herself, daring to decipher the news. "Influenza worse. Daughter taken to Newton Abbot workhouse infirmary", she read. The words blurred in front of her eyes. The infirmary was for folk who were sick, it was not the final resort for those gripped by poverty; yet it was still the workhouse. Despite her carefully crafted cloak of indifference, the vision of Daisy, institutionalised and alone was unbearable.

When Albert came in from fishing, an agitated Polly was waiting for him, the telegram still in her hand.

''Tis, the maid,' she cried. 'They've sent her to the workhouse! What's to do?'

Albert was busy easing waders from his sore feet. He flexed his cramped toes, encased in the thick woollen socks.

'Easy mother,' he said. 'Tell us again what's happened.'

'When they first sent to say she wasn't eating and couldn't leave her bed, I did think it might be the enteric. Then, when I went down and saw how thin and listless she was, I wondered about the green sickness but the whole family has gone down with it. Seems for certain it's this influenza.'

'It's been in the papers that,' said Albert. 'They say this illness is taking the young and healthy, without so much as a by your leave. 'Twas mostly overseas at first, naught to do with us but now it seems 'tis closer to home. There's been reports in the *North Devon Journal* of late, folk've been taken sick all over.'

'But she's in the workhouse, Alb,' reiterated Polly. 'I can't bear to think of it. What should we do?'

'We'll send to the workhouse and find out what's what,' said Albert. 'It may not be so bad as you be thinkin'. 'Tis probably just there was no one to see to her where she was. You said they was all poorly.'

The infirmary loomed above the other buildings that made up Newton Abbot workhouse. The smoke, tumbling from the tall incinerator chimney, eddied and rose reluctantly skyward. In the lee of the sombre stone, Albert hunched against the sharp October wind. Polly, unsettled and uncomprehending, had retreated into herself once more. It was left to Albert to send telegram after telegram to the workhouse, enquiring after his daughter's welfare; it was he who trudged to the post office and handed over the hard-earned coins to Mrs Howard. For form's sake he signed each message with Polly's name, not his own, surely such messages should come from a mother? Replies came back indicating that Daisy was able to leave, providing there was somewhere she could go to be cared for. There was no possibility of her returning to Upton Hill; she was far from being fit to work. It was the latest telegram, received twenty four hours after Daisy had arrived at the workhouse, that provoked Polly into a reaction. It spoke of "mental trouble". The sinister shroud of the madhouse descended and Polly had been adamant.

'Fetch her home Alb,' she'd said. 'They'll be putting her in the asylum else. She's not to go there. You have to fetch her back. I'll send to say you'll be coming for her tomorrow.'

So yet another telegram had been sent and here was Albert, intent on bringing his daughter home. Louisa Taylor, the superintendent nurse at the infirmary, took Albert into a cramped office. Black-covered ledgers lined the walls and untidy papers trickled over the desk. The nurse, in her sharply starched uniform, moved a pile of books from a chair and bade Albert sit down. She was a woman past middle age, with a plain but pleasing, lined face and iron grey hair. Her brisk efficiency was at odds with the state of her surroundings. She exuded capability and Albert began to feel reassured. She explained that Daisy had been quiet at first and not in the least excitable or violent. It was only yesterday that she had become volatile and unmanageable.

'And I am afraid it has been very difficult to get your daughter to take nourishment,' Nurse Taylor was saying. 'She has barely had three pints of milk since she arrived.'

'But I can take her home?' asked Albert, anxious now. It was, after all, what he had come for.

'Sir,' said Nurse Taylor, firmly, 'I beg you to reconsider. Your daughter is not fit to travel across the county. You do her a great disservice by not leaving her in our care.'

'But you said she could leave,' said Albert, bewildered now.

'That was before this latest development,' replied Nurse Taylor. 'I don't know how you would manage the journey with her how she is.'

In the face of her authority, Albert's resolve faltered but then he thought of Polly; he could not expose his wife to more torment. It was the mention of mental trouble that had brought about her change of mood. She had swung from indifference to distress. Haunted by the apparition that was the asylum, Polly had wanted her daughter to return to the shelter of her family.

'I's come to take her home,' said Albert, obdurate now, 'and takes her home I will, with respect to you ma'am.'

Albert put his arm round Daisy, steadying her, as they made their way across the platform at Barnstaple. The guard was raising his green flag. Hurriedly, Albert hoisted his daughter on to the final train of their journey and climbed the step behind her. The guard slammed the door after them and blew his whistle. Now they were nearing home, Albert relaxed a little, thankful that they had the third class carriage to themselves. They still had to get from Bideford to Clovelly but Mrs Hamlyn, through her associations with the Red Cross, had helped to organise a motor ambulance for that. It was a good job they'd managed to get this train, he thought, it wouldn't do to keep them waiting. He hoped he was doing the right thing, bringing Daisy home. He'd had some doubts himself, especially when that Nurse Taylor had advised against it but Polly had been insistent.

Daisy sat sedately opposite her father. Her eyes were focussed on the condensation that ran down the windows and she was aware of a damp, musty smell that rose from the rough seats. Her body ached with an all-consuming intensity. Her loosely-hanging clothes felt unfamiliar, irritating, chafing at her flesh. Apart from the half-remembered ride to the workhouse, it had been a fortnight since she'd worn anything but a nightgown. Her hat made her headache worse and her shoes were like leaden weights, holding her down. Albert was staring out of the window, looking for the lights of familiar stations but Daisy barely realised who she was with, where she was, or why. The recurring rhythm of the rails overlaid all meaningful thought.

The train rattled out of Fremington, heading towards Instow. Albert stood up, fighting sleep. He had worried about how he was to get Daisy as far as Bideford, sick as she was but he'd coped. Yes, she was frail but she was subdued, biddable, exhibiting no signs of the excitability that the infirmary staff had spoken of. Nonetheless, he needed to be watchful, wakeful. He released the leather strap and lowered the window. Smut-laden steam hit his face as they rounded the bend but the rush of cold air refreshed him. The screech of the whistling train stirred Daisy from her stupor. Animated, she rose from her seat with an energy that belied her weakened state. Pushing Albert to one side, she thrust her head through the window. The unheeding train ploughed on.

Daisy felt the arm of her fearful father, trying to pull her back from the unseen dangers but she twisted away. The pain in her head was excruciating. She tugged at her hat, loosening the steel hatpin. Yes, she remembered, she had been so thrilled to buy that hat with Winnie. It was only last month, yet it was an interminable lifetime ago. Dimly remembered feelings of pride flickered and were gone. The hat became her enemy. It was hurting her, imprisoning her, adding to her agony. The idea obsessed her. If she was bareheaded she would be free. Daisy flung the hat away from her. It whirled out of the window, caught in the vortex of the moving train. Now, the appalling consequence of what he had done, of what might be to come, dawned upon Albert.

It was late when the front door crashed, announcing Albert and Daisy's return. With the denial of the defeated, Polly cowered in her bed, burying her head under the faded quilt.

12
Autumn 1918

Clovelly slept. There were no sounds from the cobbled
street but the night and its attendant horrors, closed in
on Edward Collins. Even eighteen months spent
embraced in the village's serenity had not banished the
terrors that darkness could bring. He awoke from the
recurring nightmare, shaking and sweating. Curled in a
foetal position, clasping his knees, he silently sobbed. As
his distress gradually subsided, he became aware of
voices penetrating the thin wall that divided Mrs
Stanbury's cottage from its neighbour. He hadn't yet
seen her but he knew that Daisy, his shimmering
Marguerite, was home. He'd heard that her father had
brought her back from Torquay late last night. In the
morning, he thought, he might properly enquire after
her welfare, take her some tasty morsel to whet her
appetite. Thoughts of the enigmatic young woman, now
barely a touch away, calmed him. Tomorrow, he would
hear again her sweet voice, with its enchanting
Devonshire lilt. Minutes passed. The hum of
conversation from the adjoining room continued. He
could not distinguish the words but he could hear
Daisy's exclamations, interspersed with the deeper

rumble of her father's responses. Then, escalating agitation could be detected in their tones. A door banged. Silence. Edward lay flat on his back, his eyes staring into the thick blackness. Undisturbed, Amelia breathed shallowly beside him. His concern for Daisy's welfare made sleep slip further from his grasp. Finally, as the fading year's late dawn light banished the starry dark, he drifted into restless sleep.

Daybreak brought no such respite to the family in the cottage next door. A fire was lit in the tiny upstairs room and the tin bath was lugged up from the kitchen. Daisy sat submissively as her unwilling mother helped her to wash, the soap-slicked water cooled round her wasted frame. The knobs of the girl's spine protruded alarmingly and her back was covered with dark downy hair. The sting of the red carbolic soap as it penetrated the scratches on her arms and the abrasive touch of the rough flannel provoked no reaction. Daisy acquiesced as her mother slipped a clean nightdress over her head. It hung forlornly on the sharp angles of her shoulders. No remnant remained of the vivacity that had first caught Edward Collins' attention. Polly's glance took in the sunken eyes, the thinning hair and the skeletal feet peeping out from under the hem of the nightdress. The unwelcome tug at her maternal heartstrings drew upon reserves that she no longer possessed. Defeated, Polly could gaze at this unbearable travesty of her daughter no more. Everyday actions became her haven. She concentrated on tasks that did not require such an agonizing expenditure of emotion, household duties that might stop her from having to think about Daisy. Daisy as she had been. Daisy as she was now.

Mechanically, moving like an elderly woman, Polly went to heat some broth on the stove.

Resolutely, Daisy refused to eat. She writhed and thrashed, shrinking back from the nourishment that was being offered. Broth spilt on the counterpane and the spoon clattered to the floor, as Daisy flung her arm wildly. Resignedly, Polly returned downstairs, frustration and fear etched on her face. Albert looked up expectantly.

'Did the maid take any?'

Polly put the bowl down on the oil-cloth with a sigh.

'What are we to do Alb? Why won't she eat? I be so cross with her Alb. I could hit her, I really could. What's making her so blessed stubborn?'

Disregarding the rejected broth, Albert took a cup of milk up to Daisy. He tried coaxing, cajoling, begging but even for him, she resisted, gritting her teeth and twisting her head away. He did manage to get a few drops past the lips of his distraught daughter before she pushed forcefully at his hand. The sound of the cup smashing echoed ominously through the cottage. Milk dripped down the wall and seeped through the gaps in the floorboards, in an appalling parody of Daisy's hold on life, which too was ebbing away. Polly had less patience and greater fear. Her ill-disguised anxiety was more infectious than the influenza that had stolen their daughter from them, taken their beloved girl and left instead this tortured changeling. Daisy became increasingly agitated in Polly's presence. Repeatedly, Polly tucked the restraining bed sheets firmly in, only to have Daisy throw them back in an effort to leave her bed and retreat to a sanctuary that existed only in her imagination. Daisy spoke rarely but when she did, it was in random, rambling sentences, that bore no relation to the questions she was being asked. Amongst her incoherent utterances, she claimed that food would harm her, that she must not eat. Clearly distressed, convinced that her throat was closing up, Daisy refused both cup and spoon. For Polly, each failure twisted the knife of rejection ever deeper.

The doctor was sent for. The workhouse had stressed that Daisy would need to be tended to without delay. Dr Crew was a major now, away serving in India and Dr Kay had taken over his patients. When Albert asked him to call, word came that the doctor was himself unwell and that Dr Toye would travel out from Bideford instead. This news flustered Polly. Albert needed to go to sea, it would be left to her to cope with the unknown doctor alone. She could have managed if it had been Dr Kay; he was comfortingly familiar. Polly was uneasy about revealing their torment to a stranger.

Dr Toye was a tall, brusque man in his forties. When Dr Kay called, you felt that he was visiting for a cosy chat, Dr Toye was very different; he was businesslike, hurried, eager to give his verdict and to move on to the next patient.

'She says there's something in her throat Doctor,' said Polly, apprehensively, endeavouring unsuccessfully, to banish all thoughts of that other child who had struggled to swallow in the stifling May heat, in that far away time before the war began.

Dr Toye conducted a brief but competent examination. Daisy seemed docile, unresisting but the essence of her was elsewhere. The doctor tutted as he held Daisy's stick-like wrist, in order to take her pulse.

'And you say she won't eat, won't respond, that she has no energy?' he asked.

'Well, there's times she's like that doctor. Other times though, she's so strong we can't hardly hold her. Earlier she would scarce stay in her bed. 'Tis like she's a mad thing, like she hardly knows us.'

Polly crumpled, no longer able to conceal her pain.

'What are we to do doctor? I don't know as I can do all this again.' The metronome in Polly's brain beat out the refrain, not again, no, not ever again.

'She needs regular nourishment,' the doctor replied. 'Hourly feeds, plenty of warm milk. Can you manage that do you think?'

Polly nodded, abjectly but it was as if his words were the waves in the bay, washing over the sand but leaving no lasting impression. So far, they had scarcely managed to get Daisy to take anything at all; the prospect of trying to deliver hourly feeds was overwhelming.

'Either myself or Dr Ackland will call tomorrow,' Dr Toye was saying as he collected his neatly folded coat from the chair by the door. Then he was gone. The house was deserted apart from Polly and Daisy. There was nothing, nothing but Daisy to fill Polly's thoughts. She watched from the doorway as Daisy lay sleeping, shrunken against the greying pillows. Grasping the cup of warm milk resolutely, Polly inhaled deeply and approached her daughter with trepidation. She knew that somehow she must get the girl to drink but she was aware that she was not equal to the challenge. Polly could feel her heart racing, she could not quell the rising panic. What could she do if, yet again, Daisy turned her head away, jaws tightly clamped, fighting the food that would save her?

Outside, the village gossips commented on Daisy's return to Clovelly.

'Yes, fetched her home last night he did, all the way from down south.'

'What's up with the maid then?'

'I heard she be proper mazed and she was in a good 'ole state when her da tried to get her on the train.'

'No, 'tis this awful 'flu she's got.'

'There's hundreds of folk with it. 'Tis a terrible year for the influenza.'

'*Western Morning News*'as been saying 'tis goin' to take a heap more than the war!'

'Polly will need a hand. They littluns haven't been too special neither.'

'The maid just needs feedin' up a bit, plenty of good food and she'll soon pick up now she be 'ome.'

And so it went on, sympathy and concern batted back and forth from neighbour to neighbour, every sentence overlaid with a fear for their own and a barely concealed relief that this awful illness had not struck any closer to home.

Seeing the strain that Polly was under, kindly villagers came to ease the burden. Mrs Stanbury popped in from next door, vigorous, efficient, meaning well but only serving to accentuate Polly's inadequacies. She strode up to the room where Daisy was sleeping, carrying fragrant beef tea in a brown earthenware pot. Daisy looked up as Mrs Stanbury entered the room but she showed no sign of recognition. Her expression was vacant, her eyes failed to focus. Matter-of-factly Mrs Stanbury approached.

'Now then, none of this nonsense, you need to get your strength up.'

She loaded a spoon and waved it under Daisy's nose. The girl blanched but nonetheless, slowly opened her mouth. Swallowing obediently, Daisy took a sip or two. Polly stood silently in the doorway, alienated, discarded, redundant.

Each day was another battle, another desperate struggle, as Daisy weakened and retreated further behind the mask of madness. Sometimes the girl would lie passively, as if in a happier world of the past. Or they might find her manic, hysterical, summoning reserves of strength from who knew where, in order to hit out at her carers. Frequently, she complained of being imprisoned, railing against her parents' efforts to get her to rest. One frightening morning, Polly walked in the room to find Daisy astride the window sill, her hair blowing wildly in the October wind. Panic-stricken, Polly grabbed her daughter's arm and screamed for Albert, as Daisy fought to fling herself on to the cobbles below. Together, Albert and Polly dragged a resistant Daisy to safety. Sombrely, Albert screwed the window stay down but the role of captor sat uneasily on him.

Officialdom arrived in the shape of the local relieving officer, Thomas Sanders. Seemingly, Polly was unaware of his rap on the door. She remained in her chair by the Bodley, gazing into the middle distance, trapped by her memories, by her fears, lost in a world that Albert could not penetrate. A second knock, more urgent this time. Albert stirred from his doze and got wearily to his feet. He was pinning his hopes on this visit. Surely someone high up like Mr Sanders could sort things out, free them from this nightmare. They had tried the best they could to get Daisy to eat, tried persuading, tried pleading, tried shouting. Their daughter was growing weaker in mind and body, failing in front of their very eyes and they were powerless to save her.

Mr Sanders' seemed to fill the small kitchen. Ever wary of authority, Polly remained morose and monosyllabic, sensing menace in the neat suit, the clipped tones, and the proficient manner of their visitor.

'I'll need to see the girl. See how she is getting on,' Mr Sanders was saying.

Polly folded her hands on her lap and acted as if he had not spoken. It was Albert who ushered the relieving officer into the room where Daisy lay, with her face drained of all natural colour, her once bright eyes dull and her hair unkempt. She raised herself in the bed as they came into the room but did not otherwise acknowledge their presence. Instead, her bone-thin fingers picked absently at the cuff of the flannel nightgown that hung loosely on her emaciated body. Mr Sanders enquired after the state of her health. Daisy did not respond, concentrating instead on examining a neat darn on her sleeve. Mr Sanders, realising that he would not get a coherent reply from Daisy, returned downstairs, with Albert trailing after. Polly remained as they had left her, unseeing, oblivious. It fell to Albert to relate the course of their daughter's ill-health and the difficulties that they were having trying to get her to eat,

'Can she not be taken to the nursing home, sir?' queried Albert. He'd heard that Mr Sanders' wife ran such an establishment.

'No, that would not be appropriate,' responded Mr Sanders. 'The home does not take mental cases.'

At the mention of mental cases, Polly flinched and looked up sharply but still she did not speak. There were sounds from the room above and Daisy wandered into the kitchen wraith-like and wan.

Albert addressed his wife, 'You sit still mother,' he said, although Polly had not stirred.

He stepped forward to guide his daughter back up the narrow staircase. She resisted, writhing away from his grasp, her bare feet kicking out ineffectually at her father's shins. Mr Sanders went to Albert's aid, taking Daisy's other arm. The girl wrenched herself free and rushed back upstairs of her own accord. Mr Sanders smoothed his palms down his thighs, then passed his hand across his thinning hair. Albert looked at him expectantly. Surely, now he could see the difficulties they were in, the man would understand that Daisy, in her mazed state, was too much for them to cope with. Mr Sanders opened his brief-case and shuffled the papers inside but said nothing. Moments later, the sound of breaking glass shot through the uneasy silence. Polly cringed but made no attempt to move. The two men hurried to the bedroom, whilst Polly remained transfixed in her chair. She should move, she knew she should move but upstairs lay Daisy. Dealing with Daisy meant confronting all those fears and frustrations, the helplessness and the impotence. Best leave her be. If she didn't want to eat there was nothing to be done. It was as if the shards of the shattered pane had pierced Polly's heart, numbing, dehumanising, freeing her from feeling.

Albert came down and went into the back kitchen, busying himself looking for something with which to board the broken window. There was no sound from Daisy, who had presumably been persuaded by Mr Sanders to abandon her escape attempt.

'Perhaps you should hire a nurse to watch her,' Mr Sanders was saying as he re-entered the room. Polly sat, unmoving, just as she was when the window had been broken. The words of the relieving officer penetrated her thoughts. A nurse? No, that was a mother's job, she had nursed Violet, now she must nurse Daisy. An image of Nelson's fevered face flashed unbidden into her brain. Slamming the door forcefully on the past, Polly finally rose to attend to her daughter.

A small group gathered outside Ellis' shop, waiting for the newspapers to be delivered. They were hopeful of good news. It seemed that the war might soon be over and their menfolk could come home. There was no peace in the offing for Polly; her battle was just beginning. If a neighbour came to sit with Daisy, Polly could escape from the cottage but still her daughter imprisoned her, haunting her every step. She couldn't walk two yards down the street without someone asking after the girl. It was kindly meant but it took a formidable effort for Polly to respond again and again. This morning, Mr Collins was holding forth to a disinterested audience, giving his opinion on the international situation. As Polly passed the queue, Mrs Bushell stopped her.

'How be the maid now?' she asked.

Polly abandoned the attempt at platitudes, 'I can't be doing with her when she's so violent. 'Tidn't like her at all, proper mazed she be, flinging herself about and the like.'

Mr Collins looked aghast. Violent? That beautiful, moonbeam child, his Daisy. No. He could not let that pass. Mr Collins rounded on an astounded Polly with venom, his face scarlet and his voice shaking with anger.

'How dare you say such things about your daughter. You aren't tending to her properly. You're a liar,'

Polly summoned a final vestige of resistance and retaliated, her self-righteous indignation fuelled by the fact that her accuser was an outsider.

''Tis naught to do with the likes o' you,' she said, deliberately turning her back on Collins and aligning herself with her neighbours.

Moving to address Mrs Bushell, Polly pulled her shawl more tightly, as if to shut out not only the sharp wind but also Mr Collins' cutting comments.

'It seems you can't do what you like with your own children now,' Polly said loudly, defiantly but under the fine veneer of her annoyance lay a creeping worm of doubt.

Autumn had set in in earnest. Brown leaves were tumbling across the cobbles in the gusting wind. In the bay, the herring were running and Albert and Bertie were making the most of the season, silver darlings shimmering in their nets. They would fling open the cottage door at the end of each day, bringing in the scent of the cold sea, fish scales sticking to their oiled-wool jumpers and to the backs of their scarred hands. With her menfolk at work and her younger children at school, Polly was left alone in the house with Daisy for hour after unending hour. There was no one to stem the spectres of the past, or to tame the terrifying thoughts of what the future might bring. She had to steel herself to mount the stairs. If Daisy was out of sight, Polly could somehow forget for a moment that a girl lay mortally sick under the patchwork quilt, that her daughter was gradually, inexorably, slipping from life's grasp.

Weary from trying to get Daisy to eat, Polly was aware of the sonorous striking of the clock. Three o'clock. That's nigh on an hour I've been here she thought. And for what? A knock on the door heralded a temporary reprieve but when Polly saw that it was Mr Collins with his superior smile and accusatory tone, she realised that this was no respite at all.

'I have come to feed Daisy egg and milk,' he stated.

'No,' said Polly, drained of all emotion. 'No. Not now, not today. It's all too much. She doesn't want to eat. What's the use of giving food to a dying girl? She's dying, best let her die in peace.'

Stunned into speechlessness, Collins reluctantly turned away but within the hour, Mrs Stanbury was on the doorstep. This time, Polly relented, too exhausted to argue. She took her neighbour up to Daisy's room. Mrs Stanbury greeted the sick girl as if she expected to get a rational response. None came. Undaunted, she raised a cup of beef tea to Daisy's lips. Listlessly, the girl turned her head away. Polly watched from the corner of the room, resentful, yet paradoxically pleased that Daisy was refusing food from this usurper. Mrs Stanbury tried again.

Daisy moaned, 'No I must not eat. I cannot.'

Polly stepped forward swiftly and took the cup. Mrs Stanbury looked alarmed.

'What did you do that for?' she asked. 'The girl needs to eat.'

Polly looked shamefaced. 'It's killing me,' she whispered. 'Why are we doing this? She's mortal sick. Why are we punishing her by feeding her?'

Mrs Stanbury raised her eyebrows and thwarted, went downstairs where the kettle was bubbling on the stove. She filled a stone hot water bottle and wrapped it in a piece of flannel, before taking it to Daisy. The child, it was hard to think of her as a grown woman she was so slight, seemed pathetically grateful but the cup was nowhere to be seen.

Mr Caird called to present Mrs Hamlyn's good wishes and to enquire after Daisy. Remembering the last time he had visited, Polly was reluctant to invite him in. Only the thought that other people might overhear what he had to say persuaded her to grudgingly open the door wider and usher the dapper little man inside. He brushed down his immaculate, tweed plus-fours and rested the stout stick that he always carried against the chimney breast. The stick was an affectation, rather than a necessary aid; Mr Caird was fit for his fifty years.

'Well, what can we do for you?' he asked.

All this continual concern irritated Polly. If something could be done, surely she would be doing it.

'There's naught that can be done,' she said. 'It is cruel to feed a child who's going to die, a girl who wants to die. I want you to pray for Daisy's death. I don't see it's any good her being alive seeing she's mazed. In fact, she would be better dead.'

'Now don't be silly,' Mr Caird responded tersely. 'You know you don't mean that. Mrs Hamlyn's taking an interest you know. She will send food for the girl.'

Polly moaned inarticulately. She just wanted it to be over, the effort was too great.

At the end of Daisy's first week home, Polly sat, stupefied, gazing out of the front window, listening as the All Hallows' Eve wind howled down the chimney. She knew that she should be trying, yet again, to get Daisy to take food but she was frozen, unable to confront her daughter, frightened of the consequences of failure. A noise on the stairs brought Polly out of her reverie. Daisy stood in the doorway, her stained nightdress awry and an absent look on her face. The girl headed towards the front door, her bare feet dragging on the wooden floorboards. She stumbled as she reached the rag rug, seemingly unable to lift her feet. Polly sighed and turned towards her daughter.

'What you be up to now, you daft maid?' Polly said. Her tone was not unkind but there was a hint of rising panic in her voice.

If Daisy went out on to the street in the chill of the October afternoon, the whole village would know she was not right in the head. Polly's single thought was that she had to stop Daisy reaching that outer door at all costs. Little did she realise the enormity of what those costs would be; costs in pain and in dread. The aura of the asylum lurked in the deep corners of the fisherman's cottage. Uninvited, it advanced from the darkness and consumed Polly's thoughts. Polly had heard too many tales. Tales of Alb's Aunt Ellen, who had at least come home after her months away but who had never been quite the same. More alarming still, accounts of his Aunt Matilda. One minute she'd been serving teas in Bucks Mills, the next, incarcerated, abandoned, left to die alone.

'My da's down on the quay. I need to see my da,' Daisy crooned. It was a statement rather than a response to her mother's question.

Polly tried to put herself between Daisy and the door but the girl sidestepped round her.

'You can't go out like that, you'll catch your death. Da'll be home dreckly.'

Frantically, Polly looked at the clock. It would be some time before the younger ones came back from school and even longer before she could expect her husband to return to aid her. Daisy was wrestling with the door latch, as if its mechanism was foreign to her. This few moments of hesitation gave Polly the chance to clutch at the folds of her daughter's nightdress, in an attempt to forestall her. Despite her frailty, Daisy, empowered by insanity's strength, swung round, grabbing her mother by the throat. Polly struggled for breath but Daisy's superior height gave her an advantage.

'Need to get down to the quay,' Daisy muttered, tightening her hold on her mother.

Polly put her hands up to her neck and tried to get her daughter to loosen her stranglehold. In desperation she hit the back of Daisy's hand with as much force as she could muster and the girl relaxed her grip. Slumped on the floor now, Daisy was screaming eerily, uncontrollably. The front door flung open to reveal Mrs Stanbury. To Polly's eyes she was imperious, malevolent, a bringer of retribution and peering nervously over her shoulder, was Mr Collins.

'What's to do here then?' asked Mrs Stanbury, rushing to embrace Daisy.

Daisy shrugged her off, finding the touch uncomfortable but at least the shrieks had given way to whimpers. Mr Collins too was fussing round Daisy, seemingly unsure of the appropriate course of action. Polly shrunk back against the stove, one hand at her bruised throat, the other steadying herself on the mantleshelf. Breathing heavily, Polly stood, wide-eyed and silent. Attention swung from Daisy to her mother.

244

'You've hit her. You didn't ought to have hit her,' Emma Stanbury rounded on Polly, accusing, condemning, hostile.

Mr Collins began ushering Daisy back to her bed, unmindful of the impropriety. The outline of Daisy's emaciated body was all too evident as she clasped her nightdress closer to her. Mr Collins took hold of her bony elbow and steered her towards the staircase. Daisy, deflated, broken, gave no resistance.

Briskly, Emma Stanbury took charge. Later, when the children clattered back from school, she shooed them off to be minded by Mrs Harris. As the autumn day darkened, Mr Collins remained upstairs, guarding Daisy as she slept. In the kitchen, Polly went through the motions of preparing tea, her mind elsewhere. She cut huge, uneven wedges from a loaf and absently began to ladle on butter and blackberry jam. All the while, Mrs Stanbury sat silently watching her, waiting like a jailor for Albert to come up from the shore. Fortunately he came alone, Bertie was off somewhere on an errand of his own.

'You need to take your missus in hand,' the words were out of Emma Stanbury's mouth before Albert was through the door. 'She's been hitting that poor maid.'

Albert looked uncertainly at Polly, who was gazing at the floor.

'I wish she was dead,' Polly whispered, 'then all this would be finished.'

Mrs Stanbury was shocked. When she had gathered her thoughts, she called to Mr Collins and the couple left for the neighbouring house, leaving Albert staring helplessly at his wife.

'Oh, Pol,' he said. 'What have you done now?'

Mr Collins sat alone in the bedroom; his wife having declined his offer to accompany her to the Reading Rooms. The evening was darkening rapidly but Collins did not stir to light the candle. Women's voices came from next door.

He heard Daisy's shrill cry, 'Don't, don't.'

Surely that was a slap he could hear and a gasp, as if the girl had been winded. Galvanised, he jumped down the stairs, two at a time and rushed into the kitchen where Mrs Stanbury and her daughter, Hannah Davies, were encouraging young Stanley to lisp a nursery rhyme.

'It's that woman, next door. She's slapping the poor girl again. For God's sake go in to her.'

Emma Stanbury grabbed her coat and hurried to the adjoining cottage, followed by an agitated Mr Collins. Mrs Davies hovered in the street, with a grizzling Stanley in her arms. The older woman drummed loudly on the door of number 69 and without waiting for a response, flung it open. The hinges protested as the door crashed back into the wall. Mrs Stanbury mounted the stairs, whilst Collins remained hesitatingly on the doormat. As she reached the bedroom, she took in the scene. Daisy was sat on top of the quilt, her knees bent upwards, discarded food on the floor. Polly, enraged, unaware of Mrs Stanbury's presence, raised her hand as if to strike the girl. Emma grabbed her arm to restrain her.

'I will do it,' cried Polly, attempting to struggle free. Then, defeated now, she whispered, 'I wish she was dead and out of pain.'

Leaving Emma to comfort Daisy, Polly turned and hurried out of the room. Mr Collins pushed past her as she descended the stairs.

The low hum of conversation reached Polly as she stood in the kitchen, whilst her neighbours tried to settle her damaged daughter. Some phrases were louder than others and Polly clearly heard Daisy's pleading tone. The words cut to the core of her being.

'They are killing me. They are killing me. Take me away from that cruel woman.'

Horror-struck, the magnitude of the situation sunk home and Polly fell to her knees.

Up in the bedroom, Mrs Stanbury was trying to disentangle herself from Daisy's clinging arms.

'I can't take you away just now, maid,' she said. 'I will come in and sit with you when I can.'

'And I,' Edward Collins was standing awkwardly in the corner of the bedroom. He turned to his landlady, 'I could pay for a nursing home,' he said. 'Do you think the mother would allow that?'

Emma Stanbury looked askance at Collins as he moved to tuck the sheets in round Daisy with an uncharacteristic vigour. And what would your fine wife feel about that? She thought to herself.

Friday morning and the never-ending nightmare continued with a visit from Dr Ackland, who descended on the family, bringing with him a determined-looking man, wearing round spectacles and an intimidating tailored suit. The doctor swiftly made the introductions.

'This is the magistrate from Bideford, Mr Dennis,' he said, indicating his companion.

Uncomprehending, Polly looked to Albert for guidance. Why was the magistrate here?

'We don't need another doctor,' Albert said. 'Dr Toye's been coming regular while Dr Kay's ill. And,' he continued bravely, 'we don't need no magistrate. We are all right as we be.'

'I don't think you understand,' said Mr Dennis. 'We are here at Mr Sanders' behest. He is of the opinion that your daughter is a candidate for the asylum. I am here because I have the authority to certify her.'

Polly stood, mesmerised, silently appealing to Albert, her only ally, to bring about some miracle, to save their daughter, to bring an end to the horror. Powerless, Albert could do none of these things. The couple waited in the kitchen whilst the two men went upstairs, the family's deliverance or destruction within their gift.

Finally, Polly spoke in hushed tones, 'What's to do Alb? Supposing she's having one of her spells up there.'

Despite an ambivalent attitude to God, they had known too much tragedy to believe in Him unquestioningly, a life-time of chapel-going is not easily erased.

'Pray, maid,' said Alb. 'Pray to God and all his angels that today she be quiet because we can't let them take her.'

In a rare gesture of affection, Albert encircled his wife in his arms and for once, Polly did not recoil. They stood in desperation, intertwined and impotent, appealing to a deity in whom they had little faith.

'Well then,' Mr Dennis said, as he clattered down the stairs, 'your daughter is not a candidate for the asylum.'

Polly exhaled audibly, unaware that she had been holding her breath.

'She just needs good food. We will keep a watching brief, yes? Mr Sanders will visit regularly. We will see how things progress. But good food eh, remember that.'

'Yes, sir,' said Polly meekly, anxious to get the men out of the door before they could change their minds.

When they had gone, Polly turned to Albert, 'I am just so tired,' she said, 'tired of trying to get the maid to eat, tired of all the busybodies poking their noses in, tired of fighting all these posh folk, who think they know best. It seems as if no sooner one lot goes away satisfied, than the next lot is on the doorstep. You mind, there'll be someone else tomorrow.'

Polly's prophesy was fulfilled with the reappearance of Mr Sanders. Unlike the previous day, when Daisy had been sullen but compliant when Mr Sanders called, this time she was ranting incoherently and refusing all attempts to feed her.

After a quick look at Daisy, the relieving officer addressed Albert and Polly, 'She is very weak,' he said, 'and not at all rational. I think the asylum would be the best place for her.'

Polly looked at Albert in alarm, surely they had already vanquished that particular demon. Albert cleared his throat, uncertain how to respond. He was well aware of the terrors that the prospect of the asylum held for Polly.

He turned to Mr Sanders, 'That fellow from the court yesterday, he said she weren't right for the asylum,' he said indignantly. 'He said she just needed feeding. She's quieter than she were. We can manage now. We don't want her going in no asylum. We can look after her here.'

Mr Sanders looked doubtful but ever mindful of his long list of calls still to be made and of the cosy fire that would be waiting for him at home when he had finished, did nothing to try to force Albert's hand.

Before Mr Sanders left, Dr Kay arrived. The two men greeted each other.

'I'd like a word, doctor, when you've seen the girl,' Sanders said.

Albert took the opportunity to escape to the shore. Although Dr Kay was on his feet again, he was still looking drained after his illness. Daisy was one of many patients who had fallen victim to this pernicious influenza and his round was a long one. Polly accompanied him to Daisy's room, leaving Mr Sanders waiting in the kitchen. Dr Kay offered to try to get the girl to take some food.

Polly, nervous of disturbing Daisy, protested, 'Leave her be doctor, for Godsakes leave her be, she hates being fed so. Let her die in peace.'

The doctor, noting Polly's agitation, patiently explained that regular nourishment was vital.

'See if she'll drink this milk, then try her with some solids, fish perhaps. I am sure you have plenty of that. I am going to consult with Mr Sanders downstairs whilst you see what she will take.'

Daisy had already turned on her side, facing the wall. Polly stood, helpless, the cup of milk in her hand. Making no effort to feed Daisy, she strained to hear the conversation between the two men in the room below.

'I'm not happy that the girl is being looked after satisfactorily,' Dr Kay was saying.

'Well, I've suggested the asylum,' replied Mr Sanders, 'though Dennis thought otherwise. Can she be removed from the home?'

'Well she could but it will have to be local. She's in no fit state to be moved far.'

Polly shut the bedroom door firmly, her breath quickening. They said that eavesdroppers heard nothing to the good and it was true enough. Panic's noose tightened, the terror was hers alone.

Clovelly wore its party face. Despite the grey skies and churning sea, there was an air of pageantry about the village. Folk looked out bunting that had not been seen since the king's coronation. Moth-eaten flags were unearthed from chests and dangled from window frames. The war was over. Celebration. Jubilation. Relief, even though it would be many weeks before battle-weary husbands and sons came home. No such euphoria for the family at number 69. In harsh contrast to the cheers and revelry in the street, here was torment, hopelessness and despair. Daisy was slipping out of their grasp, she was further from reality, further from safety and soon she would be further from home. Worn down by the continual pestering from her neighbours and Daisy's own anguished pleas to get away, Polly had finally agreed that her daughter could be nursed elsewhere.

'Let them take her to Mrs Harris' then,' she'd said, 'get her out of my hair. They think she needs fussing over. They can do all the fussing they like over there. I'll be glad not to have to watch her die.'

Polly looked on submissively, as Daisy was bundled in a rough blanket and carried across the threshold in Mr Collins' arms. It was strange, to begin with, Polly hadn't wanted her to go, had held out against it this past week or more but now Daisy was missing from the house, all that Polly could feel was an overpowering sense of relief. It was out of her hands. The untouched milk in the cup, the uneaten food in the bowl, the sobbing and the ranting from the upstairs room; all gone. Now that there were no constant reminders that a girl lay dying, Polly could resume her life, look after her little girls, cook Albert his tea, pretend that Daisy was still away in Torquay, happy and safe.

The local wives were diligent in their care of Daisy. Mrs Stanbury, Mrs Foley, Mrs Collins, and Mrs Bushell, all took their turn as nurses. Even Mrs Hamlyn condescended to visit, alerted by Mr Caird to the state of affairs. Mr Collins dropped in so often that Mrs Harris became quite impatient with him and asked him to call less frequently. Albert took in milk and Brand's Essence but Polly stayed away.

Three days later, as the lingering stars were fading in the angry pink dawn, Daisy, alone in the borrowed bed, loosened her final, fragile grip on life.

13
November 1918

Albert grieved for his daughter alone. He had known that it was over, that their lives were irreparably dislocated, the instant he had opened the door to an ashen-faced Mrs Harris in the early hours of Thursday morning. Desperate sadness that his daughter was gone was tempered by a sense of guilty relief. At least now Daisy's torment and Polly's anguish, would be at an end. As for Polly herself, she scarcely seemed to acknowledge the news. Mrs Harris was trying to offer her stumbling condolences but Polly matter-of-factly continued to ready the younger children for school. Lily and Rosie cried a little, because they felt they should but to them, Daisy was a remote figure, a grown-up who had been long gone from the family home by the time they were old enough to take notice. Polly seemed unaware of the need for the formalities. It was Albert who summoned the undertakers and asked Dr Kay to call to sign the death certificate, Albert who walked up to Gardener's Cottage to tell Violet and Albert who went to the post office to send a telegram to Leonard, who was on board the *Hamborn* somewhere in the North Sea.

In the early afternoon, Dr Kay arrived. Mrs Harris let him in and issued a whispered warning before he ascended the stairs.

'You won't find her mother up there, doctor. Her father's been sat with the poor maid for hours but her mother's not come at all. There's no tellin' with some folk.'

In the upper room of the Clovelly cottage, Albert was bidding farewell to his firstborn. In death, Daisy looked at peace, thin still but there was a softness to her features that Albert had not seen in past weeks. As the doctor entered the room, Albert got wearily to his feet and shook the proffered hand, accepting the gesture as an expression of silent sympathy. He felt embarrassed by his wife's absence. What would the doctor think? Polly had shown no interest in seeing her daughter's body; she had already vetoed Albert's tentative suggestion that Daisy should come home to await the undertakers.

'She's gone,' Polly had said, 'and that's all there is to it. What's the use of bringing her back here? We'll get her buried and that will be that.'

Albert left the doctor to his work and went to wait in the kitchen with Mrs Harris. When he came downstairs, Dr Kay's manner was oozing embarrassment.

'I am sorry,' he said to the grief-stricken father who stood before him, 'I am unable to sign a certificate at this time. There will need to be an inquest, under the circumstances.'

Circumstances, thought Albert. What circumstances? She had been ill, she had died. What more was there to be said? Why couldn't Dr Kay give them a death certificate so that they could lay Daisy to rest? It was the last remaining duty that Albert could perform for his daughter and this was being denied him. Her precious body would be violated, laid bare on the coroner's slab like a piece of meat. It was beyond comprehension.

'It will be in the next day or so,' Dr Kay was explaining. 'The coroner will be in touch. You and your wife will have to attend.'

So the nightmare had not yet ended, thought Albert. There was no resolution, no peace. Reluctantly, he went to relay the news to Polly. He feared for her.

'Doctor says we've to go to court. 'Tis not a proper court like, 'tis the coroner and a few other folk, just tidying up loose ends. Naught to fret about. It will soon be sorted, then we can have the certificate and arrange her burying.'

For all the notice that Polly took, he might as well have remained silent.

⚖

Albert pushed open the white, wooden gate and gestured for Polly to go in front of him. Hesitantly, she walked down the wide, mossy steps to the door of the Reading Rooms. The last of the year's reddened leaves still clung to the Virginia Creeper that crawled round the

256

windows of the long, low building. Although the Reading Rooms were at the top of the village, higher even than the fountain, they passed them frequently but there was no comfort in the familiar façade. Stepping inside was daunting. Albert and Polly felt out of place, oppressed by the book-lined shelves. The Reading Rooms were for folk with time on their hands, not for fishermen and their wives. The few cushioned seats had been pushed to one side. In front of the largest reading desk were three rows of wooden chairs that ranged across the full width of the room. The newly-lit fire burned in the grate but it had not yet banished the November chill. Each time the door opened, the temperature plummeted and only those who were seated closest to the fireplace felt comfortable loosening scarves and removing gloves. Superintendent Shutler stood to one side, his hands behind his back, his peaked cap on the small, oak table beside him. His presence startled Albert; surely this was not a police matter? The coroner, Mr Brown, balding and bespectacled, was seated behind the long desk. Periodically, he whispered to the fussy little clerk who sat beside him.

Polly looked to Albert for guidance but he was as ignorant of the procedure as she. They stood uncomfortably at the back of the room. Eventually, the clerk ushered them to two vacant chairs in the centre of the front row. Albert glanced around, taking in the scene. Mrs Stanbury was there and Dr Kay and that interfering Collins from next-door. Why was he here? What was it to do with him? Surely all this was only about getting the certificate, so that Daisy could be decently buried.

The proceedings began. Mr Brown cleared his throat, motioning to Albert to step forward. Albert stood submissively, twisting the brim of his battered trilby hat round and round in his hands.

Mr Brown addressed him, 'Would you please explain the circumstances of your daughter's death.'

Albert hesitated, formulating sentences in his mind, reluctant to relive the horrors of the past weeks, uncertain where the story should begin.

Mr Brown looked at him expectantly, 'Come on man, where was she living when she became unwell?'

'She'd been working in Torquay nigh on a year,' Albert muttered.

The coroner interrupted, 'Could you speak up, so that we can all hear.'

Albert continued, imperceptibly louder, 'She'd been ill a week in her mistress's house. Then they put her in the workhouse. I fetched her home on the 25th of October.'

'And how did she seem?'

'She was quiet until we got to Barnstaple but then I had a job to hold her on the train.'

'What medical attention did she receive once she was at home?' Mr Brown asked.

Albert replied, 'Dr Kay is our doctor but he was ill, so Dr Toye came out at first but later Dr Kay and Dr Ackland both came.'

'What advice did they give you?'

'To feed her up, milk, fish, nourishing fare.'

'And did you do as you were advised?'

Albert glanced nervously at Polly before responding, 'We tried feeding her sir, both me and her mother. Sometimes she'd take it readily enough but then there were days when she'd just lie there, refuse to open her mouth. She could be very violent to us, we couldn't keep her in her bed.'

'But she was removed from your home was she not?'

'Yes sir, on the 11th of November it was, the day we got news that the war was over. She went to our neighbour, Mrs Harris.'

Mr Brown paused as the clerk turned a page in the ledger, 'And why was that?'

'I don't know who ordered it but the neighbours organised it.'

'Why did you not send her to the workhouse infirmary in Bideford if she was so sick?'

'I didn't know she could have gone to the workhouse infirmary, sir. I spoke to Mr Sanders the relieving officer. I wanted him to take her into his nursing home but he wouldn't. He said he didn't take mental cases, so that was that.'

Mr Brown's questioning continued, 'Did Mr Sanders not suggest taking her to the workhouse?'

'I didn't hear him say anything about that, sir. He knew how sick she were. He came to see her when she was proper bad. I told him she'd tried to get out of the window. He niver said about the workhouse.'

'And did you secure the windows?'

'Yes, I did but then the silly maid knocked out a pane of glass.'

'Do you consider that your daughter received proper care?'

Albert's voice cracked as he answered, 'We done our best sir, us and the neighbours that came in to help. We all tried to feed her, we couldn't do no more for her.'

Mr Brown put his hands on the arms of the wooden chair and raising himself slightly from the seat, he leaned forward towards Albert saying, deliberately, 'I want you to think very carefully before you answer. This is a very serious accusation. It is alleged that your wife ill-treated your daughter. What have you to say about this?'

Sweating now, Albert replied, 'Not when I was there. I niver saw it.'

'Did you know about this accusation?'

'There was a fuss with some of the neighbours. I was out to sea but they did say summat about them thinking she'd been ill-used. I heard about it from Mrs Stanbury when I came in from fishing. But when a poor maid is so mazed that she grabs her mother by the throat, then it is time to smack her. Mr Sanders himself had trouble trying to get her upstairs on one occasion. He seed how she be.'

Mr Brown's questioning continued, remorselessly, 'And how was your wife with the deceased?'

Albert's glance rested on Polly, who was sat in front of the desk, next to the chair that he had vacated, her gaze fixed on the storm-darkened November sky. She was watching the wheeling seagulls that were visible above the net curtains that screened the lower half of the small windows. It was as if she was in some far-away place where the coroner's words could not reach her.

Finally Albert spoke, desperation in his voice, 'She did all she could to keep her clean and comfortable, sir.'

'And did you hear your daughter cry out when her mother was attending her?'

Albert coughed, nervously, 'She did scream a time or two when we were trying to see to her; we had to call Mrs Stanbury in to help hold her.'

'Seeing the condition of your daughter, why did you not get her removed to a place where she could be restrained and properly looked after?' The coroner's tone was neutral but Albert sensed menace in the words.

'She did seem like she was getting a bit quieter. We didn't want no truck with the asylum. Not for her.'

Polly stared at the fiercely blazing fire; a log fell, sending sparks skyward. She knew Alb had been speaking but the words had washed over her, the blur of sounds failing to form coherent phrases. She looked at Albert. Inconsequential thoughts filled her head. She found herself wondering when her husband's hair had gone so very grey, when he had ceased to be the young fisherman she had first been attracted to at the temperance meeting all those years ago. Her name was called twice before she realised that she was being addressed. She rose to her feet, bewildered. Slowly, mechanically, her thoughts elsewhere, Polly answered the coroner's questions about Daisy's time in Torquay. Didn't this man know how hard it was to watch your child slowly dying? Did he not understand how Daisy had been? Surely he should have been told that Daisy had rejected all her mother's efforts and violently too.

'She ill-used me sir, for all I tried to help, she ill-used me. I have six other children to see to but she lacked nothing that money could buy. Sometimes she took food, then other times she would clench her teeth and scream.'

'Now,' said Mr Brown firmly, 'we come to the matter of the ill-treatment.'

For the first time, Polly seemed to realise that the proceedings might be more than a formality. Heat swept through her body, her face flushed and she was left perspiring and breathless.

The coroner went inexorably on, 'I caution you to answer honestly,' he said, peering at Polly over the top of his spectacles. 'Anything that you tell us may form evidence in a magistrates' court.'

Polly was gabbling now. It was as if she had reasoned that the speed of her words would obscure their meaning, 'In all her life sir I only struck her the once. I was desperate sir. I couldn't hold her on my own. Her father was at sea and she said she was going down to the quay. Well I couldn't have that sir, not the way she was, not in her night clothes and all. I didn't know how to stop her sir. Not by myself. So I did strike her, just that once. She had her hand to my throat sir. All I did was strike the back of her hand to get her to release me.'

The clerk's frenzied scribbling seared the silence. Then the fire hissed as a damp, mossy log was thrown on to the flames. Polly looked round frantically, she was feeling dizzy now. If only she could have a sip of the water that stood in the cut-glass decanter on the coroner's desk but she dared not ask for a cooling drink. Seconds ticked by, unfolding like hours, as Polly stood exposed and disparaged.

Oblivious of Polly's discomfiture, Mr Brown resumed his questioning, 'And do you remember your neighbour, Mrs Stanbury, coming in at that point?'

'Yes sir. I told her then the girl was violent, that I was obliged to do something.'

'And did your daughter complain to Mrs Stanbury about your treatment of her?'

'Not in my presence sir. There was naught to complain of. I deny ill-treating her.'

Relentlessly, the questioning continued, 'Did you refuse to let Mr Collins come in and give her eggs and milk?'

Polly looked angrily at Mr Collins but gave her answer faintly, 'No. He did come in a time or two and feed her. Mrs Stanbury was the person who gave food to her mostly. I didn't refuse anyone giving her food.'

'Did you express yourself that you wished she was dead?'

'No. I did say how thankful I should be to God, if He were to take her from her suffering.'

Mr Brown consulted the papers in front of him, running his fingers under a line of writing, 'Did you say. "What is the use of giving food to a dying girl. She is dying, best let her die"?'

'No. I never used that expression. I never gave up feeding her,' said Polly firmly, deluded self-conviction blurring her memory.

'And when your daughter was removed to a neighbour's house, did you object?'

'I said naught. Folk said she should go, so she went. I thought she would get more attention there. 'Twas better than the asylum.'

'That will be all for now,' said Mr Brown, dismissively.

Polly sunk in her chair, her face grey and strained, no longer buoyed by adrenalin. When she refocussed on what was going on around her, Dr Kay was speaking, saying that Daisy was out of her mind. Well, that was true enough, thought Polly.

'She died from her mental condition and want of food,' Dr Kay stated, 'I told the mother to feed her hourly but the next day it did not appear that she had been fed.'

'I tried,' Polly cried out, 'I tried to do what the doctor said.'

The coroner ignored the interruption.

'In your professional opinion, Dr Kay, has there been such neglect as to accelerate the death?'

Albert gasped. Surely they could not think that it was their fault. He had never anticipated this. Dr Kay had said the inquest was for form's sake, the doctor would have explained to the coroner that they had done nothing wrong. Wouldn't he? The clock ticked loudly through the oppressive silence. It seemed like an eternity before the doctor replied.

His words hit like a storm, 'Yes. I should say so.'

In the hushed room, Mr Collins could be heard exhaling triumphantly.

Mr Brown tapped the papers on the desk into a neat pile, 'I fear I shall have to adjourn this inquest,' he said, getting to his feet. 'We need to gather more evidence. We will set the date for Wednesday next and we will empanel a jury.'

⚖

The days before the inquest reconvened passed in a haze for Albert and for Polly; their lives suspended in an unfathomable limbo between an unspeakable past and an uncertain future. Albert forewent the height of the herring season and remained at home, unwilling to run the gamut of the gossiping neighbours. Bertie failed to appreciate the enormity of the situation and was unsettled away from the familiarity of the fishing boat. At least though, thought Albert, Violet and Leonard were away working, safe from the accusatory stares, the turned backs and the conversations that halted abruptly when they passed. He had debated keeping the younger children home from school but reasoned that Mark was big enough to take care of himself. Surely, the little girls were too small to understand any teasing that they might encounter, as harsh children taunted with phrases they'd heard from their parents. It was good to have them out of the house all day, their presence only served to fuel Polly's dark mood. It seemed that he was right about Mark. The boy returned home from school on Monday with a bloody nose and bruised knuckles, suggesting that he had dealt with the bullies in his own way.

Perfunctorily, Polly paid lip-service to her normal routine. She put meals in front of the family but ate little herself. Although she dreaded the empty expanse of each sleepless night, instead of relief, dawn brought a renewed struggle to rise from her bed and face the day. She embarked on a cleaning regime of an intensity better suited to spring. The neighbours shook their heads when they saw her hanging rugs over the line and beating them vigorously, unconscious of the drizzle. Anything to keep her mind occupied, to keep the demons at bay, to stop the doctor's accusations from crushing her.

⚖

The inquest resumed on Wednesday morning in the club room of the Red Lion, the space in the Reading Rooms being inadequate for a jury and additional witnesses. Albert and Polly walked down the street to the quay, their steps dragging and their anxiety unquelled. As they entered the crowded room, heads turned and murmurings ceased. The jury were seated together on one side, uncomfortable in their role as adjudicators. Damp coats gently steamed in the heat of the fire and raindrops trickled from furled umbrellas on to the polished floor. The claustrophobic press of too many bodies in a confined space made Polly feel light-headed. Why were all these people here? Why were they all looking at her? This time it was not only Mr Brown who sat in judgement but a jury of their peers, folk who were known to them, friends and neighbours. Polly looked at the fifteen men who held the power to free her, or to condemn. At their head was Mr Cruse, no longer the farmer up the road, someone she had known for decades but now formidable in his role as foreman of the jury that was to decide her fate. She could not return his half-smile of acknowledgement.

Mr Brown called the room to order. After much coughing and scuffling, an uneasy silence fell. The jury were sworn in and the evidence from the previous Saturday was summarised for their benefit. It seemed to Albert that, at second hearing, every phrase took on ominous overtones. The examination of the witnesses began. Mrs Stanbury studiously avoided Polly's eye as she was invited to stand and walk to the front of the room. The two women had not spoken since Daisy's death. Too much had passed between them, eroding years of guarded neighbourliness.

'Mrs Stanbury, in your own words, please tell the jury about the alleged ill-treatment of the deceased,' said Mr Brown.

'She was not being properly fed. I went to take her beef tea but her mother wouldn't have me there, said we was punishing the girl by feeding her. Then, on another occasion, her husband was there that time, the mother took the cup away from me and said she wouldn't have anyone in the house feeding her daughter that day. She said, "What's the use of feeding a dying girl?".'

Albert interposed, heatedly, 'I was there. She didn't say that.'

'Please continue Mrs Stanbury,' said Mr Brown, frowning at Albert.

Albert dropped, helplessly, back in his chair, his face reddening. Polly sat stiffly at his side.

Mrs Stanbury bridled, shooting an indignant glance in Albert's direction, 'The girl would beg me to take her away. She would say, "They are killing me". There were red marks on her thigh. Mrs Hamlyn wanted her moved where she could be looked after, so we arranged for her to go to Mrs Harris' house. I helped to feed her when she was there. She had to be fed, she was too weak to take food herself by then. Sometimes it would take three-quarters of an hour to get anything down her, other times she would take small amounts readily.'

'And what of her demeanour?' queried Mr Brown.

'Sometimes she was excitable.'

'Was she violent?'

'No. She was never violent.'

On and on went the questions. To Polly's tormented mind, the images that Mrs Stanbury's statement conjured up sounded unfamiliar, as if the woman was talking of another girl, another time. Then it was the turn of Mr Sanders to add yet more weight to the evidence that was amassing against Polly.

'How did you find the girl when you visited the family?' Mr Brown asked the relieving officer.

'I found her restless and pre-occupied. She would not respond when spoken to. They did ask if she could be taken to my wife's nursing home but I explained that that was not appropriate.'

'And do you think she was a fit patient for a workhouse infirmary?'

'Not ours,' said Mr Sanders, firmly, 'because there was no accommodation.'

'In your opinion though, was it right, her being left at home?'

'Well, if she was properly looked after,' Mr Sanders appeared to be on the defensive. 'I gave instructions accordingly and suggested that the family got a nurse in. When I returned on November the 2nd I said she would need to be removed to the asylum. The parents protested. They said they did not want her taken away.'

At this, Mr Sanders looked disapprovingly at Albert and Polly who sat in their adjacent chairs, not touching, not moving, not acknowledging each other's presence.

'Was the girl being fed properly at this time?'

'The mother said that the girl would not take food from her as she would from other people,' Mr Sanders answered.

'At that time,' persisted the coroner, 'did you, or did you not, think it a proper case for the asylum?'

'Yes, if she was not being looked after, although by then she was more settled. I got the doctor to look at her and Mr Dennis, the magistrate but she was not certified insane.'

'Was she, as her father suggests, violent?'

Mr Sanders' response echoed round the small room, 'No. She was not.'

There was a gasp of horror. It was too much for Albert. All this and now they were saying he was a liar. 'My evidence was correct,' he cried despairingly but his words evaporated like the puddles on the floor by the fire.

Mr Sanders resumed his seat and Mr Collins was called upon to take his place.

'You are Mr Edward Laurence Collins?' asked the coroner, rhetorically. 'Please state your occupation and residence.'

'I am a consulting engineer, currently residing in Independent Street, Clovelly.'

'And what is your connection to the deceased?'

Mr Collins was giving his responses rapidly, his words tripping over each other. 'I have resided next door to the family of the deceased for the past eighteen months. My bedroom adjoins that in which the girl was nursed.'

'Tell us of your concerns for the girl.'

'The partition walls are very thin. I suffer from insomnia and I was awake during the night following the girl's arrival home. The girl was quite quiet but I could hear her father talking to her. Next morning, I was awoken by a commotion and I saw her mother pass below my window at about 7.30am. I heard her and her father talking rather excitedly. I heard the mother telling neighbours that the girl had been very agitated and violent all night. A few days later, I heard a conversation between the defendants. They were grumbling that people could not do what they liked with their own child without interference from strangers. I believe that I was meant to overhear and that they were referring to a strong conversation I had had with the mother, reprimanding her for thrashing the girl the previous night.'

Mr Collins paused to draw breath and Mr Brown interjected, 'Please tell us, in your own words, about the incident when the defendant allegedly thrashed her daughter.'

When had a little tap become a thrashing? wondered Albert.

Mr Collins went on, swiftly, 'I heard an uproar in the girl's bedroom and the sound of blows being struck. The girl called out "Don't. Don't." The cries stopped suddenly, as if she had been prevented from making a noise.'

'And whom was the girl addressing?'

Mr Collins, flustered now, hands flapping and face scarlet, replied, 'It is my belief that she was speaking to her mother. I could hear the mother speaking.'

'What action did you take?'

'I fetched Mrs Stanbury, in whose house I am lodging and her daughter, Mrs Davies and we went next door. The door was locked and we banged on the door waiting to be admitted. I went straight up to see the victim but I could hear Mrs Stanbury saying to the defendant, "You shall not strike her".'

Imperceptibly, Daisy was no longer just the deceased, she had assumed the victim's role.

Mr Brown, half-heartedly, attempted to re-establish impartiality, 'How did you find the deceased?'

'She was sobbing piteously. She begged Mrs Stanbury not to leave her at the mercy of her mother. I remonstrated with the mother and she said she had done it, she had hit her daughter but would not do so again. The father was called in and Mr Sanders the relieving officer. The father said the girl had been very violent and Mr Sanders himself said he was obliged to carry the girl back indoors, as she had broken away. The father was very aggrieved that I had spoken out. He stormed out of the house saying those who wanted the girl to have so much fuss and attention had better pay for it as he could not.'

'And what course of action did you take?'

Self-righteous now, Collins said, 'I tried to act in the girl's interest. I saw Mrs Hamlyn about the matter. I urged her to use her influence, which indeed she did and rightly so.'

Others were called to give their versions of the events, accounts that Polly barely recognised. Polly wondered how her own recollections could be so unlike the evidence that she was hearing from the lips of her neighbours. The morning was interminable. Albert was slumped forward now, his head in his hands. Reality was suspended.

⚖️

The coroner began reviewing the evidence, clarifying matters for the jury, 'It is my opinion,' he said, 'that the magistrate was correct in not certifying her insane.'

'What is clear in this unfortunate case is that it is evident that some skilled person was required to nurse the girl and properly feed her. The doctor,' he turned to acknowledge Dr Kay, 'has said that her death was accelerated by neglect and want of food and that he thought that she must have been underfed for some time. You must consider if Mr Sanders did all he could to prevent this.'

Sanders huffed indignantly and sat upright in his chair.

Mr Brown was still speaking, 'The mother is alleged to have remarked, "What is the use of giving food to a dying girl?".'

'My wife denied that!' cried Albert.

'You must not interrupt,' said Mr Brown, 'or I will hold you in contempt of court. The alleged remark,' he continued, firmly, 'was a most extraordinary one. If everyone adopted that attitude towards anyone likely to die, I am afraid that I should be occupied all day long. I have examined the body, which was terribly emaciated, with the bones protruding through the skin.'

Albert flinched, recalling that painfully thin body, with the essence of Daisy reduced to a fleeting echo.

The coroner continued, 'By the intervention of Mrs Hamlyn and other kind people, the girl was removed to a place where she could get rest and quiet but I am afraid it was, by then, too late and she got weaker and died.'

Turning to the jury, Mr Brown said, 'It is your duty to determine the cause of this unfortunate young woman's death and to ascertain if her end was hastened by neglect. You must reach a verdict upon which at least twelve of you are agreed.'

Solemnly, the men filed out to consider the evidence that had been put before them.

⚖

Twenty minutes later, the jury resumed their seats, their deliberations over.

Mr Brown addressed the foreman, 'What was the cause of death of this young woman?'

Mr Cruse stood to present the findings of the jury, 'It is our belief that she died from weakness, due to insanity and want of adequate nourishment.'

'Was her death accelerated by the neglect of her mother and her failure to provide her with sufficient food?'

Mr Cruse looked regretfully at Polly, 'Yes. It was.'

'And did the mother ill-treat her daughter, in such a manner as to accelerate her death?'

Mr Cruse replied emphatically, 'No. She did not.'

Mr Brown pressed on with the questioning, 'Did the father know the mother neglected the deceased and failed to give her proper nourishment and to care for her sufficiently?'

Mr Cruse's single word reply, resounded like a death knell, 'Yes.'

'And is it your belief that the mother prevented Mrs Stanbury from nursing the deceased?'

'Yes, on one occasion.'

'Do you find that Mr Sanders was neglectful in his duties in not removing the girl from her parents' house, or in not providing a responsible person to care for her?'

'We do believe that when he saw her condition, he should have taken some action to get the girl removed.'

Mr Sanders interjected, 'I took all the steps that I could in the matter. There is no provision for lunatics at the workhouse and the girl was not destitute.' His voice rose several tones in his annoyance.

Mr Brown turned to address Mr Sanders, 'The jury consider that she was helpless, whether her parents were wealthy or not. It was your duty as relieving officer, to see that she was being cared for.'

Mr Sanders drew himself up to his full height, a personification of righteous indignation, 'I reported the matter to the magistrates at the earliest convenience.'

Albert was glad that the attention had swung away from them but the reprieve was short-lived.

Mr Brown was speaking again, 'As coroner, it is my painful duty to say that this verdict amounts to one of manslaughter against the mother and against the father, in a lesser degree. I therefore issue warrants of arrest against them both.' He stood and rapped a polished gavel on the desk. 'Bail is allowed.'

Uncomprehending, Polly and Albert gazed at each other. A rumble of voices rose up around them. Mr Caird stepped forward. He must have been a latecomer, as they had not been aware of his presence before the jury retired to deliberate. He took two white five-pound notes from his inside pocket and laid them on the desk in front of the coroner.

'There's your surety,' he said.

The press of people parted, allowing the bewildered couple to make their way out of the room and return home. They climbed the hill in silence, oblivious to the implications of the coroner's verdict.

⚖

Two days after the turmoil and confusion of the inquest, Mr Sanders called, just as Albert was about to head down to the quay. This time, Sanders' visit was in his capacity as registrar. Albert took the thick, cream envelope held out by Mr Sanders. It was unsealed. He lifted the flap and extracted the contents. Hands shaking slightly, he unfolded the single sheet and stared at the certificate that lay across his palm. The sharp creases stood out, maiming the paper's surface. Albert rubbed his scarred thumb gently across his daughter's name. The writing was cramped and the thick black ink stark against the flimsy background. The purple tinge to the paper shrieked of loss. Tears touched Albert's eyes as he read the cause of death, "Asthenia due to insanity and want of sufficient food" and then, in darker lettering, as if the writer had pressed more firmly with the spluttering pen, the single word "Manslaughter". Despite everything that had happened, until now, it had somehow been possible to shut out the awfulness of the past few weeks, to believe for fleeting seconds that Daisy was simply away working and that they would see her again. Standing there, with the death certificate in his hand, the finality hit home. Daisy was gone, all her bright promise extinguished. Was this piece of paper to be the only reminder of his daughter, her only testament, her only legacy?

He called to his wife, 'Pol, 'tis Mr Sanders. He's brought the certificate. It's over. We can bury the maid.'

And bury the maid they did, or rather Albert did, laying her in the frozen November earth next to her brother. Nelson's passing seemed to belong to another time. It wasn't that he was forgotten exactly but it was hard now to recall his features, or his voice, as he called after his older brothers in play. Lichen was already forming on the cross that marked the boy's last resting place. As the rain intensified, Daisy was lowered into the shallow grave that had been hollowed out in the ground by her brother's memorial. Albert stepped forward and a handful of reddish earth rattled on the top of the plain deal coffin. Circled behind him were a scattering of villagers, amongst them Mr Pengilly, Oscar Abbott, Mr Tuke and Mr Caird, representing the estate. Most had stayed away, confused by the revelations of the inquest and unsure how to approach the grieving family. Mr Collins was absent; Albert had made it clear that he was not welcome, that his interference had done enough.

Braving the steady drizzle, a robin perched on the overhanging bough of the ancient yew tree, its bright breast enlivening the endless grey. The bird's liquid carolling formed an incongruous accompaniment to the vicar's intonations. The sexton did his melancholic work and a pitiful mound of sodden earth marred the virgin soil.

14
New Year's Day 1919

Throughout the confusion of the days that followed Daisy's death, Polly focussed on the imminent return of her eldest son. To have Leonard back would be a symbol of normality, an indication that life held hope. Christmas came and went, with no news that the *Hamborn* had docked after eight tumultuous, war-torn months at sea. Alb had tried to convince Polly that all must be well, that there was peace now and Leonard would be home but she needed to see her son, to know for herself that he was safe. It was Leonard's first voyage under Captain Jenn and Polly was glad that there were several Clovelly men on the *Hamborn*; men who could support Leonard, as those who were left behind sustained each other when times were bad. Catherine Bate's husband Tommy was part of the crew, a sober chap, only five years Leonard's senior but already taking command when Captain Jenn was ashore. Will Harding was another, known to Leonard from childhood.

Waiting was the lot of the seaman's family. So, with her neighbours, Polly assumed a stoical patience, yet she was aware of an illogical rising panic that intensified with each passing day. She did not usually feel like this when she was expecting the ship to dock; she was a fisherman's wife, she had trained herself to quell her anxiety, had to really. The only way the women could survive was to push all thoughts of the perils and uncertainties of the sea to one side, to disregard their fears and close their minds to the dangers.

Finally the news came, sent by telegram to Mrs Jenn and reverberating up and down the echoing street until all the watchers, the waiters, were told.

'Them be on their way, Mrs Harding,' called Mrs Bate, as they encountered each other outside Ellis' shop, smiling, anticipating, relieved.

The *Hamborn* had docked up country and the Clovelly men would be heading for home when the last few onboard tasks were complete. The gossip speculated on how soon that would be, on when their menfolk might alight from the station at Bideford and commence the last leg of their journey.

It was New Year's Eve when Captain Jenn sent word for Eli to bring out his cart and collect the Clovelly crew members from the train. Weary and apprehensive, Leonard hauled his kit bag on to the cart and hunched down next to Will Harding, an experienced sailor who looked older than his thirty four years, with weather-hewn face and prematurely balding pate hidden under a cap. Will was a family man, eager to get back to his pretty wife, his near-grown son Billy and three little girls. He was unusually talkative, proud that his Billy would soon be going to sea too. Leonard grunted in what he hoped was a fitting manner but he longed to be alone with his thoughts.

They'd telegraphed of course, with the awful news about Daisy. Captain Jenn had told him, kindly but gruff, so he was spared the embarrassment of his parents trying to explain; that was a relief. Leonard was uncertain how he should feel. Like most of his contemporaries he was used to the tragedies of war, was numb to bereavement, hardened even. He knew he should be, well, sad perhaps. He should at least feel something. He had been closer to Daisy than to his other sisters. They were the nearest in age, they even shared a birthday. He hadn't really expected to spend time with Daisy when he came on leave. They were both adults now, ploughing their own furrow, as his da said. He hadn't seen Daisy for nearly a year. She had left to work down south and he had only had two weeks at home since the previous January. To know she wasn't there, wasn't anywhere, that he would never see her again was different. Final. Confusing. Leonard was dreading seeing his parents. How should he react? He was now the eldest child in the family; the responsibility was burdensome. It was his ma he worried about. He remembered how she had been after they'd lost Nelson, morose and moody, lurching from screaming and sobbing to seeming indifference.

The cart dropped them at Head the Hill, the furthest into the village that wheeled transport could venture. The men flung their possessions on a tethered sledge for the ongoing journey down the cobbled street. The sky was darkening early, even for December. Seamen all, they could smell uncertain weather in the air. They tightened mufflers, pulled caps lower over their brows and stooped against the lively wind. Spiralling smoke rose, acrid yet comforting, from the chimneys in the valley below. Captain Jenn lit his pipe, cramming the last of his tobacco down into the bowl, reassured that, now they were ashore for a few weeks, he could replenish his supply. The sledge lightened as each man reached their home and removed his bag, leaving the others to stride closer to the harbour. Leonard's turn was approaching with fearful rapidity. He was reluctant to leave the camaraderie of his shipmates and head into the unknown upheaval that awaited him.

'Happy New Year lad,' said Captain Jenn, making the conventional salutation, oblivious of the irony. 'See you at the service tomorrow.'

Raising his hand to the Captain, Leonard gulped in the winter's air and exhaled heavily, his breath making patterns in the gloom. He discarded his half-smoked Woodbine, grinding its glow into the cobbles with more vigour than was necessary. He could feel his heart-rate quickening as he stepped towards the front door. He wanted to rehearse his opening sentences but words eluded him. Should he knock? The door would be unlocked. He never knocked but somehow he felt that there should be some warning of his intrusion into the household of sorrow. In the end, the decision was taken out of his hands. Rosie had been at the window awaiting his arrival. At not yet six years old, she was unconstrained by any sense of propriety or mourning.

''Tis Lennie,' she exclaimed, struggling with the heavy wooden door and uninhibited, flinging her arms round his thighs, almost knocking him off balance.

'Aye, let the lad come in maid,' said their father, quietly.

Albert clasped his eldest son's hand between his own and pumped it up and down.

'Good to see ee boy, good to see ee. Especially, well, you know. Your ma's been worried. We've all been worried. All this talk of torpedoes and such. Shame you weren't in time for Christmas. Not that it's been much of a Christmas, what with... .' His sentence trailed momentarily. Then, 'We did the best we could for the young uns, they don't really understand. None of us really understand. As for the war, can't believe it's all over, they said it wouldn't last beyond that first Christmas. Over, lad. Over and you be back, praise be.'

Albert was rambling uncharacteristically, trying to fill any awkward silences, taking up the conversation, perhaps to prevent his son saying anything inappropriate. Leonard was aware that his mother had come into the room, black-clad and unsmiling, hands wringing and eyes moistening. Never one for physical or verbal displays of affection, Polly merely nodded in Leonard's direction.

'You'll be wanting your supper,' she said, taking refuge in the daily routine.

Rosie was still prattling about her own concerns, excitement oozing from her restless body.

'Me and Lily, we're going to the treat up at the Court tomorrow,' she said. 'There's to be tea and decorations and a big tree and presents and all.'

Leonard raised his eyebrows at his father over Rosie's bouncing head. The annual New Year's treat, given by Mrs Hamlyn, was reserved for the Anglican Sunday scholars.

'She's right lad,' acknowledged Albert. 'They was asked special. Under the circumstances, you know.'

Leonard wondered if they would forever skirt round the issue, whether Daisy's name would now be unmentionable. Was she to be consigned to that never-to-be-visited compartment in their consciousness, as Nelson had been? Polly was busying herself at the stove. She wielded a spoon vigorously and it clanged against the enamel pan; her rigid back discouraged interaction.

Home, Leonard sighed to himself. Six weeks ago, he had been longing for this leave, for a chance to abandon the unremitting clamour of shipboard life in favour of chilly walks with Annie along the cliff path. He could not then have anticipated the tragedy that he would find back in Clovelly. He had considered himself a man for the past seven years but he felt as if his childhood had been ripped from him, leaving him without a past that he recognised. Nothing would ever be the same again.

The winter's daylight was already illuminating the room when Leonard woke on the first morning of his leave. He glanced at his brothers, still soundly sleeping, safe in the knowledge that this was not a day for work or school. In recognition of Leonard's seniority, Mark had vacated his narrow bed to join Bertie in the larger one, leaving Leonard to sleep alone on Mark's hard stuffed mattress in the corner. Leonard would have been happy to share the large bed, with its reassuring lumps and faded quilt but he was now the adult and adults had the privilege of a bed to themselves. He gazed at the ceiling, observing that new cracks had joined the ones that were comfortingly familiar. He puzzled over the events of the previous evening. Everyone had been wary, quiet, embarrassed perhaps. His mother had barely spoken, whilst his da uttered half sentences that trailed off and went nowhere, conveying nothing. Bertie had sat by the Bodley rigging a longline, head bowed, uncommunicative, whilst Lily and Rosie squabbled over a doll. Finding the atmosphere oppressive, Leonard had slipped out to join Mark in the scullery, where he was applying dubbin to the family's footwear; an essential task if they were to be ready to face the scrutiny of their neighbours. Unsaid phrases had hung in the air, as if his family were oppressed by some awful secret.

Leonard knew that his day was not his own. Firstly, he would be expected to go to church. For Leonard, religious observance was no longer an integral part of his routine and was unaccompanied by deep conviction. The New Year's Day Club Service though was not to be missed. It was always held in the church and was attended by Anglicans and Methodists alike. Members of the Rechabites and The Mariners' Union friendly societies entertained a healthy rivalry. New Year's Day was a chance to acknowledge your affiliation and parade to and from church, banners unfurling and in the case of the Rechabites, regalia proudly worn. Leonard was not yet a paid-up member of either friendly society, not on his wage but he and the other lads were encouraged to march with the older men and to be honest, he quite enjoyed the ritual. It was a man's affair this, he would have to wait until later to see Annie. He'd written to her a time or two from the ship. Not as much as he should have and not as often as she had written to him. He felt bad about that but there never seemed to be the time and what could he say? She sent news of home, of trivia and domesticity. He could hardly respond with the stark realities of a merchant ship in wartime; a raw and brutal world of steam and oil, of men's sweat, blood and if you were sure no one could see you, tears.

The Club Service was a day for best clothes, for spit and polish, for forsaking the cap for a bowler hat, should you possess such a sign of respectability. Leonard scraped his razor across his foam-laden chin cursorily. Even at twenty-one, he rarely needed to shave. It was a source of self-consciousness; that and his short stature, sparked good-natured ribbing from his shipmates. The men of the family jostled for space by the back door, grabbing scarves from pegs and tightening boot laces. Unsatisfied with Mark's washing technique, Polly scrubbed his face with a piece of rough, red flannel before tweaking Albert's collar and deeming them fit to be seen in public, on what was an important occasion in the Clovelly calendar.

The Mariners' Union assembled at the Red Lion but Leonard, his father and brothers were to march with the Rechabites from the New Inn, up the back road through the Court gardens to the church. As they assembled in the street outside the inn, persistent drizzle curtailed conviviality and the men were keen to be on their way before their best clothes were spoiled. The heavy cloth flag of the Rechabites, proudly borne by young Billy Harding, was becoming sodden.

'Where's your da?' Leonard asked Billy. 'I thought he'd be here.'

'Fishin',' replied Billy laconically. 'Times 'as been 'ard while he's been at sea. Ma had naught to give him for supper last night. We all be fair starved at home. 'Tis late for herrin' but he's hopeful.'

Leonard realised that matters must be bad if Will was missing the service.

'Who's he gone out with then?' asked Leonard, looking around for another missing face.

'He's out in the *Annie Salome* with Frank Badcock,' said Billy. 'I'd be out too if I weren't chosen to carry the banner.'

Leonard understood. Carrying the flag was a great honour. No one would miss the chance to head the parade, however hungry they were.

'Frank's back too then,' stated Leonard.

'Ay,' said Billy, struggling to hold the flag upright in the gusts that funnelled down the street. 'Back on leave from the *Albion* until the end of January. He's hoping for his discharge from the reserve now war is done. That do in the Dardenelles took it out of him. He's not been himself since. Just wants to be home with

Mrs Badcock and the boys. Can't be much fun being a gunner when all you want to do is fish.'

At that point, The Mariners' Union parade, coming up from the quay, reached the New Inn. Billy hoisted the flag aloft and the Rechabites fell in behind, swelling the procession to nearly one hundred men.

'Tis coming in proper dirty over the Bar,' muttered Tom Pengilly, who had been to check that his fishing boat was secure on its mooring, before joining his fellow Rechabites.

Tom was coxswain of the lifeboat, he could read the weather better than he could the *Western Morning News*. Leonard bent his head against the freshening south-westerly wind and began the slow march up the street. Folk were watching and waving from their doorways. Leonard was conscious that some of the spectators cast sidelong glances at his family as they walked past. There were occasional sly nudges and whispered comments, as hands shielded mouths. Was this all to do with Daisy? he wondered.

There was no sign of Annie. This was not unexpected. Granny Smale's was one of the tea-rooms where the Rechabites would be served their refreshments after the service, so she would be laying out pasties, saffron buns and scones. Later she would be busy serving of course but he would catch a glimpse of her as the men tucked in. It would be too soon to give Annie her birthday gift, that would wait until the proper day tomorrow but he hadn't seen her since Easter and Daisy's passing had suddenly made it all the more important. He realised that he could take nothing for granted. It could have been Annie. Leonard was thankful that it was not but that made it seem as if he was glad that Daisy had died, so Annie could be spared. He tried to put such thoughts from his mind. The procession wound its way up the muddy path by the side of the walled garden of the Court and into the church. The wind whipped through the churchyard's turbulent trees. Leonard averted his eyes in an attempt to avoid looking at the freshly dug grave that was his sister's. In the space next to Nelson's memorial, the bare earth cleaved a scar in the rain-drenched grass.

All Saints lacked the security and familiarity of the Methodist Chapel. Even with every seat filled it was cold and unwelcoming; the hard, wooden pews dug uncomfortably into Leonard's spine. Sandwiched between his father and a self-important Mark, who was attending the service for the first time, Leonard shifted his body to gain himself a few extra inches of space and clutched the slightly damp, well-worn hymn book. The distinctive smell of steaming wet worsted pervaded the air. Reverend Simkin sonorously announced the first hymn. Tom Finch, during the week the rector's gardener but proud organist on a Sunday, began to play, with more regard to volume than melody. *Oh God our Help in Ages Past*, comfortably recognisable to Methodists and Anglicans alike. The congregation sung with gusto, the sounds eerily deep in the absence of lighter female voices.

'Our hope in years to come.'

Hope. There was hope then? Hope of a dawning year, hope of a newly peaceful world, hope of pursuing his relationship with Annie. Leonard took a sideways glance at his father, who was surreptitiously wiping his nose on a greying handkerchief. Did he feel hope on this dark day? Did his mother feel hope? What had she to hope for? As was traditional at the Club Service, the chosen Psalm was 107, known as the sailors' Psalm. The men shuffled to their feet self-consciously as the minister began to utter the familiar words.

'They that go down to the sea in ships, that do business in great waters; these see the works of the Lord and his wonders in the deep.'

Leonard wasn't so sure about wonders. His shipboard experiences were mostly hard work, dirt, fear and a good dose of boredom. Reverend Simkin's voice rose, as if for emphasis.

'For He commandeth and raiseth the stormy wind, which lifteth up the waves thereof.'

The congregation was aware of the wind that was gaining momentum outside, as if to reinforce the clergyman's words. Reverend Simkin began to preach, taking as his text, "Now the Lord is that Spirit: and where the Spirit of the Lord is, there is liberty." Leonard knew he wasn't learned like Reverend Simkin but he found himself wondering where liberty was for those of his friends who would never return from war.

The service finally over, the men clattered down the street, with much less solemnity than their upward journey. The Rechabites, mostly Methodists and non-drinkers, bundled into the New Inn, who were as happy to serve teetotallers as drinkers. Those the New Inn could not accommodate, crowded into the tea-rooms, put their wet coats on the backs of the wooden chairs, smelled Granny Smale's flavoursome hot pasties and waited for the heavy teapots to circulate. Leonard spotted Annie and found it hard to suppress a broad grin, as he clasped his hands and bowed his head for grace. She'd blossomed while he'd been away, proper grown-up she was now, eighteen she'd be tomorrow. Here was his hope. Here was his liberty.

The members of the Mariners' Union repaired to The Red Lion for their repast, which would be accompanied by beer, or even whisky. The Club Room had been suitably decorated with garlands of greenery and candles for the occasion. Mr Moss' staff were on hand to serve a roast dinner, befitting of the status of those on the top table. Reverend Simkin, as an honorary member, opened with a grace that seemed overly long to many, who had, after all, already sat through a fulsome sermon. The silence to remember members lost during the previous year seemed particularly poignant, as most had not died after long lives lived to the full but had perished in the obscenity that was war. At last, steaming bowls of oxtail soup were carried up from the kitchens and set before anticipatory diners. Talk turned to the fishing, to the weather, which was turning fierce and to what the peace would bring.

Up at Granny Smale's, pasties eaten and cakes on the table, Eli saw Oscar Abbott pat the breast pocket of his jacket and excuse himself from the corner table. Eli smiled and followed the younger man.

'So you felt like a pipe of baccy too then?' remarked Eli, companionably.

'Aye,' replied Oscar. 'And I needed a breather. It be too hot in there. If they baint talking politics, then they be talking religion. Me, I just worry about me fishin'.'

'Won't be no fishing for a day or two with this weather,' said Eli.

'No,' agreed Oscar. 'Frank was a rare fool to go out today in this. I told him as much. Not that he didn't know. But go he would. Off before daybreak to catch the tide. Still, he must be back now as the tide's turned. Just as well, this sou-wester be proper keen.'

The men paused on the Look-out and chewed on their pipe stems, peering through the gloom and unrelenting drizzle, looking towards Bucks Mills. With the keen sight and instinct of a fisherman, Oscar was the first to spot the speck on the lurching waves.

'Oh, God,' he groaned, the rare blasphemy a sign of his anguish. ''Tis the *Annie Salome*, right proud of that boat Frank be. Named for his mother it were. Why the hell baint they back. They will never get into harbour now.'

Even Eli, the landsman of the two, was fully aware that Clovelly tides meant that there was a window of time during which boats could re-enter the harbour. If the fishermen missed that, they would have to remain at sea for several hours, until the state of the tide allowed them to return safely.

'Raise the lifeboat,' screamed Eli, his voice whipped away by the wind but Oscar was already running for the Red Lion, where many of the crew would be lifting fluffy roast potatoes to their mouths.

Eli pounded down the back steps two at a time, intent on ringing the bell outside the lifeboat house that would summon the crew. This was two of their own out there. It gave an added frisson to the rescue that was absent when they were called out to strangers.

Oscar flung back the doors to the Red Lion's Club Room. Breathless, it took a moment for him to be heard above the hubbub of voices.

'Boat in distress,' he yelled, just as the bell began to sound.

Galvanised, men pushed back their chairs, eager to be amongst the crew. Even those whose days on the lifeboat were long since gone instinctively hurried for oilskins and boots, hoping to be one of the launching party.

The sound of the alarm reached the Rechabites; Leonard shuddered as his father got up to volunteer. The first to reach the boat would form the crew and several of the older men went to hold Albert back.

'Don't put your missus through this Alb,' cautioned Tom Pengilly. 'There's plenty to man the boat, younger men and those who can be better spared right now. 'Tidden cowardice, 'tis common sense. You and the lad here can help with the launch.'

Leonard held his breath, hoping that his father would see reason but Albert's eyes were gleaming with a sense of purpose as he prepared himself to join the rescuers. This was something Albert understood. This was something he could do. He hadn't been able to save Daisy, he hadn't been able to save Nelson but perhaps his life could have a meaning again if he went to the aid of these men.

By 1.30pm, the lifeboat, the *Elinor Roget*, affectionately known as the *Elinor Rocket*, was sliding on to the swirling sea and Albert was amongst the fourteen men with oars at the ready, cork lifejackets tightened. The watching crowd, apprehensive and fearful, strained to see the struggling fishing boat dipping and tossing in the distance. The lifeboat listed alarmingly as the oarsmen fought to maintain a steady path through the waves. Albert's expression was grim, as he and the rest of the crew attempted to master the elements in a one-sided battle. The mist had thickened rapidly and obscured the *Annie Salome* from view.

'The *Rocket*'s going to struggle to get her,' said Eli, stating a fact that was obvious to all. 'Frank's only been back from war these four days past, Will's hardly even been home. Why the hell did they go out today?'

Before long, the lifeboat was hidden from those hoisting telescopes and frantically scanning the sea for their friends, their neighbours. There was silence as Merelda Badcock and Rose Harding arrived at the lifeboat house, hands clasped, faces white and strained. The women had grown up together on the quay and were well used to the tragedies of the sea. Now they were united in fearfulness, husbands in danger and brothers attempting the rescue. Billy Harding supported his mother as she pushed through the crowd. He had pleaded to be allowed in the lifeboat but his age and family ties precluded this. His three sisters, far too young to comprehend the seriousness of the situation, had been left with a neighbour. The Badcock boys glanced nervously at Billy, who they looked up to, who they had waved eagerly to only a few hours before as he had passed with the flag in the parade. The events of the morning were now an eternity ago, had dulled into distant memory.

Up the street in her cottage, Polly had heard the lifeboat bell. She realised that Albert could be one of those risking his life on the heaving sea. She knew that the cries she could hear from the cobbles meant that local men were in peril; men whose faces she knew, men whose children played with her own. This was not just another rescue. Normally, she would have been amongst the crowd on the Look-out, waiting for the safe return of the lifeboat. She would be concerned for her husband and eldest son, who could be amongst the rescuers. Her mind told her that she should join her neighbours in their anxiety but her body remained immobile. There was no danger, this was just another Club Service day, she told herself. Her menfolk would soon be home full of tales of the feast. Tragedy was held at bay.

The waiting villagers were well aware that the chances of the missing men returning safely to shore were slender. Fishermen scoffed at the idea of wearing lifejackets; lifejackets were not for real men. Few of them could swim, believing that, if tragedy struck, attempts to reach safety would merely prolong the inevitable. Harding wasn't even a fisherman, he was a member of the mercantile marine. Crewing a merchant ship was very different from a small open fishing boat like a Clovelly picarooner. The watchers tried to reassure themselves, focussing on Frank Badcock's experience, rather than the foolhardiness of setting to sea when it was clear that a storm was threatening.

'Been fishing this bay since he was no more than a tacker, Frank. He knows what's what.'

'If anyone can hold firm in a storm it's Frank. He'll be waiting it out 'til the tide turns.'

Soon there was nothing left to say, the same, oft repeated, platitudes no longer gave comfort and the crowd fell silent. Mark began to fidget, too embarrassed to speak to young Wilf Badcock, who was one of his greatest friends. He understood now why people had mumbled and failed to meet his eye in the days since Daisy died. Some of his classmates had lost fathers or brothers in the war but this was different, lacking in that heroic veneer that somehow made communicating with the bereaved easier.

'I'm off,' said Mark to his brothers, as he began the climb up from the quay, to tell his mother and sisters the news that was no news.

The family's own Daisy-induced heartache was subsumed by this latest ordeal that had been unleashed on the tight-knit community. Leonard and Bertie remained on the shoreline, knowing that it served no purpose but somehow feeling that returning home would be a sign that they had bowed to the inevitable.

They needed to see their father step safely back on dry land. After an eternity of watching, eyes squinting through the rain that was now lashing across the bay, the cry went up.

'She's coming in,' and the *Elinor Roget* turned from a mirage to a certainty.

The wave of anticipation rolled from the end of the harbour wall to the quayside and on to envelop those who had decided that the Look-out, high on the cliff, was the better vantage point. Cottage doors opened, shawls were donned and the waiting crowd swelled. Whispered conversations started up, half smiles were exchanged. There was a communal stiffening of shoulders as the villagers braced themselves for the lifeboat's return. Hopes were raised as the *Elinor Roget* entered the harbour but as the crew became distinguishable, the gloomy countenances and hunched shoulders of the weary men told their own story. An unearthly wail, scarcely human, went up from Rose Harding, as her father and brothers climbed out of the boat. Normally, they wouldn't all be part of the same lifeboat crew, the village liked to spread its risk and its grief but this had been different. Captain Jenn enveloped his sister in his arms and lowered his face to her hair to hide his despair.

'Go back Jim,' sobbed Rose to her brother. 'You must go back, I can't do without Will. He must be out there somewhere.'

Her plea was taken up by others on the quayside. 'We still have light for another hour, we must go back out. We can't give up.'

The unspoken thought that it could be them, their husband, their son, added vehemence to their entreaties. Tom Pengilly turned ruefully to his exhausted crew and shrugged his shoulders. The older men were clearly past setting out to sea again. Albert was in his fifties and Captain Jenn's father older still. With no sign of the *Annie Salome*, or the two men, Tom had made the common-sense decision to return to land. To his mind he had already put the lives of his crew in more danger than was wise, spurred on by the thought that they sought brothers-in-law and friends. The weather was dirty and the sea looming; deep down, Tom knew there was little chance of finding Frank or Will alive. He knew too that those who were begging for the lifeboat to go back out to sea were desperate, that they needed to feel that something was being done, however futile. Albert had sunk to the quayside, his head between his knees and old Mr Jenn could barely stand. Tom resigned himself to the inescapable truth and quickly assessed the remainder of his crew.

'I'll need four new men,' he sighed.

Sid Abbott, Dick Cruse, Richard Foley and Steve Headon were the first to step forward and join the younger crewmen, who were already shaking off exhaustion and returning to their stations on the boat.

Albert protested that he could go back out, he must go back out, he was good for a few more hours yet. Tom Pengilly understood but was resolute; Albert was amongst those who had done their share. Fatigue finally won the battle with resentment in Albert's mind and he shrugged his acceptance. He turned to his eldest son.

'Is ma down?' he asked.

'I've not seen her,' Leonard replied. 'Mark went to tell her you was out.'

Albert accepted Polly's uncharacteristic absence as he had had to accept many other unusual aspects of her behaviour lately. He went to hang his lifejacket in the station but despite being wet and weary, he showed no sign of wanting to return home. Leonard wondered if it was from a genuine desire to continue the vigil, or if it was a welcome opportunity to escape from Polly's unpredictability. His few brief hours at home had already shown Leonard that his mother was not coping with the loss of another child. All thoughts of seeing Annie that afternoon had gone and Leonard decided that he should stay with his father, at least until the lifeboat returned.

Hope died with the dusk, the lifeboat's second journey proved as fruitless as its first. Mrs Badcock and Mrs Harding were led away by their friends. Merelda Badcock's silent, trance-like stare a contrast to Rose's racking sobs. Did this put a new perspective on Daisy's death? Leonard wondered. She left grieving parents and siblings certainly but no spouse or child had depended on her for their bread and board. Leonard knew Daisy had died of the influenza but no one had told him more. His father had fetched her on the train, he knew that too but how had she felt? Had she been scared? Had she known that she was going to die? As he headed for home, Leonard tried to understand his parents' silences and the furtive glances of the neighbours. He could not help feeling that there was something that he was not being told, something ethereal, beyond his grasp.

Overnight, the wind dropped but the skies were still clad in iron-grey clouds. The community was drained. Drained of energy. Drained of emotion. Brave faces were to the fore and some semblance of normal routine was followed but no one felt like working. In the past, Polly would have been one of the first to offer help and comfort to the grieving families but she seemed listless, almost unconcerned, unaware. It was left to other neighbours to provide pasties, or to offer to mind silent children whilst their mothers mourned.

Albert and Leonard walked towards the harbour, still undecided whether or not to put out to sea. Leonard wondered why his father had been so insistent that Bertie did not accompany them. They had almost reached the Red Lion when Albert pulled his son to one side.

'You need to know,' he said. 'You're a man now. I didn't want to say before with the young 'uns about and all that business yesterday. There's naught to worry about. 'Tis all sorted but there was a bit of bother over Daisy. Folks said things they shouldn't have. Your ma was upset. Your ma and me, we errr,' Albert paused and cleared his throat, 'we had to go up in front of the coroner before they'd give us the death certificate. Some such fuss that never should have been. I don't know no sense to it.'

Leonard was unsure how to respond.

'But there's nothing to worry about now?' he ventured, struggling to picture his parents in court.

No wonder it had all been so odd since he came home. He had sensed that it was more than just Daisy succumbing to the influenza, which the papers said was taking so many lives.

'Coroner's done the certificate now,' said Albert. 'All done and dusted.'

Leonard took his father's statement at face value and turned his thoughts to the tragedy of the previous day. This morning, the lifeboat had launched again but all knew that this was now a search for bodies and a boat and not in the hope of returning the men to their families.

The news came that afternoon, as Leonard was tidying the cellar and anticipating finally meeting Annie on what was her birthday. The *Annie Salome* had been found on the pebble ridge at Westward Ho!. With not a scratch on the boat, it was hard to comprehend how the men had lost their lives. The empty nets had washed up some hundred yards further on. Whatever awful incident had occurred in that tiny open boat, on that forsaken sea, it was before the men had hauled in a catch. Apart from a single conger eel, there was no fish in the boat. All the families could do now was to wait and hope that the tide would return the bodies to the shore, so they could lay their menfolk to rest. It would be ten days or so before this was likely. An image of that new grave in All Saints' churchyard flashed into Leonard's mind. In spring there would be snowdrops, daffodils, renewal. In time there would be a headstone. His father had said that the estate and the chapel might help with the cost; so that Daisy would have a permanent memorial, as Nelson did. If Leonard wanted, he could sit in solitude at the graveside, or at least acknowledge his siblings if he walked that way. The Hardings and the Badcocks may not be so fortunate. If they could not find the bodies there could be no closure, no funeral, no place to mourn.

15
January 1919

In the wake of the loss of the *Annie Salome*, Clovelly folk rallied to protect their own. The women fussed round the new widows, baked them cakes, proffered sugary tea, exchanged sympathetic smiles in the street. They were not only driven by altruism. The support that they offered to the bereaved was a talisman, a way of somehow protecting their own families from tragedy. In the mind of every fisherman's wife, lurking frighteningly close to the surface, was the thought that on another day, in another storm, it could be their husbands who did not return, their children who were left fatherless.

Polly remained aloof, trammelled by her own sorrow. She was no longer the recipient of the villagers' compassion. They had moved on; this latest catastrophe had eclipsed Daisy's passing. In the early days of the new year, the new peace, men began returning home. They had escaped from the battlefield, yet they could not evade the memories of what they'd endured. Although there were stark gaps left at tables by those who were gone forever, families adjusted, made room for the haunted men who had survived and began to look forward. For Polly, there was no eager anticipation of a peacetime future; neither did Polly look back. She lived day to day, performing the necessary tasks in a listless fashion, largely ignoring her younger children unless they addressed her directly, which gradually they ceased to do. Albert fretted about her. In the weeks since Daisy's death she had not cried, had not raged as she had when they lost Nelson. Instead, she had withdrawn from reality, devoid of all emotion, an impenetrable husk, unreachable and empty.

Busy with the remnants of the herring season, Albert found it easier to resume a semblance of a normal life. Just before Christmas, a notice had appeared in the papers, saying that Mr Sanders had been cleared of all blame in the matter of Daisy's death. Albert had absorbed this news with equanimity. As far as he understood, the issuing of the death certificate had drawn an indelible line under the upheaval of the inquest. They would hear no more of it, they could put the events of the preceding weeks behind them and instead, devote their energies to coping with the latest village tragedy.

⚖

Sharp hail stones clattered on the blemished glass of Polly's kitchen window. The continuing gales had kept Albert and Bertie indoors. Leonard, bored with inactivity, announced that he was going to see if he could help Annie in the tea-rooms. The younger children, wrapped against the winter weather, set off up the hill to Wrinkleberry for the second day of the school term. The deep chimes of the clock on the mantleshelf above the flickering fire sounded nine times. A dark knocking on the door echoed back.

'Who be that at this time?' grumbled Albert, as he crossed the room in response.

Outside stood Police Sergeant Ashby from Bucks Cross. The rain ran down his black oiled cape and puddled at his feet. Droplets clung to his drooping moustache. Albert blanched, unsure why the officer would be calling. Neither man spoke; the silence stretched uncomfortably between them. After several slow seconds, Albert shuddered, suddenly aware that something was required of him and reluctantly, he ushered Ashby in. Catching sight of their visitor, Bertie, with a young man's distrust of authority, backed out of the room. Polly scarcely glanced up in acknowledgement. Ashby removed his dripping cloak and unbidden, hung it on a wooden peg just inside the door, next to fishermen's waterproofs and Polly's shawl. Unhurriedly, the policeman took off his helmet and lay it on the scrubbed table. Ashby was an impressively built man, even bare-headed he towered over Albert. He addressed Polly first.

'I am arresting you for the manslaughter of your daughter. Do you wish to say anything in answer to the charge? You are not obliged to say anything but anything you do say, may be given in evidence.'

Polly was unable to raise her gaze above the middle of the policeman's chest. Her mind was captivated by insignificant details, the shiny buttons that marched down Ashby's tunic, the red weal on his neck, left by the chin strap of his helmet. Everything about the man's attire seemed too small for his formidable frame. His collar was tight, the leather belt with its metal clasp, was stretched across his ample stomach, even his boots were taut and misshapen by the bunions that were a legacy of past years on the beat. The officer was evidently waiting for her to respond in some way. There was only one thing that she could say.

'I am innocent,' the three words were softly spoken.

Ashby turned to Albert and repeated the same caution. Albert was quicker to reply.

'Of course I am innocent,' he said heatedly. 'I don't know no sense to all this. We've got the certificate now. I thought that that was an end to it.'

'Your attendance is required at the court in Bideford,' Ashby was saying. 'Likely it won't take long. They're bound to adjourn the proceedings in order to call witnesses and so that you can get legal representation.'

The knot of panic that had been building in Albert's body crescendoed and crashed with the policeman's words. Every deep-buried fear surfaced, every nightmare was made manifest. As for Polly, she retreated once more into the past. Her thoughts hovering and alighting somewhere in the depths of those halcyon times before the horrors began.

⚖️

As Ashby had predicted, the hearing had been brief. Mr Carnegie, who was presiding at the Bideford County Sessions on the day of Albert and Polly's first appearance, had declared that they were charged with manslaughter by neglect. Ashby's superior, Superintendent Shutler, explained that the matter had been put before the Public Prosecutor, who had ordered proceedings to be brought.

Then Carnegie had announced, 'There are some twenty witnesses to be called. We are not ready to go on with the case today and the defendants will, I understand, be legally represented. It is only fair that they should have time to prepare their case.'

When asked, Albert and Polly had again protested their innocence. Then the hearing was over, yet, in so many ways, the worry and the dread had barely begun.

For Polly, all conscious thought was suspended during the week before the case resumed. The days of purgatory were punctuated by flustered preparations of which Polly was barely aware. At Mrs Hamlyn's instigation and through the efforts of Mr Caird, Mr Lefroy was engaged to put Albert and Polly's case. He came to the cottage to discuss their defence but Albert was confused and Polly incoherent. The solicitor left, despairing, with very little that he could put forward in their favour.

⚖️

Polly sat stiffly in Dymond and Sons' mail brake, next to an ashen-faced Albert. The early morning journey from Clovelly seemed interminable. There were no words to say. Neither looked back as they left the track to the village and turned left on to the main Bideford road. Familiar sights slipped by. The smithy at Bucks Cross, the lane leading to Peppercombe, Hoops Inn cradled in the bend of the road at the bottom of a sharp incline, Handy Cross, Catshole Lane. Nervously, Albert wondered how long it might be before he would see these comforting landmarks again. The road grew busier as they reached the outskirts of the town. They caught a glimpse of the workhouse as they passed the end of Meddon Street; Polly shivered involuntarily. Then there was the old cemetery, the school, and the site of the house where it was said the witches used to live. Polly was not the only parent who had threatened her recalcitrant small children with tales of how Goody Lloyd would cast a spell on them if they did not behave. Temperance Lloyd and her co-accused had been hanged outside Exeter jail. Reminders of capital punishment were hardly reassuring.

Yellow, snow-laden skies threatened to the west. As they descended Bridge Street, the river below them was mercurial, its molten surface gleaming as the sun struggled to break through. Polly glanced up to the villas at Chudleigh, on the far side of the Torridge. It was inconceivable that it was nigh on thirty years since an eager girl, whom Polly no longer recognised as her younger self, had set off from Peppercombe to work there. So much had happened in the years between. Love and loss. War and worry. Joy too there had been and simple pleasures; the cries of her newborn children, the blooming of the hollyhocks round her door and the clasp of Alb's hand as they left Bethesda Baptist Chapel in Gunstone Street as man and wife.

Polly went cautiously through the open door of the imposing red-bricked building on the corner of Bridge Street. Albert was beside her, yet they had never been more achingly apart. As she entered the courtroom, the smell of beeswax on the highly polished wood assailed her and the gas lamps hissed and flickered. Sitting in judgement were the magistrates, with their intimidating air of officialdom; Mr Duncan in the chair with Mr Cock and Mr Fulford flanking him. Mr Warlow was there to speak for the Director of Public Prosecutions. Polly supposed that she should fear him, regard him as her enemy perhaps but she was numbed beyond feeling. She looked up to the spectators' gallery and gasped. Crowded together, filling every available space allowed to them, were people that she knew. Abbotts, Jenns, Foleys, Perhams, Dunns and so many more. Clovelly folk had turned out in force, some motivated by a salacious curiosity, others sympathetic to the plight of their neighbours. As she stepped forward, it appeared to Polly that everyone's attention was upon her. She scanned the faces, unequal to the struggle of distinguishing friend from foe.

Then the court was called to order. Mr Lefroy was on his feet requesting that the room be cleared of all the witnesses. Polly jerked to attention when the charge against her was read. The use of her full name compounded the unreality of the situation. It was as if her identity had been stripped away. She was Polly, no one ever called her Mary Elizabeth, except here, except now, in these unfamiliar surroundings where consolation was absent and reassurance was gone.

'You are charged, under coroner's warrant, with the manslaughter of your daughter on the 14th of November 1918. How do you plead?'

Someone, somewhere, was saying the word "innocent" but Polly did not identify the voice as her own.

Mr Warlow was speaking, 'There is a body of fresh evidence that was not put before the coroner. The prosecution deem it to be manifestly fair that the defendants should have an opportunity of seeing and hearing the witnesses. The charge of manslaughter is based on the fact of the allegation that the defendants each had an active part in the care of their daughter, who was, in body and in mind, in a helpless condition.'

Odd phrases resonated with Polly. Helpless condition? Yes, that certainly was true but death had put Daisy beyond helplessness, her suffering was over. Whereas, for Polly herself, the torment was now, was immediate, was unending.

'The deceased was twenty four years of age,' Mr Warlow went on. 'There was no legal obligation upon them to render her any assistance, any more than a stranger would be bound to do. But the law states that if a person takes upon himself or herself, the charge of a helpless person, they owe a duty to that person and if they fail in the performance of it and the person dies as a result, it is manslaughter. The charge against the defendants before us today is that they did not act in discharge of that duty in an ordinary and reasonable manner.'

What was ordinary? thought Polly. What was reasonable? They had done all they could. She flinched as she realised that she was now the subject of Mr Warlow's attention.

'One cannot expect from people in a fishing cottage the same luxury and comfort that anyone would get in the houses of the rich,' he was saying disparagingly, 'but there are certain things that anyone with ordinary intelligence would know that they were bound to do. They are bound to supply sufficient food and drink beyond other things. The broad outstanding fact of the case is that, unfortunately, within three weeks of the time that the girl was taken home by her father, she died. With regard to the wife only, we are looking at an additional allegation of actual ill-usage.'

Polly stood, head down, twisting her hands together. She felt desperately alone, unaware that Albert wanted to reach out to her, to take her hand, to offer solace. She could not know that his inability to reassure her left her husband tortured by his own impotence, defeated, in an agony that matched her own.

Mr Warlow visibly swelled as he resumed his case, confident now, 'On the medical evidence alone we could rest our case, but we shall bring witnesses to show pretty conclusively that, although the victim was in a state in which she would object to receiving food, she was in fact fed by numerous people during the days which were material to this case.'

Mr Lefroy rearranged his papers. He wanted this strange little lady to go free and not just because it would enhance his professional reputation. He prided himself on his ability to represent and take seriously, the cases of the downtrodden and Polly was certainly that. Pity he couldn't plead puerperal madness, that usually worked but it was six years since Polly had last given birth and Daisy was no newborn infant. This was going to be harder. The main witness for the prosecution was articulate, convincing, a Cambridge man, far removed from an overawed fisherman and his wife. Lefroy had hopes of getting the husband off. The charge was less serious and the evidence against him was circumstantial at best. The woman was a different matter. All the magistrates' sympathy would be with the fresh faced young girl who had lost her life, not with this prickly, diffident woman, with her whispered monosyllables and constant glances to her husband, as if she were checking her story. He wondered if he could exploit Polly's manner to strengthen the defence. Even the land agent, Mr Caird, had commented that the lady was regarded as odd by her community. Yes, thought Mr Lefroy, he would make the most of her recent past, the hardships she had suffered, the tragedy she had known.

⚖️

As the morning ticked relentlessly into afternoon, witness followed witness on to the stand. Sat with his fellow journalists, Richard Ottley found that, in his absorption, he had written very few notes. He could not remember when he had last felt an emotional

312

investment in the outcome of a trial. Objective observance was his second-nature but the drama that was playing out in front of him had awakened something deeper, had demanded that detachment be put to one side. He found that his long-forsaken fascination with human nature, which had first attracted him to journalism, was piqued.

'Call Mrs Cornelius.'

Mrs Cornelius pulled her fox-fur necklet tighter and tottered forward, her new snakeskin shoes pressing on her incipient corns.

'Please state your full name and address.'

Mrs Cornelius spoke slowly, taking care that her vowels should not betray her humble origins, 'Mrs Kate Cornelius, 48 Upton Hill, Torquay.'

'What is your relationship to the deceased?' asked Mr Warlow in bored tones; to him this was routine.

'She came to work for my husband and myself as a gardener and parlourmaid on the 12th of January last, sir.'

'Did she give satisfaction?'

Mrs Cornelius paused, 'Yes,' she said, wonderingly, as if she had only just come to that conclusion.

'And when did she first become ill?'

This was easier, facts she could deal with, 'Up until the 15th of October she appeared to enjoy the usual health. On the 16th she came down with influenza, along with the rest of the household.'

The testimony went on. Mr Lefroy began questioning on behalf of the defence, 'What would you say relations were like between the deceased and her parents?'

Mrs Cornelius looked uncertain, how was she supposed to respond? Non-committal, surely that was best.

'She did not talk to me about her parents but as far as I know, she was on the best of terms with them. Her mother visited her at our home on the 21st of October, when the girl was ill. She returned to Bideford the same day, as she had other children who were unwell.'

Then it was the turn of Louisa Taylor. Gravely confident, she faced Mr Warlow, her uniform adding to her air of authority.

'I am the Superintendent Nurse at the workhouse infirmary in Newton Abbot,' she said crisply, in response to the request to state her name and occupation.

'And what is your connection with the deceased?'

'She was brought to us from her place of work in Torquay on the 23rd of October, on the orders of Dr Cook. There were seven in the house and only one elderly gentleman to care for those who were taken sick.'

'And how long did the deceased remain in your care?'

'The father took her away on the 25th of October, sir.'

Mr Warlow continued with his questioning, 'How did you find the deceased? Did she exhibit any signs of violence?'

'I myself found her to be quiet, sir and not at all excited or violent.'

There was a pause, Mr Warlow seemed to be expecting something more.

Nurse Taylor was less assured now and anxious to provide a suitable answer, 'I was informed that she had been violent overnight.'

'And were there any marks of violence on her body at that time?'

'No sir.'

Still more questions followed, 'How was the deceased's appetite?'

'She was on a milk diet, sir.'

'And why was that?'

'She was suffering from gastritis.'

It seemed that Warlow was not yet done, 'How did she take her nourishment?'

'It was only with difficulty that she took food at all, sir. She only took three pints of milk in the two days she was with us.'

'When her father said he was going to remove her from your care, what did you advise?'

On surer ground now, Miss Taylor replied, 'I begged him not to, sir, on account of her weakened state.'

'So she was removed against your advice, the advice of a medical professional?' said Warlow, with a triumphant glance in Mr Lefroy's direction.

'Well, yes sir, she was.'

Unwittingly, Nurse Taylor had strengthened the prosecution's case but then Mr Lefroy began his examination. Ottley found that he was willing the counsel to offer something that would stem the flow of detrimental evidence against the couple whose cause, incongruously, he had found himself championing.

'Miss Taylor, when the deceased arrived at your institution, what were the arrangements? How long were you expecting her to stay?'

'She was admitted as a temporary case, sir.'

'So you would not have expected her to stay indefinitely? You would anticipate that some other arrangements would be made?'

Louisa Taylor appeared to take this as a criticism, 'Indeed sir,' she said, indignantly, 'but arrangements that were in the best interests of the patient.'

Sensing that pursuing this line of questioning was not going to be helpful to his clients, Mr Lefroy changed tack. 'Whilst the deceased was with you, what communication was there with her family at home?'

Still on the defensive, Miss Taylor responded, 'I received six telegrams from the mother sir and I replied to them all.'

'And what was the nature of the messages that passed between you?'

'I told her about the deceased's mental trouble.'

Mr Lefroy persisted, 'Did you describe the course of this mental trouble?'

'I said it remained unchanged.'

'Did the defendant at any time ask if her daughter could go home?'

'Yes sir.'

'And,' asked Mr Lefroy, 'how did you respond?'

'I said that she could go as soon as she liked.'

Mr Lefroy cut in, repeating each word deliberately and with emphasis, 'You said she could go as soon as she liked.' His tone made this a statement not a question.

Miss Taylor glanced anxiously at Mr Warlow but his expression gave her no indication as to how she should proceed.

'Yes sir but that was before I realised that she was such a mental case,' she said, speaking as she might to a not very bright child.

Mr Lefroy pressed home his advantage, 'Members of the bench, you will recall that Miss Taylor told the mother that the deceased's condition was unchanged. Now she would have us believe that she, a trained nurse, was unable to recognise the full extent of the debility of a patient in her care.'

He turned again to Louisa Taylor, who was now less sure of herself. 'Did you at any time cancel the permission to remove the patient?'

'No sir, I did not but I did write to the mother the night before the father came, explaining the seriousness of her condition. The next morning, I received a telegram from Bideford saying that the father was on his way.'

'That will be all thank you Miss Taylor,' said Mr Lefroy, dismissing the witness.

⚖️

Polly was struggling to concentrate on the testimonies that were being given. It was as if they were reading a tale in a book. She could not relate the characters that were being described to her own family, or to her acquaintances.

An elderly man wearily took the stand. He gave his name as Dr Cook, his Northumbrian burr outlandish to west country ears.

'I was first called to attend the deceased at her place of work in Torquay on the 23rd of October last. I diagnosed her to be suffering from influenza and gastritis. I advised her removal to the workhouse infirmary forthwith.'

'Was there no one in the household who could attend her?' asked Mr Warlow.

'No. She was troublesome and took an aversion to those who were trying to help her. It was difficult, they were not well themselves. I gave a certificate that the patient was fit to be moved.'

'And did you attend her in the workhouse?'

'The influenza has given me many patients. Once she was at the infirmary, the staff there were responsible and well qualified to care for her but yes, I did see her before she left the workhouse.'

'At that time, Dr Cook,' said Mr Warlow, his manner suggesting that his examination was reaching its climax, 'did you see any injuries on the body of the deceased?'

Dr Cook's reply was damning, 'There were no bruises on her body when she left the workhouse.'

Bruises, thought Polly. Of course there were bruises. When she'd been at home the poor maid would scarce stay in her bed. She had to be kept there somehow and she was so hauntingly thin that every finger you laid upon her left its purple stain.

Mr Lefroy rose to his feet, hoping to divert the magistrates' attention to aspects of the case that would show his clients in a more favourable light.

'Is mental trouble a feature of influenza?' he asked.

'Yes, it is,' Dr Cook replied, 'I have seen several such cases.'

'And isn't it also a common feature that people take aversion to other people?'

The small scufflings from the gallery ceased, those whose attention had not wandered could see where this was heading. Richard Ottley leaned forward, eager to hear how Lefroy would develop his argument.

'Yes,' responded Dr Cook, 'it is a common thing.'

One medical man was replaced on the stand by another. This time it was Dr Kay but Polly drew no reassurance from the fact that it was now someone known to her who was giving evidence.

'You were the medical attendant in this case?' Mr Warlow was saying.

'Yes indeed.'

'What was your assessment of her condition?'

Dr Kay gave his testimony in ringing tones, 'I visited the girl several times. When I first saw her on November the 3rd she was of unsound mind and was suffering from great weakness. She was too frail to be moved and I gave instructions for her to be fed hourly.'

'Did you notice any particular aversion to her parents?'

'I did not.'

When the time came for the cross-examination, Mr Lefroy took the opportunity to deflect some of the blame from the defendants, 'Why did you not certify her as insane on the 8th of November, so that she could be admitted to the workhouse?' he asked Dr Kay.

'I am sorry now that I did not but the parents then said she was taking her food better and it was dangerous to move her until she was stronger. On the 9th of November the parents said that they had again been unable to feed the girl but I was able to get her to take nourishment, in spite of the mother's protests. She said it was hopeless and it would be better not to disturb the girl. She said if her daughter wanted to die, she should be left alone.'

'Do you find it a fairly common thing amongst country people, to dislike forcing their children to do anything?'

Doctor Kay looked at Lefroy. He appreciated this line of questioning. They were both professionals whose working lives were made more difficult by the rustic attitudes that they encountered.

'I am afraid it is a common weakness.'

'Why was a nurse not obtained?'

'With so much illness in the locality, it would have been very difficult to secure the services of a nurse. On the 11th I thought the girl was a little better and could be moved to a neighbour's house. I was disappointed to find two days later that she had not rallied.'

'Would you say that when insanity occurs in this type of influenza, death invariably follows?'

'I cannot confirm that view.'

Lefroy was building up to his final questions. He took a surreptitious look at the magistrates but they sat, implacable, giving no indication of where their sympathies lay.

'In your professional opinion, Dr Kay, to what do you attribute this unfortunate girl's death?'

'She was mentally affected by influenza and this weakness, together with want of proper feeding, led to her death.'

'How did want of food contribute to her demise?'

Dr Kay replied firmly, 'I am quite sure that the insufficiency of food accelerated her end.'

'And if she had been ill-used, what would be the effect on her condition?'

'Ill-usage would have had a bad effect on the girl and depressed her vitality. The mother refused to allow any other treatment that I suggested, on the grounds that it would be cruelty. A post mortem examination disclosed extreme emaciation due to lack of nourishment. All her organs were healthy. There were a few fading bruises about her legs.'

'And what of the allegations that the mother had ill-used the girl? Was there any evidence of this?'

Dr Kay inclined his head towards the bench, 'There is no foundation whatever for certain rumours which have been mentioned,' he said, incisively.

Ottley looked at the defendants. Had they realised how crucial this statement by the doctor was? Albert, who had been standing dejectedly, with his head bowed, jumped, suddenly alert. It was Dr Kay who had started all this fuss, well, him and that interfering Collins

⚖

from next door. Had he heard aright? Was the doctor now, after all this, on their side? Polly remained impassive, giving no indication that she had grasped the importance of the doctor's last words. Polly sighed. She didn't understand all this, what they were doing there, what she was supposed to have done. Mr Lefroy had tried to explain it to her but she had been unable to take it in. She needed it to be over, regardless of what over might mean.

Polly stood silently during Mrs Stanbury's lengthy cross-examination. At just one point did she show any awareness of what was being said.

'I saw her hit the girl when she was in bed,' Mrs Stanbury was saying. 'The girl was crying and said her mother had been beating her. She said that her parents were going to kill her. I pushed the mother back from the bed and told her that she must not do it.'

'How severe was the blow?' Mr Warlow asked.

'It was not a very hard blow.'

'And what gave you cause for concern?'

Emma Stanbury stole a look at Polly and continued, reluctantly, 'The defendant said she would do it and that she wished her daughter was dead.'

At this, Polly became animated and cried out, 'I didn't. It's a wilful lie.'

Mr Warlow frowned but passed no comment, returning instead to questioning Mrs Stanbury, 'What attempts were being made to feed the girl?'

'I gave some bread to the girl and the defendant said she would not have food given to a dying girl.'

The inquisition went on but Polly had sunk back into her daydream, once again oblivious to the words of her neighbour.

⚖

Outside, the winter's day was darkening; the trial had gone on for several hours, with the magistrates taking only a short break for refreshment. During this time, someone had given Polly a cup of scarcely-brewed tea and some stale biscuits but now she felt weak from hunger and enfeebled by the long hours of standing.

Mr Caird was giving evidence, responding to Mr Warlow's questions, 'I knew the defendant well. She would come to see me frequently. In her daughter's last illness, she asked me to pray that the girl would die and said that she would be better off dead than mazed.'

No. No. That was not how it had been, thought Polly. She must say something, she could not let that pass, 'I did not wish her dead,' she cried.

She had never really taken to Mr Caird. He was, after all, not one of them. Then there was that business when he'd spoken to her about Bertie. Well, that just wasn't right and she really hadn't wanted aught to do with the man since. Why couldn't folk just mind their own business and let her alone?

Mr Warlow was pressing on, ignoring her interruption.

'What is your opinion of the defendant?'

'She is rather eccentric. In fact, I would go further...'

Polly was no longer listening to Mr Caird's opinion of her. She was back in the Peppercombe Valley of her childhood, squabbling with her sisters, walking the Devon lanes in search of blackberries or sloes. Then she could visualise her time in Bideford, exciting for the young girl she had then been but she preferred the quiet of the country and the scents of the sea. Next, she was watching the rush of the Clovelly tide, relieved that Albert's boat was safely ashore, clasping a small girl's hand in hers, feeling her second child quicken in her womb.

⚖️

The prosecution had just called their key witness. Ottley was intrigued. What had motivated such a man, one who was clearly of the professional classes, to become embroiled in the goings on of an insignificant fisherman's family? Ah but perhaps that was the point, Ottley began to mentally debate with himself, maybe the defendants were not so insignificant after all. If he could only understand what motivated them, would he then be able to unravel how this tragedy had come about? He wished he knew more of the dead girl; was she the key to all this?

Edward Collins took a deep breath and tried to compose himself as he walked towards the stand. This was very different from the coroner's court where he had been full of self-righteous confidence, assured that he was acting as every good citizen should. Recently, it had become increasingly clear to him that he was not at one with the villagers of Clovelly. Although Collins struggled to interpret the subtleties of social interaction, even he had noticed a distinct cooling in his neighbours' attitude to him since the inquest and this had intensified over the past week. Folk barely grunted when they met him in the street, or they hastened in the opposite direction when he approached. His belief that he had been accepted, that he fitted in, had been a delusion.

Edward glanced up at the Clovelly villagers in the crowded gallery, intimidating, condemning, as if it were he who was on trial. He responded to Mr Warlow's questioning as best he could but all the brash conviction that he had felt when giving evidence to the coroner had deserted him. He found that he couldn't remember things, that he was muddling the order of the events that he was trying to describe. On several occasions, Mr Warlow had to ask him to clarify a point. Collins shook his head from side to side, trying to marshal his thoughts and banish his confusion. It was difficult to recall what his initial answers had been. With Mr Warlow's guidance he stumblingly reached the point in his rambling and repetitive narrative where Daisy was taken from her parents' home.

'They moved her from her father's house to Mrs Harris'. I, my wife and other neighbours, attended to her there,' he said.

'To whom did you express your concerns about the defendants' treatment of their daughter? Did you complain to the police?' asked Mr Warlow.

Once again, Edward Collins felt as if it were he who was the accused. 'No. I did not complain to the police. I felt that friendly pressure was more effective. About two weeks before this incident I did speak to Mr Caird and then to Mrs Hamlyn, who is the local agent for the NSPCC, about the defendants' treatment of their mentally weak son.'

Collins was wondering how much longer he would have to endure this interrogation. He was deeply regretting his interference. All he had wanted was justice for Daisy, a girl who had held an inexplicable attraction for him, an appeal that he was unable to define. Now it was Mr Lefroy who was bewildering him, trying to confuse him, to trip him up. Why wasn't his wife here? Amelia had not been called as a witness and had chosen not to attend. He needed her now. She kept him sane. There was a roaring in his ears, surely he wasn't going to have one of his turns. Not here. Not now. Not in front of all these hostile people. He breathed deeply and slowly, closing his eyes for a moment, trying to remember the calming techniques that he had been taught in the sanatorium at Netley.

'Who paid for the girl's care when she was removed from her home?'

Here was a chance to redeem himself, 'I myself paid for a great deal.'

'Did her parents refuse to pay for her care?'

'Not that I am aware,' replied Collins, wishing he could say differently.

'Did you at any time hear the defendant say that her daughter had taken hold of her?' Mr Lefroy asked.

Edward did not stop to consider his response, 'Yes, it is true, she did say that her daughter had taken hold of her before she struck her.'

'Can you swear that any of the blows were struck by the victim's mother. They might have been struck by the girl herself?'

'They might have been,' replied Edward, 'but it is hardly likely. The girl would not cry out if she was striking herself.'

'Do you have anything else to say about the defendants' treatment of their daughter?'

'The mother told me she had smacked the back of her hand once but later she said she had hit her several times.'

This jerked Polly from her reverie once more, 'I did not,' she exclaimed, vehemently.

'Did the defendant tell you it was because the girl had her hands round her mother's throat?' Mr Lefroy persisted.

'She certainly did mention that the girl had hold of her.'

'I put it to you Mr Collins,' said Mr Lefroy, sensing victory, 'that this evidence differs materially from that which you presented at the coroner's inquest.'

'No, sir,' the response was meek, no longer defiant.

⚖

Mr Lefroy was reviewing the evidence.

'I cannot recall a single witness who has said that the victim's father has done anything which, even in the most indirect way, could possibly have accelerated the girl's death. There is no evidence that food was short but on the contrary, there is every indication that food was abundant. There was farm produce to be had and the father was a fisherman; their diet was not noticeably restricted by rationing. If anything was asked for it was provided. I cannot see what more there was that the father could have done in respect of his daughter. There is in fact no evidence of breach of duty on the father's part.'

Albert looked up at this. Did this mean that he was free, that for him at least the ordeal was over? But what of Polly?

'As regards the female prisoner, there is no evidence of gross neglect. There is no chance of a jury convicting either of them, should the case to be sent to the Assizes. The parents took steps to have the girl removed to a nursing home but this was not deemed appropriate. With regard to the story of ill-treatment, this all rests on the testimony of Mr Edward Collins, who I do not think, by any stretch of the imagination, can be called a reliable witness. The tale of ill-usage did not lose anything in the telling. Often it is found that a mother is a poor nurse but this is very different to criminal neglect. I do not suggest that the mother is dismissed without any stain. She has been foolish but I put it to the bench that there has not been such evidence brought forward by the prosecution that would justify her or her husband standing trial at the Assizes.'

A smattering of applause from the gallery was hushed by Mr Duncan and the magistrates retired to discuss their verdict. Although he still cut a forlorn figure, Albert was looking a little more relaxed, the colour had returned to his cheeks. Polly, drained and haggard, was still weighed down by the enormity of her predicament. She had no comprehension that Mr Lefroy's words might lead to her release.

The watching crowds shuffled restlessly and murmured conversations buzzed and hummed. They did not have to wait long for the verdict. The magistrates returned and Mr Duncan rose to address to the room; an anticipatory hush descended.

'I have to inform you that, with very little discussion, we have decided to dismiss the evidence against both defendants.'

A feeling of relief astonished Richard Ottley by its intensity. It seemed that he was not the only spectator who had been craving a not guilty verdict. A few isolated claps coalesced and surged into a ringing ovation.

For Albert, this was a closure but subconsciously, Polly was aware that she would never escape from the past, that it could not be obliterated by the magistrate's words. Her burdens would never leave her. All that she had endured remained, lurking within, threatening her equanimity and corroding her future. The room swirled, Polly's body burned, nausea threatened. She was vaguely aware that someone was calling for three cheers for Mr Lefroy. Before the final hurrah died away, the load that she carried finally overwhelmed her and she fell to the floor.

Epilogue
20 August 1962

The summer season was at its zenith and Clovelly was awash with carefree strangers. Unrestrained holidaymakers, brightly dressed and exhilarated, exclaimed over the quaintness of the scene and cooed at the donkeys. In recent years, the patient animals' role as beasts of burden had been exchanged for the task of wooing the tourists. Girls in twin-sets, slacks and unsuitable sandals, interlinked arms and giggled as they steadied each other on the steep slope. They stopped to wonder at the sturdy, grey haired woman, in a worn blue cardigan, who was feeding the herring gull that relentlessly begged for bread on the wall by the Lookout. Although she was not diverted from the bird's demands, the lady greeted the visitors cheerily and invited them to put pennies in her proudly displayed box, that collected funds for the Lifeboat Association. A bent little man passed by, accompanied by a tall youth.

'Hello Auntie Lil,' called the lad, eager to be off to the shore.

The woman finally ignored the gull's importunities and addressed the boy, who fidgeted awkwardly in front of her, ungainly as he hovered on the threshold of manhood.

'Good to see you lad. You've brought your granfer down to visit us on his birthday then.'

The boy was already clattering unheedingly down the street. The man responded in his stead, 'We thought we'd look in on mother,' he said, 'She's always pleased to see the youngsters but she's not answering.'

'Not like her to go far,' the woman replied, 'I've not had sight of her since I popped in first thing.'

'I'd best be off after the boy,' said the man. 'He'll be hoping to earn a tanner or two rowing the visitors out.'

'Well, happy birthday to you brother, that's another year gone and none of us getting any younger.' The woman paused, 'How is Annie these days?'

'She can't get about much on account of her arthritis but we gets by,' the man answered, with a rueful smile.

He headed after his grandson and the woman watched his rolling gait until he disappeared from view.

Unnoticed amongst the uproar, an elderly lady, stooped and careworn, was making her way down to the shore. She rarely went beyond the Look-out now but on this particular day, it seemed important. She needed to put her feet on the sea-smoothed stones one final time. Only today, just for a few brief moments, would she allow herself to remember. It was as if the August sun, that had burned off the early morning mists, had scorched through the protective layer that the old woman had erected around her. Nobody spoke of the dark days long gone; folk barely recalled them now. Why was she still here when so many had passed on? Her beloved Albert, laid in the graveyard these past five years. Mark, Mrs Hamlyn, Mrs Stanbury, all dead. Another war had come and gone; the Great War, their war, had not, as they'd said, been the war to end all wars. Rosie and Lily, both widows, with grown children of their own. Sometimes she would look at Rosie's daughter and catch a glimpse of a darker child, flittering through shafts of sunlight, laughing at the waves, running barefoot over the cobbles. The few who were left never mentioned the matters that plagued her soul. It was as if there had been no accusations, no courtroom, no anguish. After a few moments, she turned her back on the sea, turned her back on the past and buried her memories deeply once more.

The weather-wise locals muttered that they would have to pay for this spell of hot sunshine, that the winter was set to be a harsh one. Unwary visitors, unused to the seaside heat, displayed pink cheeks and sun-sore arms. Children swung sandy buckets and fruitlessly searched for crabs in all the wrong places. The latest hits blared from transistor radios; Frank Ifield crooning *I Remember You*. The old woman on the beach did not recognise the song. The irony of its title was lost on her. On the quay, the adults sat and supped sweet tea and pretended to relish the unfamiliar clotted cream that was liberally smeared on their scones. Their offspring clamoured for yet one more ice cream in its wafered cone, which always went soft before the last of the treat was consumed. Those heading up the street, unused to the steepness of the slope, panted and puffed, all speech suspended for the duration of the climb. Self-absorbed, their thoughts were of guest house teas and sending postcards home. They were villagers for a day, for a brief stay, for a season. The worries of the locals, the secrets of their pasts, were of no concern to these transient strangers. As they paused on the Look-out to regain their breath, they watched the tiny figures on the shore below. Careful observers spotted a drab little woman, lost in thought, with her shoes and wrinkled stockings in her hand, hobbling up the slipway, barefoot on the cobbles.

Barefoot on the Cobbles

The pretty white cottages, the thatch and the slate,
Hide many stories of life, love and hate.
The sea and the church and the woods on the hill,
The stories that happened are living there still.

Maybe a murder or maybe a storm,
The wreck of a ship on a cold winter's morn,
The pages of history turn every day,
Stories of colour amongst all the grey.

The ghost of a girl trying to find her way home,
Running barefoot on the wet cobblestones.
The cries of the fishermen lost in the storm,
Mix with cries of a baby, new born.

The sailor the squire and the scullery maid,
All lived their lives with the cards they were laid,
The echoes of deeds and the tales long past,
Shine through the mist like a light on the mast.

The tourists have left now the evening is chill,
The pretty white cottages climb up the hill.
The fires are lit and the hearths are all warm,
But the weathercock warns of a westerly storm.

Dan Britton

About the Author

Janet Few inhabits the past. You may find her lurking in her four hundred year old North Devon cottage, or spot her thinly disguised as the formidable Mistress Agnes. This alter ego is a goodwife of a certain age, who leads a somewhat chaotic life during the mid-seventeenth century. One way or another, most of Janet's time is spent working to inspire others with a love of history, heritage and the written word.

In a vain effort to support her incurable book buying habit, in the past, Janet has been known to pull the odd pint or two, sell hamsters and support very special schoolchildren. Somewhere along the way, she acquired a doctorate in community history 'for fun'. Janet has an international reputation as a family historian, giving presentations across the English-speaking world. She has written several non-fiction history books but *Barefoot on the Cobbles* is her first published novel. A second novel, investigating an earlier North Devon tragedy, is being carefully nurtured.

Any time that Janet can carve from her history-obsessed existence, is spent embarrassing her descendants, travelling and trying to make her garden behave itself. Janet is fascinated by human behaviour, past and present, real and fictional. She loves the wonderful Devon landscape and leading her grandchildren astray.

If you have enjoyed reading *Barefoot*, it would make a decidedly eccentric author very happy if you were to leave a few words on the reviewing platform of your choice.

Keep in touch with Janet Few via her website and blog thehistoryinterpreter.wordpress.com or by following her on Twitter @janetfew

A request from Blue Poppy Publishing

We sincerely hope you enjoyed this book as much as we enjoyed producing it.

On behalf of the author, we would encourage you to write a review of this book. Every author writes for different reasons but, when we publish our work, what we desire most of all is for it to be read.

As much as it may seem like a small thing, every review, especially those on goodreads.com and on Amazon helps towards getting the book noticed by potential new readers.

We especially appreciate sincere reviews with a few words of explanation as to what you enjoyed and even what you did not enjoy about the book. Something which one reader may not have enjoyed might in fact be the very thing another reader is looking for.

Thank you

You can find out more about Blue Poppy Publishing, including our other authors and titles, as well as how we help aspiring authors to self-publish their work, by visiting our website at www.bluepoppypublishing.co.uk.

By the same author

Remember Then: women's memories of 1946-1969 and how to write your own (Family History Partnership 2015)

'I have laughed and cried reading all the memories. It just transports me back to that period.'

Coffers, Clysters, Comfrey and Coifs: the lives of our seventeenth century ancestors (Family History Partnership 2012)

'Whether you like to read a book cover to cover, or dip into random chapters, this book presents a rich flavour and a well-balanced portrait of seventeenth century life.'

The Family Historian's Enquire Within (Family History Partnership 2014)

Shortlisted for a Chartered Institute of Library and Information Professionals award

'If you only have one Family History reference book on your shelf, this is the one you need'

Putting your Ancestors in their Place: a guide to one place studies (Family History Partnership (2014)

'It's Marvellous!'